SWING!

SWING!

Swapping, Swinging, and Other Sinful Stories

Edited by
Sage Vivant

Venus Book Club
Garden City, New York

Published by Venus Book Club, 401 Franklin Avenue, Garden City, New York 11530.

Book design by Christos Peterson

ISBN: 1-58288-085-9

Printed in the United States of America

For Chris,
with whom all things are possible

Contents

Introduction by Sage Vivant ix

Bob & Carol & Ted (But Not Alice) by M. Christian 1
How I Became a Swinger by Randy Panache 11
Shoe Shines by Debra Gray De Noux 21
Sausage Making for Couples by Joy VanNuys 31
Anything for You by Odysseus Eleftherios 41
Under the Bridge in Warsaw by Jason Rubis 51
More Sunscreen, Please by Julia Rebecca 63
Group Sex, Once Removed by Chris Bridges 81
Meet Maureen by Florence Hoard 91
The Arbitrageur by Bill Noble 101
Jessie's Girl by Jayden Blake 113
Agua by Jennifer Maer 127
Sharing What I Borrow and Coveting What Is Mine
    by Stacy Reed 137
His Scene by Elizabeth Coldwell 153
Birthday Girl by Ludmilla Kryzmska 163
In at the Deep End by Bryn Colvin 171
Balance by Helena Settimana 187
Sex with His Ex by Jennifer Whitlock 193
Burn by Tenille Brown 203
How Can I Help You? by Sage Vivant 213

Author Biographies 221
Swinging Resources 225

Introduction

After operating Custom Erotica Source for nearly six years, it's been impossible for me not to notice how often people want additional sex partners in their stories. Though orgies and sex parties are a popular choice, the most requested story element is the addition of just one person to the sex between themselves and their partners. Still other clients like me to write another couple into their story.

Would these clients call their desire for sexual variety "swinging"? In many cases, no—they are merely interested in exploring the erotic possibilities posed by adding a new person (or two or three or more) to their sex lives.

What is swinging, anyway? Depends who you talk to. Swingers clubs define swinging as a form of recreational social sex among consenting adults. Most are male/female couples meeting other male/female couples for sex and/or ongoing intimate friendships. Typically, these sexy meetings occur at preplanned parties, either at someone's home who is a member of an official swinging organization (or an unofficial one) or any space where free, polyamorous sex is accepted and encouraged.

The Lifestyle is the term commonly used to describe the sharing of partners as a way of life. This occurs when both partners—the man and the woman—are equally enamored of the concept and both are ready, willing and eager to participate. People living The Lifestyle attend recreational sex parties with some regularity.

But these are not the only folks who swing. Labels, as we all know, can be misleading.

Other people have never joined a club (sexual or otherwise) in their lives and don't plan to—they seize the opportunity to explore sexual sharing whenever it arises. These opportunities don't present themselves all that often and finding like-minded people can be extremely difficult—which is probably how clubs evolved—but they prefer to take life and sexual serendipity as it comes. Organized swinging isn't for everyone; the desire to experiment sexually with new people appeals even to less party-oriented souls.

Another contingent of sexual adventurers wants a third person to complete their long-term living arrangement. They seek sexy fun, most definitely, but they believe that three people living and loving together is bound to multiply the bliss experienced by two. These couples want to add a third to their relationship on a daily, ongoing basis. Shopping for the right person is the only time when "recreational" sex might truly describe what they're doing.

And then there are the people who fantasize about swinging. They may find themselves in the happy circumstance of being able to experience it for one unforgettable time, or they may allow the fantasy to enhance their traditional lovemaking or masturbation activities.

What do all of these swingers have in common, aside from a sexual penchant that society condemns? They share a certain degree of bisexuality, a need to diversify their sexual palette, and, much to the general public's surprise, a profound and abiding love and respect for their primary partners. A person has to have exceptional faith in the enduring commitment of the other partner to not only agree to but also enjoy sharing them with someone else. Those who swing acknowledge that swinging is an abysmal failure when half a couple isn't completely sold on the idea or is dragged to a swinging event by an overzealous or insensitive partner.

This anthology attempts to present the full spectrum of

experience that results from adding to a twosome. From Randy Panache's marvelous essay on her experiences with The Lifestyle to Chris Bridges's hilarious guide to the pratfalls of multipartnered sex, you'll get an idea of how beautifully it all can work as well as how comically it can fail. Bryn Colvin looks at swinging in captivity, while M. Christian brings his usual warmth and storytelling finesse to the topic.

Some of these stories and essays are told from the couple's perspective and others are told from the point of view of the third party. Because these perspectives vary wildly, as might your place in a third-party situation, they are presented here for your enjoyment and consideration.

If swinging (or introducing new people into your sex life) is an idea that has intrigued but intimidated you, perhaps these stories and essays will help you understand the potentially satisfying, confusing, and erotic possibilities that await you. Be sure to review the resource list at the end of this book for more information on swinging and polyamory. But most of all, do what feels right for you.

—Sage Vivant
San Francisco, 2003

Bob & Carol & Ted (But Not Alice)

by M. Christian

What are you afraid of?" Not spoken with scorn; with challenge, though. This was Carol, after all. His Carol. The question was sweet, sincere, one lover to another: Really, honestly, what are you frightened of?

Robert fiddled with his glass of ice tea, gathering his thoughts. He trusted Carol—hell, he'd been happily married to her for five years so he'd better—but even so, it was a door he hadn't opened in a long time.

They were sitting in their living room. A gentle rain tapping at the big glass doors to the patio, dancing on the pale blue surface of the pool beyond. In the big stone fireplace, a gentle fire licked at the glowing embers of a log.

Carol smiled—and, as always, when she did Bob felt himself sort of melt, deep inside. Carol . . . it shocked him sometimes how much he loved her, trusted her, loved to simply be with her. He counted himself so fortunate to have found the other half of himself in the tall, slim, brown-haired woman. They laughed at the same jokes, they appreciated the same ear of jazz, they both could eat endless platters of sashimi, and—in the bedroom, the garage, the kitchen, in the pool, in the car, and everywhere else the mood struck them —their lovemaking was always delightful, often spectacular.

"I don't know," Bob finally said, taking a long sip of his drink (needs more sugar, he thought absently). "I mean I think about it sometimes. Not like I don't like what we do, but sometimes it crops up. A lot of the time it's hot, but other times it's kinda . . . fuck, disconcerting, you know? Like I should be thinking of what we're doing, what I want to do with you—" a sly smile, a hand on her thigh, kneading gently "—instead of thinking about, well, another guy."

Carol leaned forward, grazing her silken lips across his. As always, just that simple act—one sweeping kiss—made his body, especially his cock, stiff with desire. "Sweet," she said, whispering hoarsely into his ear, "I don't mind. I think it's hot. I really do."

Bob smiled, flexing his jean-clad thighs to relish in his spontaneous stiffness. "I know. It just feels weird sometimes. I can't explain it."

"What do you think about? Talk to me about it. Maybe that'll help a little bit." Her hand landed in his lap, curled around his shaft. "Pretend I'm not here," she added, with a low laugh.

He responded with a matching chuckle. "Oh, yeah, right," he said, leaning forward to meet her lips. They stayed together, lips on lips, tongues dancing in hot mouths. Bob didn't know how to respond, so he just followed his instincts—his hand drifted up to cup Carol's firm, large breasts. Five years and she still had the power to reach down into his sexual self, to get to him at a cock and balls level. But there was something else.

"I think it's hot," Carol said, breaking the kiss with a soft smack of moisture. "I think about it a lot, really. The thought of you with—what was his name again?"

Bob doubted Carol had really forgotten, but he smiled and played again. "Charley. College friend." Charley: brown curls, blue eyes, broad shoulders, football, basketball, geology, math, made a wicked margarita. Charley: late one night in their dorm room, both drunk on those wicked margaritas, Charley's hand on Bob's knee, then on his hard cock. "We fooled around for most of the semester, then his father died. Left him the business. We stayed in touch for a year or so, then, well, drifted away. You know."

"I think it's wonderful," Carol said, smiling, laughing, but also tender, caring, knowing there was a Charley-shaped hole somewhere deep inside Bob. Carefully, slowly, she inched down the zipper on his shorts until the tent of his underwear was clearly visible, a small dot of pre-come marking the so-hard tip of his cock. "I think about it when we play. When we fuck."

Bob suspected, but hearing Carol say it added extra iron to his already throbbing hard-on. Carol normally wasn't one to talk during sex. This new, rough, voice was even more of a turn on.

Bob felt a glow start, deep down. Even to Carol, Charley was something private—but hearing Carol's voice, he felt like he could, really, finally share it. "He was something else, Charley was. Big guy, never would have thought it to look at him. That sounds stupid, doesn't it?"

"No it doesn't. You're speaking from the heart, sexy. Since when is anyone's heart logical or fair?" Carol had gotten his shorts down, quickly followed by his underwear. Bob's cock had never seemed so big or so hard in his life. It was like two parts of his life had met, with the force of both working to make him hard . . . so damned hard. Carol kissed the tip, carefully savoring the bead of come just starting to form again at the tip.

He smiled down at her, taking a moment to playfully ruffle her hair before allowing himself to melt down into the sofa. "I wouldn't call him 'sweet' or 'nice,' but he could be sometimes. He just liked . . . fuck . . ." The words slipped from his mind as Carol opened her mouth and, at first—slowly, carefully—started to suck on his cock. "Fuck . . . yeah, he liked life, I guess. I don't even think he thought of himself as gay or anything. He just liked to fuck, to suck, to get laid, you know. But it was special. I can't really explain it."

"You loved him, didn't you—at least a little bit?" Carol said, taking her lips off his cock for a moment to speak. As she did, she stroked him, each word a downward or upward stroke.

Bob didn't say anything. He just leaned back and closed his eyes. He knew she was right but that was one thing he wasn't quite willing to say—not yet. He'd come a long way, but that was still in the distance.

Carol smiled, sweetly, hotly, and dropped her mouth onto his cock again. This time her sucking, licking, stroking of his cock was faster, more earnest, and Bob could tell that she was aching to fuck, to climb on top of him and ride herself to a shattering, glorious orgasm. But she didn't. Instead, she kept sucking, kept stroking his cock, occasionally breaking to whisper, then say in a raw, hungry voice: "I think it's hot . . . not him just sucking your cock . . . but that you have had that. Bet sometimes . . . we look at the same guy . . . and want to know what he'd be like . . . to suck . . . to fuck."

Even though Bob was . . . somewhere else, damned near where Carol wanted to be, he knew she was right. It was hot, it was special, and he recognized that. He wanted to haul her off her knees, get dressed, and bolt out the door to do just that. The kid who bagged their groceries sometimes at the Piggly Wiggly, that one linebacker, Russell Crowe—he wanted to take them home, take off their shirts, lick their nipples, suck their cocks, suck their cocks, suck their cocks—

Then something went wrong. Just on the edge of orgasm, Carol stopped. Bob felt slapped, like ice water had just been dumped into his lap. He opened his eyes and looked, goggle-eyed as Carol got up off the floor, straightening her T-shirt over very hard nipples. "Didn't you hear that? Of all times for some-one to ring the fucking doorbell."

Tugging up his pants, Bob rehearsed what he'd say: Mormons? Slam the door in their faces. Door-to-door salesman? The same. Someone needing directions? "Sorry, but you're *way* off," then do the same . . .

Just as Bob got to the living room door, he heard Carol,

who'd been a lot more dressed to start with, saying. "Ted! How's it hanging?"

Bob rounded the corner, a smile already spreading across his face. Of all the people to have knocked on their front door, Ted was probably the only one who would have understood.

Ted and his charming wife, Alice, lived just across town. Normally, Bob and Carol would never in a million years have crossed paths with them, but it so happened that Ted worked in the coffee place right across the street from where Bob worked. After six months of going back and forth, Bob finally struck up a conversation with Ted and found out, much to his delight, that the tall, sandy-haired young man and he had a lot in common: the Denver Broncos, weekend sailing, and Russell Crowe movies. Bob and Carol felt very relaxed and even sometimes sexually playful around Ted and Alice—even going so far as to having a kind of sex party one night, when they all got way too wasted on tequila and some primo greenbud that Ted had scored the night before. All they'd done was watch each other fuck, but it had been more than enough to blast Bob and Carol into happy voyeuristic bliss and fuel their erotic fantasies for weeks afterward.

"Low and to the right," Ted answered, smiling wide and broad and planting a quick kiss on Carol's cheek. Bob gave Ted his own quick greeting—a full body hug that, only until he finished did Bob realize had probably given Ted more than he expected with regard to Bob's still rock-hard dick.

Bob and Carol smiled at each other, feeling relaxed and still playful in the presence of their friend. "Where's Alice at, Teddy? Somewhere in the depths of Columbia?" Bob asked. Alice was the other half of Bean Seeing You, their little coffee house, and was often away trying to wrangle up all kinds of stimulating delicacies, not all of them coffee-related.

"Worse than that," Ted said, playfully ruffling his friend's brown locks. "Deepest, darkest Bakersfield. I'm kinda worried about her—the last expedition down there vanished without a trace."

Everyone laughing, more out of released tension than Ted's weird brand of humor, they retreated back to the living room and the couch. As Bob and Ted sprawled out on the couch while Carol got some drinks, Bob couldn't help but wonder if their friend had figured out that they'd been almost screwing their brains out a few minutes before. The thought of it made Bob grin wildly.

"Come on, bro," Ted said, picking up on the smile. "Out with it."

Suddenly tongue-tied, Bob was glad when Carol walked in with three tall, cool drinks. "One for the man of the house"— Bob—"one for the handsome stranger"—Ted—"and one for the horny housewife." Carol. "Cheers!" she concluded, taking a hefty swallow of her own drink.

Bob and Ted toasted her, Bob almost coughing as he drank—the drinks were stiff and then some. He smiled to himself again as he sank back into the sofa. Talking about Charley made him feel like a secret had been released from some dark, compressed part of his mind. He felt light, airy, almost like he was hovering over his body, looking down at Ted—tall, curly-haired, quick and bright Ted—and Carol. Carol, who even just thinking of made his body and mind recall their wonderful lovemaking.

Sneaking a furtive glance at Ted, Bob looked his friend over more carefully. In his new, unburdened vision, Ted looked . . . well, he wasn't like Charley, but there was still something about Ted that made Bob think of his college friend—no, his college lover. Something about their height, their insatiable appetite for life, their humor.

"Is it hot in here or is it just me?" Carol piped up, laughing at her own cliché. Bob and Ted laughed, too, but then the sound dropped away to a compressed silence as Carol lifted off her T-shirt and theatrically mopped her brow.

Bob's mind bounced from Carol's beautiful breasts, and her obviously very erect nipples, to Ted's rapt attention on them. He was proud of Carol, proud that she was so lovely, so sexy. He wanted to reach out and grab her, pull her to him. He wanted to kiss her nipples as Ted watched. He wanted to sit her down on the couch, spread her strong thighs and lick her cunt until she screamed, moaned and held onto Bob's hair as orgasm after orgasm rocketed through her as Ted watched. He wanted to bend her over, slide his painfully hard cock into her, and then fuck her till she moaned, and bucked against him as Ted watched. He wanted Ted . . .

Carol's shorts came off next. Naked, she stood in front of them. Like a goddess, she rocked, back and forth, showing off her voluptuous form. But even though he loved her, and thought she was probably the most beautiful women he'd ever seen, Bob turned to look at Ted.

Ted, with the beautiful Carol standing right there in the room with him, was, instead, looking at Bob.

Bob felt his face grow flushed with . . . no, not with what he expected. It wasn't embarrassment. Dimly, he was aware of Carol walking toward him, getting down on her hands and knees again, and in a direct repeat of only minutes before, playfully tugging his cock out of her shorts and starting to suck on it.

Still watching Ted watching him—and Carol sucking his cock—Bob smiled at him. In Carol's mouth, his cock jumped with a sudden influx of pure lust.

Carol, breaking her hungry relishing of his dick, said. "Bob, I really think Ted would like you to suck his cock."

Now Bob was embarrassed, but not enough to keep him from silently nodding agreement.

"I'd love that," Ted said, his voice low and rumbling. "I really would."

"Take your pants off, Ted," Carol said, stroking Bob's cock. "I want to watch."

Ted did, quickly shucking his shirt as well as his threadbare jeans. He stood for a moment, letting Carol and Bob look at him. Bob had seen his friend's cock before, but for the first time he really looked at it. Ted was tall and thin, his chest bare and smooth. His cock was big—though maybe not as big as Bob's (a secret little smirk at that)—but handsome. It wasn't soft, but it also wasn't completely hard. As Carol and Bob watched, Ted's cock grew firmer, harder, larger, until it stuck out from his lean frame at an urgent 45-degree angle.

"Bob . . ." Carol said, her voice purring with lust, ". . . suck Ted's cock. Please, suck it."

Ted crawled up on the sofa, lying down so that his head was on one armrest, his cock sticking straight up. His eyes were half-closed, and a sweet, sexy, smile played on his lips.

Bob reached down, turning just enough to reach his friend and not dislodge Carol from her earnest sucking of his own dick, and gently took hold of Ted's cock. It was warm, almost hot, and slightly slick with a fine sheen of sweat. He could have looked at it for hours, days, but with Carol working hard on his own dick, he felt his pulse racing, his own hunger beating hard in his heart.

At first he just kissed it, tasting salty pre-come. With a flash of worry that he wouldn't be good, first he licked the tip, exploring the shape of the head with his lips and then his tongue. As his heart hammered heavier and his own cock pulsed with sensation, he finally took the head into his mouth and gently sucked and licked. Ted, bless him, gave wonderful feedback, gently moaning and bucking his slims hips just enough to let Bob know that he was doing a good job.

As Carol worked him, he worked Ted. They were a long train of pleasure, a circuit of moans and sighs. Time seemed to stretch, and distance compress until the whole world was just Ted's dick in Bob's mouth, Bob's dick in Carol's mouth—all on that wonderful afternoon.

Then, before he was even aware it was happening, Bob felt his orgasm pushing, heavy and wonderfully leaden, down through his body, down through his balls, down through his cock, and, in a spasming orgasm that made him break his earnest sucking of Ted's cock to moan, sigh, almost scream with pleasure. Smiling at his friend, Ted followed quickly behind, with only a few quick jerks of his cock as Bob rested his head on Ted's knee.

Bob felt . . . good, like something important, magical, and special had happened. The world had grown, by just a little bit, but in a very special way. Resting on his friend's knee, Carol kissing his belly, he smiled. Everything all right with the world.

Later, the sun set, and everyone very much exhausted by many more hours of play, Ted stumbled to the front door, with Carol helping him navigate through the dim house. "Thanks for coming," she said with a sweet coo, almost a whisper, so as not to wake the heavily slumbering Bob in the next room. She kissed him, soft and sweet, smiling to herself at the variety of tastes on his lips.

"I was happy to. Very. Thanks for asking me to . . . come," Ted said, smiling, as he opened the front door.

Carol smiled. "Thank you for giving him such a wonderful gift. Next weekend then?"

"Definitely. Next time I'll bring Alice."

Another gentle kiss, a mutual "Good night" and the door was closed.

How I Became a Swinger

by Randy Panache

Blindfolded on my back, my legs wide open, knees hanging in soft cloth restraints, I reach out to touch Jens' shaved head. Definitely: the way he uses his tongue and teeth, the intensity with which he applies himself to the least sign of my increasing excitement—it can be no other. But there are other candidates around.

It was the first gangbang we hosted: four, later five women, more than twenty men. Enough men to go around, enough so that each of us could feel surrounded by male flesh, male hard-ons, sheer maleness. Jens had built a surprise for me, a flat swing covered in black shiny material, attached overhead with sturdy bolts to the metal pedestal supporting our top floor. Before I was blindfolded, the men introduced themselves—an interesting ritual in itself: The guys I'd already played with on other occasions kissed me tenderly, those new to me shook my hand. Everyone intensely checked out everyone else. I felt able to assess each guy's sexual style in the way he looked at me. When my husband announced that the party was officially opened, a silk scarf was wrapped around my eyes and two nice guys—warm smiles (quickly gone from my sight), attentive touches, gentle voices—were given the task of entertaining me while Jens hung up the swing for its inaugural deployment. They kissed me, unzipped my black wet-look dress from above and kissed my breasts, unzipped it from below *and stroked my legs—and then lifted me onto the swing.*

At the perfect orgy, I constitute the center of attention for an indistinctly large group of civilized men with prominent hard-ons and quiet voices. Other attractive women also make them feel desirable; my husband is close by, enjoying my excitement, the sight and touch of the other women, and the overall openness, suggestiveness, lewdness.

Men are all around me, gentle and demanding at the same time. Always someone between my legs, probing with his tongue or pulling a condom over his cock from a conveniently situated bowl and pushing it into me. One on either side, one pushing his dick into my mouth, more or less aggressively depending on character and sexual urgency, and one watching my actions, my reactions, soaking up everything. The watcher takes my hand and shows me how he likes to be squeezed. Some men hold my head so they can thrust deeper into me, others let me set the tempo. I bathe in the sensations, the attention, and come again and again.

The "I" in this scene is really me. I'm not fantasizing or making up things. For three years, virtually since we met, my second husband and I have been exploring the world of swinging, starting with meetings with other couples, progressing to visits to swinger clubs, occasional encounters with several men— and in recent months, our sex parties.

His fantasies revolve around horny, excitable women who enjoy sex, women excited by men, most good-looking men, simply the fact of their maleness. He's a charter member of an Internet community that translates as "wives fucked by other men." I dream of having my body, my orgasms the center of all attention. Before we met—my first phase as a single woman in a decade, early years for the Internet—I cruised the net for pictures of three- or more-somes with a predominance of men, looking at the women's ecstatic expressions as they reveled in the men surrounding them. I love men, how they feel, how they move, how they laugh, how they make love. And in the right mood, I can find every touch I receive fabulous.

Perhaps you imagine my position on the swing to be help-less, vulnerable, but what I feel at such moments is power: My sensations control the scene. My lust determines the tempo and intensity of what goes on. And I can't call up lust at will: The atmosphere has to be conducive to it, I need to feel attrac-tive and well turned out, Jens and I need to be attuned to each other. At parties like these, no one gets what they've come for if I don't enjoy myself, so they're all attentive to my every inhalation and moan. And I have what may be a new response to the feminist questions: "Is someone getting used here? Is someone objectifying someone else?" Having enjoyed myself at quite a few parties, hoping there are more to come, my take is that at an orgy—at the ones I prefer there are several men to each woman—the traditional tables are turned: Female excite-ment, female desires set the tempo, determine the mood. Men become interchangeable. If one can't keep going any more, having shot his load early on or overwhelmed by the insignifi-cance of his own personal sexuality in the larger scheme of things, another takes his place. There are minimum standards: The man needs to be clean, polite, and not physically unpleas-ant. Once he has met these criteria, a man just needs to fit into the crowd without much ado. Of course the male candidates suitable for these parties have personalities and lives outside this place—but for the length of the party, they have in fact been turned into objects. They need to be willing to let female sexuality, female response take front stage. They need to func-tion—and not be unpleasant.

I'm a sexual being, very heterosexual, fascinated by men's bodies and their sexuality, practically insatiable. As long as I can remember I've been saying to my lovers "Do it again" right after they come in or on me. I've also repeatedly fantasized about being the center of attention in a room full of men. A starting point was often the scene from Woody Allen's *Sleeper* where Woody and Diane Keaton stand around the surgical table in an operating theater, compelled to pretend they're surgeons but totally clueless, and repeat the nonsensical formula "cloning the nose, cloning the nose." I substitute myself naked with legs bound open for the nose on the operating table, a sexualized atmosphere for the clinical (and silly) one. Observers in both the room itself and the upper galleries behind glass are all riveted to watching my unending stream of response to sexual stimuli, my orgasms.

Before I met Jens, I had for several years a colorful, sometimes exciting, often lonely sex life. You could say the same about my college and postcollege years. In between these two periods, I lived unhappily (and monogamously) with one man for more than nine years. All this time, my fantasies revolved around two, often three unidentified men who were attentive to my excitement and good to me. This was not something I had an easy or self-assured hold on. I've often imposed rules on my fantasies. As a teenager, I trained myself to depersonify the guys in them: I'd decided it was too dangerous to think of specific high school boys—after all, something could happen. Later, I tried to ban fantasies from the marriage bed. I decided it was morally reprehensible if I ever thought of anyone else (neighbor or movie star) while touching my husband. I took to masturbating in secret when he'd fallen asleep next to me. He didn't see why I might want to play with myself after he'd just come inside me—"Wasn't I good enough for you?" Nor was I comfortable with the one-night stands or flings over several weeks I had in the years before and after. Repeatedly, I'd followed a whim, a mood, an exchange of flirty looks and remarks, had great sex, and awakened to the knowledge: I shouldn't have done this. This reaction was not religious or even ethical, nor was it some kind of disgust at lust. It was just that I usually had a boyfriend—often working in another city, sometimes across the ocean. Usually we had an unspoken pact of fidelity. Often I broke it. Never did I feel good about myself afterward. My underlying thought was . . . my partner will be upset with me; I'm no longer worthy of his trust. And when I was single, my sexual partners tended to be friends, colleagues, acquaintances—I'm no devotee of singles bars. I never knew how I was going to face the colleague at work the next day, how the old friend and I would work this one through.

What confused me most about the adventures I had was my nagging feeling that I had to examine each attraction I acted on to determine whether this could be a great relationship. I hated the uncomfortable talks around the subject in the days and weeks that followed. I wrote letters about longing to be with someone again. I filled journal entries with tormented effusions about trying to choose between the out-of-town boyfriend and the old friend who'd become a local lover. Had there been a permissible modus for occasionally landing in bed with someone I liked, I would have been so much happier with myself!

In my partnership with my husband, I have been wonderfully surprised about our sharing and intimacy. Everything we undertake we do together. The space we've created between us is quiet and safe, easy. It's probably unusual that one intrinsic component of our intimacy is an open approach to sharing our sexuality with others. Of course we love when it's just the two of us. But every six weeks or so we find the time and the inclination to undertake something with others. In between we talk a lot about what we've experienced, the candidates he has dug up for me on the Internet, our fantasies, fragments of our shared sexual experience that don't let us go. And we make love, of course, sometimes one of us with a gentle persistence if the other is already falling asleep, sometimes both with the wild abandon of when we just met.

We have found some similarities among couples who are active on the swinging scene. He is not jealous of her past boyfriends but rather intrigued by the richness of what she has experienced. He likes horny women in general and is confident of his sexual prowess, quite sure it won't let him down. He often uses certain organizational skills, since there's lots to be done with maintaining mailing lists, screening candidates, setting up websites, keeping up a network. She has an uncomplicated relationship to her own sexuality, comes easily and

often, is open to new experience. She has few hang-ups; if
there are practices she doesn't like, she clearly articulates that.
I haven't observed many perfectly accessorized classic beau-
ties, but many women confident of their attractiveness, at ease
in their bodies. These are often second marriages, and the partners have reached a certain maturity about themselves and
each other. All involved may be between forty and fifty, sometimes younger, the men occasionally older.

In our early days on the scene we heard about "women
who've been talked into it" or "wives whose arms have been
twisted." We kept our eyes open for these creatures, these suf-
fering women, putting up with alien pawing men to rescue
their marriages . . . until we determined they were a myth,
propagated perhaps by lonely men inhabiting the fringes of
the scene. If a couple chooses to go to clubs, meet other couples they've communicated with on the Internet, attend or
throw sex parties—it's fine with her. Most of the men have a
dominant side, a joy in seeing their women in a state of excitement caused by others. This may in fact be a strategy to cope
with the women's lively sexuality: "I'd rather be with her while
she fools around and gets off on new men than have her go
behind my back."

In real life it's not that I dream of sleeping with every man
I meet. I'm very discerning about people's use of words, their
interest in what I have to say, their responsiveness, their self-
awareness and ability to notice how they affect others. I'm
more often instinctively turned off by strangers than turned-
on. I first observe how they interact, not necessarily with me,
but with others—at a meeting, on the bus, wherever. I also
watch how men look at women, where their gaze lingers, what
sort of looks they exchange among themselves. Unless something convinces me otherwise, I'm not interested in
overweight or sloppy or loud men. But this discerning
thoughtfulness, this self-conscious filtering, gets turned off in
the right sexually exciting situation. And that's how it's been
since I was seventeen—I'm so responsive to sexual attention

that hits me the right way that I stop the excessive thinking.

A friend has asked me: Do you become friends with these couples, these men that you allow to touch your body? She was quite upset when I said, "No, friendship works differently. These are acquaintances of convenience, people we share one set of interests with. That doesn't mean I want to invite them to dinner parties and Sunday tea." She found it hard to picture one would even spend time with people one wouldn't want to meet in a café, that one didn't even really like. Her other question was expressed with even more consternation: "How could you possibly let a man touch you if you're not in love with him, if you don't at least think you could love him? Men can separate love and sex, but women can't—it's not in their nature!" Oh, but we can!

What if I hadn't met Jens? What if I'd stumbled from one mediocre relationship to the next, gradually making better choices about whose arms I landed in, until I decided to live with someone or get married again? Even if he was able to tolerate my past (it's hard to imagine now I thought I'd found someone progressive a few years back where the guy said, "I don't care if you slept with one hundred men before we met, the main thing is that you're with me now"), it's rather unlikely that he would have Jens' proclivities. If I could be open about loving sex with this imaginary partner, make sexual innuendoes, occasionally admit I found someone attractive— would that be enough of a sex focus so I could get what I need?

I'm not sure anymore. I love that we jointly discovered the swinger world. If he had pushed me into it, I'm not sure it would have worked. His angle, of course, is somewhat different from mine: He's constantly on the Internet describing how hot I am. As a result, he's in contact with the male halves of couples or the single men intrigued by horny women in general. I don't go through pictures on the Internet—I'm not very visual anyway. But I do love that my partner is fascinated with my sexuality, with women's sexuality in general. I've known many men for whom their own erections and orgasms *were* sexuality: Looking at breasts or touching a woman was a nice way to trigger their own responses, but what made women hot was not particularly interesting.

Sometimes we attend others' parties. There's much less ado about setting up the place and organizing enough guys (as there are always no-shows at the last minute), much less say in the overall atmosphere and the overall selection of people. We know a couple who charge a fair amount of money for an open-ended evening at their home that starts with an elegant, several-course dinner, usually eaten on one's lap in the living room in a state of half-undress, and ends with sessions in the heated outdoor pool, the sauna, the specially prepared oil room, or in the two party cellars, mattresses wall-to-wall, dim, slightly orange lighting, several wall mirrors, a "stretcher" covered in leather.

A warm swimming pool in a big backyard with hedges blocking it from the neighbors. A cool summer evening with many stars above. Temperature difference between air and water great enough that it's delightful to climb into the pool. I lean on my husband, my back to his chest, and observe the action around us: One man is providing support to a young woman so she can lean back and let another man bury his face between her legs. The two together are combining forces to bring her to a peak of excitement. Looking in my eyes to see if it's okay, the first guy reaches out toward me. Once I've wriggled Jens' growing cock between my legs, my ass cheeks firmly in his hands, I turn so the other guy's hand is around my left breast and reach to squeeze his cock. He immediately starts moving in my hand, setting a tempo faster than I would have at first and rapidly swelling up. When he has ceased holding up the other woman, he gives me his full attention and is soon finger-fucking me. As my excitement arises, Jens plays with my breasts, the other guy opens my legs and pulls me toward him. Because this is all taking place underwater, the moves are not sudden, but rather smooth and purposeful. The concentrated attention of the two of them has a wild effect on me: I'm full of abandon, concentrating only on pushing over the edge to orgasm. The visitor pushes himself between my legs and moves fast in a muffled underwater way. I come through his sheer presence inside me, then he does, and we nuzzle a bit at each other's necks. I turn my body to my husband, who's throbbing with excitement, eager to mingle his cock with the juices of the unknown lover. After his orgasm—rapid and intense, a third man, a huge guy named Peter, climbs into the pool and purposely walks toward me. He is quickly inside me, and he goes on for a tremendously long time. I don't understand it myself but I have one orgasm after another, like a string of firecrackers. Three men are around me, delighting in my intensity, whispering I should try to stay a bit quiet not to awaken the neighbors . . .

Shoe Shines

by Debra Gray De Noux

my wife loves to flash strange men. Since our wedding, I have taken a bunch of sexy pictures of Donna, in various states of undress, in various public places around town. We always started with her dressed up, then she would end up half naked, sitting on a park bench, flashing her breasts and panties to strangers. Then we'd go home, make love, and talk about the men who had been watching her.

Living in the big city provided us with the right atmosphere for sexy photography, and an ample supply of public places. One bright spring day, we strolled into a small, out-of-the-way park, on another of our jaunts. Donna was wearing her shortest denim miniskirt with a white blouse she'd unbuttoned to reveal a healthy view of her ample cleavage. My new Nikon was dangling from my shoulder.

Donna looked especially pretty that day. Applying a little more makeup than usual, she'd curled her long dark brown hair. At twenty-four, she never looked better. Her body had matured enough that her breasts were fuller now, and her legs were as fine as they were when I met her at nineteen.

Walking across the bridge just inside the park, we passed a shoe shiner. The young man gave Donna a good look up and down before asking, "Shine?"

It was like a light bulb going off above my head. I grabbed my wife's hand and told the man, "Yeah. Shine her shoes."

We went under the bridge to a wrought-iron bench next to one of the park's canals, where Donna sat. Even with her knees together, I could see right up her skirt to her white panties. The shoe shiner, whose name was Eddie, noticed too. He was a thin man, twenty-two years old, with large brown eyes behind a pair of black-framed glasses.

Donna gave me a sly wink, when I positioned Eddie's shoe-shine box very close to my wife's knees, so she'd have to lift her knee extra high in order to place her foot on the box. Backing up, I grabbed my camera and said, "All right, now put your foot up and Eddie can do his thing."

As soon as Donna lifted her right knee, the entire front of her panties came clearly into view. I moved around and snapped pictures. I watched Eddie, whose face was only a few feet from Donna's panties. My wife leaned back and smiled at me. I photographed the growing pleasure on Donna's face as the bulge in my pants grew. Donna's panties were very sheer, enough to give a generous view of her dark pubic hair.

When Eddie finished her right shoe, Donna dropped her foot and replaced it with her left. I motioned for her to move her right leg more to the right. Leaning her arms along the back of the bench, Donna slowly opened her legs. Her panties were so skimpy, a great deal of her dark, silky pubic hair was sticking out the sides. I was getting very hot.

So was Donna. Eddie, who was no longer pretending not to look, was staring right between her legs.

Just as I snapped another shot, Donna lifted her right leg and threw it over the arm of the bench. She had to readjust her butt, and worked at pulling up the sides of her tight denim skirt. Then she slowly unbuttoned her blouse.

She was at the last button when a homeless man walked by and stopped behind Eddie. The homeless man blinked several times and said, "Damn, that's a good lookin' woman."

"Thank you," Donna said as she undid her last button and opened her blouse.

Eddie had stopped shining. The homeless man nearly

stopped breathing. I quickly focused on my wife's exposed breasts and snapped away. I told her not to move, as I stepped around and shot her from different angles, careful to make sure I got the two excited faces in the pictures.

Donna was on a roll now. No longer looking at me, she stared at Eddie's face as she slightly leaned forward and completely removed her blouse, dropping it on the bench. I clicked away, my erection throbbing in my pants. The large round nipples of my wife's full breasts looked hard and pointy.

Donna was far from finished. Leaning back, she reached down and worked her skirt up. Then she tucked her fingers into the top of her panties and began to pull them down. She had to close her knees to get them off. But two seconds later, she had her legs open again, her right leg tossed over the bench's arm, her left leg dangling on the far side of the shoe-shine box.

I was taking pictures at a furious pace as my wife sat there, naked except for the skirt bunched up at her waist, and spread-eagled, in front of the two men. Moving in close, I took several pictures of her pink slit, of her large bush and her erect nipples, of the turned-on look on my wife's face.

Then I heard something overhead and saw a policeman crossing the bridge.

"Donna," I said, running my index finger across my throat in our prearranged cutthroat signal. I headed directly for the cop, to cut him off, in case he came around the side of the bridge. I planned to ask enough stupid questions to give Donna time to dress. The policeman went in the opposite direction. When I stepped back, my wife was standing and buttoning up her blouse.

It was a close call. I grabbed Donna's hand and thanked the men for posing with her.

"My pleasure," the homeless man said, still blinking.

Eddie stepped closer and said, "My Uncle Felix owns that shoe-shine parlor right over there." He pointed across St. Philip Street to a brown wooden building.

We were moving away. Donna turned back and told Eddie, "We'll pay him a visit, someday."

"But you owe me five dollars for the shine."

Donna and I both laughed and Eddie agreed, adding, "Just kiddin'. But please come by my Uncle Felix's. Okay?"

Donna waved and nodded.

"Where are your panties?" I asked Donna when she climbed in and I could see was still naked beneath her skirt.

"I gave them to Eddie."

God, that made me so HOT! It had the same effect on Donna, who grabbed my crotch several times on our way back home. We didn't wait to get into bed. We made love on the living room floor. Donna was a wild woman, especially when I started telling her stuff like, "This is what Eddie wanted to do to your, right on the bench."

She grabbed my butt and rocked against me.

"You'd like Eddie to be doing this to you right now."

She continued to nod.

I pulled my erection out of her and she gasped.

"They were looking right here." I pushed myself back in and she cried out.

After, we talked about Eddie and the homeless man and how their eyes had roamed over every pore of her naked body. Climbing atop me, for seconds, Donna said, "We should visit Uncle Felix's. Soon."

We went the next Saturday. Donna put on the mocha lipstick that I like so much. She climbed into a slinky white dress that had buttons running down the entire front. She let me unbutton the dress to make it low cut and high enough to almost see her bush. She also wore black high heels and nothing else. In the bright sun, I could see her nipples clearly through the dress, as well as the dark hair between her legs.

Uncle Felix's Shoe Shine Parlor was in a beat-up wooden building alongside Armstrong Park. It had two benches inside, next to several shoe-shine boxes. It also had an interior courtyard. When Donna and I stepped in, we were met by Eddie. His face was priceless. He looked like a little boy at Mardi Gras. His mouth was in a wide "O," his eyes nearly as wide.

He introduced us to his Uncle Felix and I shook the man's large hand. Felix was a huge man, about 6'5" tall, and muscular. His hand nearly completely engulfed mine. He appeared to be in his forties, but was in great shape. He was also completely bald. Felix was wearing a pair of blue jeans. That's it. He was bare-chested and barefoot.

I began to explain how we wanted to take some pictures, but I don't know if Felix was listening. He was hawking out Donna, looking her up and down as she walked by.

"Oh," my wife cooed, "this is perfect." She moved straight into the courtyard, to a large barber's chair. Donna put her purse aside and climbed into the chair.

Felix grabbed a shoe-shine box and walked into the courtyard. I followed, removing the lens cap of my camera as I moved. Donna sat up straight and uncrossed her legs. Felix sat on his shoebox and tapped the metal foot brace with his hand.

Donna lifted her right knee high and placed her foot on the metal brace. I was about to tell her to unbutton her dress more, when she did it on her own. She didn't stop at one button; she undid her dress all the way, dropping the dress from her shoulders. Then she leaned back.

I moved around to get some good shots, when Eddie tapped my shoulder. He pointed to several high windows overlooking the courtyard and said, "People live there."

"Let them look." I went back to my camera. Eddie moved next to his uncle, as I photographed the entire scene, the dark faces of the men as they leered at my wife's body, the excited look on Donna's face as she sat there naked in that sunny courtyard on that high barber's chair.

Slowly, Felix shined my wife's right shoe, his eyes moving from the shoe up her legs to her bush and then up to her breasts and back again, as if each part of Donna held a special magnetism for his eyes.

Eddie's eyes were also roaming over my wife's body. Donna's

eyes moved from Eddie's face to his uncle's and back again.

When Felix finished Donna's right shoe, he lightly touched her calf. Donna moved her right leg aside and put her left foot on the foot brace. In one smooth movement she continued moving her right leg, draping it over the arm of the chair. Felix, his face remaining stiff and serious, stared right between Donna's legs, at her pink, wide-open slit. Eddie continued smiling. I could see he was breathing heavier. I know I was, as I snapped away.

When Felix finished buffing Donna's left shoe, he leaned back. Donna moved her left knee aside, raising it to drape her left leg over the left arm of the chair. MY GOD! My erection was throbbing as I photographed my wide-open wife and the two faces only a few feet away.

Donna was biting her lower lip now as she squirmed. I looked at Felix and his face hadn't changed. He looked so serious as he stared at Donna's slit. Eddie was acting as jumpy as I was.

Then Donna lifted her butt and looked up at Eddie and told him to pull her dress out from under her. He did eagerly. As Donna let her butt back down, Felix reached his hands under her butt, his palms open.

Donna hesitated a second before sinking down on Felix's hands. I watched this large man kneading my wife's ass and ever so slowly, pulling her toward him.

Donna edged forward. Felix nodded and said, "Don't let your knees fall."

My wife grabbed the arms of the chair and sank back as Felix continued to pull her ass to the front edge of the chair. Then he stopped. I inched around for a better shot, tapping Eddie on the shoulder so we could both get a good view of the action.

Donna's eyes were watching Felix's stern face as he continued kneading her butt. Then, I noticed his thumbs moving around to rub against the bottom of my wife's pussy. Donna bit her lower lip again. I readjusted my erection and gave it a good rub. Eddie noticed and began rubbing his crotch also.

"You like this?" Felix asked, his stare moving up to Donna's face.

My wife nodded as her chest rose and her breathing increased.

"You like this better?" Felix has moved his thumbs to the front of her pussy and began massaging her.

Donna closed her eyes and nodded. Her hips moved against Felix's thumbs. I was so hot I wanted to yank myself out and impale my wife right there. But this was Felix and Donna's show.

Felix pulled his left hand out from under Donna, leaving his right hand beneath her, his thumb sinking into her now. He stood and unzipped his jeans and worked them off his hips. He had a huge erection, which was standing straight up. When I say huge, I mean it. It was the thickest penis I'd ever seen. As his jeans fell to his knees, he leaned forward and began to rub his long shaft up and down the outside of Donna's pussy.

The man was going to fuck my wife right there. I swear, I couldn't breathe. My heart was pounding in my ears. Our game had gone full circle. I was about to watch, to photograph this stranger screw Donna. I thought I'd cum in my jeans!

"You like this?" Felix asked, his voice deepening.

"OH, YES!"

Donna opened her eyes and nodded. She rubbed herself back against him. I photographed Felix's cock as it slid up and down the mouth of Donna's wet pussy.

Dipping slightly, Felix pulled back and then moved forward, pressing the tip of his swollen cock into Donna. I got a clear picture of the long shaft as it sank into her. My wife cried out and stopped her gyrating. Slowly, Felix worked himself into Donna, until his black pubic hair was pressed against hers. Then he began a long grinding ride of my wife.

Donna began to grind back, gasping as this huge man fucked her. Felix grabbed Donna's breasts, squeezing them as he screwed her. My wife bounced, her mouth open. When she cried out again and shuddered, I knew she'd climaxed. Felix

continued his long grind. Donna pushed her hair out of her
eyes and moved to catch up with Felix.

"I'm gonna cum in you, baby!"

"YES. YES!"

"OHHH!" Felix began to move his ass in spasms as he shot
his load into Donna. It was fantastic, watching this, being able
to photograph it and not missing a shot. I still had two expo-
sures left on my 36-exposure roll when Felix pulled himself out
of Donna. I passed my camera to Eddie and moved between
my wife's legs. Unzipping myself quickly, I pulled my cock out
and sank it into her soaking pussy.

Donna moved her legs from atop the arms as I sank on her
and rode her good and hard. I kissed her mouth and sucked
her breasts and kissed her neck. She was still breathing heavy
and came again as she made love to me, and I exploded in her.
"Oh, baby," I cried.

She didn't have a chance to catch her breath. As soon as I
moved off, Eddie stepped up. He was enormous too. He
moved himself between my wife's legs and slowly impaled her.
Donna gasped, reached around to grab Eddie's butt and
smiled at him. I could see perspiration along the sides of her
face. She looked so sexy!

I had to hurry to change the film, so I wouldn't miss Eddie
and Donna. Looking up a moment, I saw several faces in the
high windows overhead, faces half hidden in shadow. It gave
me an extra thrill.

Unlike his uncle, Eddie was much more loving in his lovemaking. He kissed my wife and played with her breasts and her
ass with his fingers as he made love to her.

When he came, I got a good shot of the cum oozing from
Donna as his balls slammed against her butt. Eddie gently
climbed off Donna and immediately asked if he could get her
something to drink.

"And a towel," my wife gasped, closing her eyes.

I snapped a picture of her lying in the large chair, spread-
eagle.

Eddie returned with a hot towel and several cold soft drinks. We each had a cold drink as Donna wiped herself. I took more pictures of the scene, of the two naked men and my naked wife, sipping their drinks in the sunny courtyard.

I noticed Donna trying to get up. Felix stood and moved to her. He already had a half erection. He helped my wife from the chair and, with his hands on her hips, he turned her around and bent Donna over at the waist. Then he began to rub his long shaft up and down the crack of her butt. I moved to get a better shot. Donna craned her neck back and closed her eyes.

When Felix was hard enough, he bent his knees and sank into my wife's pussy, making love to her doggie-style. Donna grabbed the arm of the barber chair and spread her feet for balance.

"Come here," Felix said to his nephew. Eddie obeyed.

"Get under there and suck this girl's titties while I'm fuckin' her."

Eddie slipped under my wife and began to suck her nipples. Felix's large hands had a lock on my Donna's waist as he pounded against her. I was getting hard as I took pictures of this scene. It was quite a sight, those three at it. In the middle of the action, Donna turned to my camera and smiled.

This time Felix cried out and grunted as he came. Pulling away, he stumbled back and sank to the ground. Donna moved to me and draped her arms around my neck and said, "Let's go."

"But I want seconds," I said.

She laughed, "Later."

I helped her to the barber chair and then gathered my clothes. Donna didn't move. As I dressed, I looked again at the windows and they were now filled with faces beaming down at my naked wife. Once dressed, I picked up my wife's dress. Eddie, who had also dressed, scooped Donna into his arms and carried her out to the car. Still naked, she wrapped her arms around his neck and kissed him as he carried her.

I hurried out and unlocked the door. People were coming

out of the house next-door now. I saw several men and some women leaning out to look.

Eddie gingerly placed Donna into the front passenger seat. When he stepped back, Donna reached over and unlocked the back door.

"Get in," she told Eddie.

I moved to the driver's side, started up our car, and drove home. Parking in our garage, I unlocked the door as Eddie carried my naked wife into our house. Thank God we have a garage. I couldn't imagine our neighbors catching sight of Eddie and Donna.

Once inside, Donna immediately began to remove Eddie's clothes. I put a new roll of film in my Nikon. Donna brought Eddie into our bedroom, sat him on our bed and then went down on him. I moved around to get some good shots of his shaft moving in and out of my wife's mouth. Then I moved around and unzipped my pants and put it to Donna doggie-style. I couldn't wait. Eddie came first, and I pulled out so I wouldn't miss the picture of the cum dripping from Donna's mouth. Then I rolled her on the bed next to Eddie and made love to her face to face, French-kissing her sweet mouth.

Eddie spent the night and Sunday with us. He screwed my wife six more times, in various positions, in different rooms of our house. I made love to Donna six more times also. It was the most exhausting, exciting, satisfying weekend of our sex life. Nothing has ever excited me more than Donna having two men in her at once, me in her mouth while Eddie was in her pussy, and then vice versa.

Later, with Donna in my arms, my wife told me how much she loved every titillating second of that weekend. When I looked at her face, she never looked lovelier.

Sausage Making for Couples

by Joy VanNuys

Really, why does anyone get married? Leaving aside the religious, the old-fashioned, the head-over-heels, in this age of living together, marriage is usually a way out. A way to ensure that the sleeping around will stop, or won't start. A promise that there's something beyond picking up his dirty socks and clipping her ingrown toenails and fighting over the pay-per-view porn bill. A good excuse, in that long stretch between valentines and anniversary, for sudden, fierce romance. And everyone else seems to think that it's time, that in fact it's long overdue, so you spend two weeks in mad love with your secret plans, hustle your best friends out of work, and take the subway down to city hall. He brings flowers, and there are tears in your eyes when you make those promises. You're off the market. There is a piece of paper that confirms your love. Back in the apartment you've shared for four years, is there a special sheen to the face in the mirror? Are the sheets extra soft for your wedding night? As you gobble the leftover carrot cake your impromptu maid of honor has baked, the taste of jealousy in every bite, do you look into his eyes and wonder if this is the man you wanted? How is the sex that night, with your wife? Is she suddenly laundry and bills and insurance policies or is she tastier than ever because she's all yours? Will this bring back the spark that's been missing for months, maybe even years?

Why does anyone sign up for a Sausage Making for Couples class? See above. Because, face it, the nights are long.

I meet him outside the school. He gives me a tiny, dry kiss.

"Hi, honey, how was your day?" I choke out this sentence every night without flinching.

"Okay. Busy. How long does this thing go on? I have a ton of paperwork."

"It's three hours, including eating time."

"Jesus. Okay. Where do we go?"

"Can you at least try to have a good time, Josh?"

Josh. It must be the worst name in the world. It's not sexy. It sounds stupid when you cry it out in passion. Josh. It means to joke around, to josh someone. He might as well be named Ignore, Browbeat, Pout. No rhythm, no syllables, no long *iiis* or *eees* to stretch out. *Jo-o-o-o-o-sh* sounds like a car motor that won't turn over. Joshua is slightly better, at least for vowel content, but he won't allow this, so Josh it is. Mostly I just avoid saying his name at all. Yet this name is the one that for four years has meant: him. Lover, boyfriend, other, and now, suddenly, husband.

I stopped home to put on jeans and a T-shirt. Josh is still in his suit from the office, but I have a pair of jeans and a T-shirt for him to change into. Actually, they're mine, but who would know? We both have the same no-hips, no-ass bodies and the very slight bulge of my non-bosom is made up for by the some-what broadness of his shoulders. Our hair is blond, our eyes are blue. We have been accused of looking like a Gap ad. On the subway once, a drunk asked us, "Are you brother and sister?" "Nope," I told him. "Well, then, are you farmers?" "Yes, we're farmers. Fuck off," Josh said. "What's the big deal?" I murmured. "Whatever," he told me, opening his newspaper.

As soon as we step out of the elevator, I realize that I have guessed wrong. All the women in the room have done their hair, put on makeup, slipped into low-cut blouses, short skirts, heels. To make sausage? The men are mostly in suits, ties untied and white shirts open a few buttons. I look like a dock worker. Dammit.

A large man with a salt-and-pepper beard and a tall white hat steps over to us. "I'm Chef Harvey! Welcome to Sausage Making for Couples!"

"Thanks. I'm Jane and this is . . ." Josh has already moved toward the bar that is set up in one corner of the room. "That's my husband, Josh."

"It'll take awhile before our sausage is made, but we've got lots of varieties for you to try if you're hungry," Chef Harvey says.

Confession. I'm actually squeamish about anything other than white-meat chicken. I've always pretended to be more adventurous about food than I really am. After all these years, Josh doesn't know that I don't eat red meat. I'll come home and say oh yeah, I ate a meatball hero for lunch, think I'll just have salad tonight, tell tales of pepperoni pizzas consumed while he was away on a business trip. Reading the course catalog, I was hypnotized by the exotic names: andouille, braunschweiger, chorizo. It never occurred to me that I'd have to touch it, much less eat it.

"C'mon, just try a slice of salami. Made it myself," he tells me.

I smile and take a tiny sliver from the tray he's holding out. "Thanks!" I slip it under my tongue and look around for a napkin to spit it into.

Greasy. Slick. And who would have thought that beards were so sexy? I bring a finger to his lips and tickle them gently, caress the prickly edge of his moustache. I slide off his checked chef's pants and stroke his hairy ass, reach beneath his generous belly to hold the solid eggs of his balls. His pubic hair is gray and soft as fur, and as I pet it, I feel his prick gently perk from soft to hard, filling up with meat. A drop of saliva falls from my open mouth onto the tip, instantly lubricating him as I smooth his wrinkles, letting every bit of cock harden to its full potential. Encircling the base with two firm fingers, my other hand begins to tease, working up, over, and down. "Chicken salad, I'll make for you every night," he tells me, panting. "The breast poached in spring water, homemade mayonnaise, celery like pearls . . ." I work him faster, pump-

ing hard, the meat of his cock expanding to stretch and fill the
space. Driven by the need to make him harder, ever harder,
my other hand cups his balls, teases his thighs, and explores
the crack of his ass. "On sourdough toast . . . a slice of ripe
*August tomato . . . baby butter lettuce . . ."

I guess I swallowed it. My mouth is empty, and he is gone,
moved on to another couple. Okay. Never felt quite that way
about old fat cooks before. A short dry spell in the bedroom,
and now I have a Chef Boyardee fetish?

I join Josh at the bar and accept an apron from a waitress,
happy to cover my stiff nipples. I cross my legs, willing away
the rush of warmth. We stand and stare out at the room, watching other people interact.

A woman struggles to tie her apron in back. A tall man in
shirtsleeves comes up behind her. He smoothes her skirt over
her hips, then finishes the knot for her. She turns.

"Hi, I'm Brenda."

"Bob. Nice to meet you." They kiss each other's cheeks.

"How's it going?" two women ask each other, and sink into
a long, lingering hug. Fingers stroke buttocks, wine flows from
one mouth to another.

Okay, who, exactly, is with whom here? Is "for couples" a
code that I don't know about? This is a cooking school, for
god's sake. But there is something in the air, lust and meat. I
wonder at the wisdom of having an open wine bar in the same
room with a mammoth meat grinder. Is there something more
dangerous than the possibility of trichinosis going on here?

A young woman in a chef's jacket and checked pants joins
us. "I'm Kim, the sous chef." I take in her spiky black hair, note
the pink undertone. Her face has several telltale holes, unfilled
piercings. Must be some kind of kitchen regulation.

"This one is mortadella," she tells us, holding out a tray of
what looks like baloney speckled with nuts and peppercorns.
"It's very smooth. I think you'll like it."

Josh takes two rolled slices.

"I'll just take a nibble of his," I tell her, hoping to avoid this odd lunchmeat, but he holds it to my mouth and she stands there, waiting.

The tiniest nibble, like a mouse. Reaching inside her white jacket, I slide down her red satin camisole, lick the pale pink of her nipple. It is pierced with a hard stud, faceted like a peppercorn, pricking my taste buds. I knock the metal rod between my teeth as I suck her whole tit into my mouth, making her beg me to stop, to go slower. "Jesus, be gentle with me." I slide the jacket off her shoulders, and pull off the camisole. "Raise your arms over your head," I tell her. "Show me your tits." Cupping both in my hands, I weigh them, bouncing them up and down, then twist the tips just until she squeals. Seeking flavor, I slide off her pants, shuck off her panties. She is afraid, so I have to hold her hands down. "Jane, please. I don't know if I . . ." Those red silk panties look so hot in her mouth, not a gag exactly, but they shut her up for now. I move my face between her thighs, spread her lips gently. I inhale her scent, brush her thighs with my soft cheek. Her salty flesh is so yielding between my sharp incisors, the tiny bud of her erection so sweet. I lay my tongue flat and lap at her like a cow at a brook, drinking in my pale-lipped goddess drop by drop.

I turn and look at Josh. Is he tasting what I'm tasting?

"Josh, are you . . . ?"

"Hi, I'm Omar," I hear. I look—yes, this large, tan hunk is talking to me.

"Jane," I say, reaching out my hand and crashing it into his solid pecs, which have suddenly come lower, closer. He kisses my cheek, rubs it roughly with stubble, leaving his scent behind in my nostrils. I check to see if Josh has noticed, but he is being hello-hugged by a woman with big brown eyes, soft hips in a single-sleeved shirt. From one side it looks as if she wears nothing under her apron. She is Charlene, Omar's girl-friend.

"Okay, class, let's gather around," Chef Harvey tells us. I pour another quick glass of wine, and join the class, circling around a large stainless-steel table. "Now we're all here to have a good time, right? So what I'd like to do is give you a quick rundown of how sausage is made, then I'll assign groups to take over the different tasks at hand." Josh pulls out a notebook and begins to write down everything Chef Harvey says.

"Forcemeat," I watch him write. "Progressive grinding. Emulsification. Fat 25-30 percent."

Is that doodle in the margin a sausage? "Josh," I whisper in his ear. "You know, that kind of looks like . . ."

Chef Harvey clears his throat loudly and glares at me. "TCM, or tinted cure mix," he explains, "is used as a preservative in fresh sausages. It keeps the color nice, prevents browning. It's also known as saltpeter, a popular seasoning in prisons and prep schools. Keeps your pecker soft, they say." The class roars, and I flush, glancing at Josh. "TCM," he writes. "AKA saltpeter."

Funny how married sex turns into shorthand for real sex. You put your hand here, and I'll put my lips there, and five minutes later, we'll switch. Put it in, oh that feels so good, do it, do it, good night, sleep tight. The word newlywed used to be sexy. Not when you're newly wed after four years of living together.

Josh, Jane, Omar, and Charlene. We are the fat mincers. I had pictured Josh and me working together from start to finish, the two of us making something happen for a change. This class is supposed to be a metaphor, a way to add spice to the disgusting ground pork fat and stinking meat of our relationship, force it into a stiff skin, tie it up tight and let it poach until it becomes something else, something palatable, even tasty. It could have been worse, I guess. Another foursome has been assigned the liver grinding. I grab a cutting board and begin to mince the thick white pork fat. It's lettuce, I tell myself. It's jicama. It's . . . disgusting. The grinders pass by with a large container of what looks like a thick pink liver milkshake.

"I'm going to grab a cracker," I tell Josh. The snack table is crowded with people. Who knew there were still so many carnivores in this fat-phobic city? A room of twenty people and no one is demurring, asking for a salad, dressing on the side.

Everyone is in love with meat. I search for cheese, tofu, carrot sticks, among the varying sizes and shapes of sausage laid out before me.

Omar has followed me. I crane my neck to see past the vast planes of his chest, up to his vaguely Asian almond eyes, wide smile.

"Nice ass," he tells me, as I lean over the table.

"I have no ass. Just like my husband," I tell him.

"Yeah, but it looks better on you. Close your eyes and open your mouth," he tells me.

The idea of being fed anything brings back the specter of wedding cake, makes me want to choke. Okay, I can handle anything for a second. I can always just swallow it. It's just meat. Don't complain. Don't tell him you don't want it.

I put my head back, close my eyes, open my mouth in what I hope is a non-dental-exam way.

His hand brushes my breast as he reaches for my mouth. "Soppressata," he whispers, as I feel my tongue begin to sting. "Hot Italian sausage."

A platter of cocks is presented to me, garnished with cornichons, pickled onions, and ramekins of mustard. Straight and curved, narrow and thick, they beckon to me. Do me, baby. Suck it, bitch. Take it, Jane. Take me all the way. I select a meaty specimen, firm and strong, suckably lean. I sink to my knees, cup it in my hand, feel its heft. Raising it to my tongue, I lick, long and slow. Tease the knot at the tip, then press it past my lips. I feel the hot pepper burning my gums, and I push it in deeper, hoping to work up some cooling saliva. Rub it on my inner cheek, scraping and grinding, working it down my throat. I gag a little, then realize that this meat is alive, attached, sprouting hard from between two smooth tan thighs. "Oh, you have an ass all right, girl. Don't make me prove it to you," Omar tells me. "Shake it for me. Show me." I twitch my hips back and forth, draw harder on the shaft, trying to resist the temptation to bite, to chew. I feel a gush of hot fluid down my throat, unctuous, fatty, hot. Swallow, swallow, swallow.

I shake my head, clearing the vision, though my tongue is still filmed with fat. I catch Chef Harvey's eye and he smiles.

"Jane? Would you and Charlene be our stuffers, please?" Chef Harvey asks. I look down at the large bowl of mottled pink meat he is offering me, and feel the hot pepper of the sausage I've just eaten reenter the back of my throat.

"I'll do the yucky part," Charlene says, smiling at me.

"Okay, I guess," I say, looking around for Josh. He is at the snack table, his back to me.

"Sausage stuffing is a two-person operation," Chef Harvey begins, handing us both latex gloves. "You need a pusher and a receiver." He positions us at either end of a tabletop metal device. "Now, Charlene, all you need to do is scoop the force-meat into the top and push it down with the pusher. Jane, your job is a little harder." He holds up two long, flat tubes. "Who knows what these are?"

"Guts?" someone answers.

"Yup. The fat one is pig, the skinny one is lamb. Lamb's harder to stuff, but makes a more delicate product. Which one do you want, Jane?"

Jesus Christ. "Pig, I guess."

"Thought you might pick that one," he says. Everyone laughs.

"Now just open up the end there and slide it down that long metal shaft. Then just keep sliding down the slack."

It's plastic, I tell myself. Just like a hose. Every woman in the room is giggling.

"Look familiar?" Charlene asks me, and only then do I realize that I'm rolling a ten-foot-long condom onto a metal penis.

"Ha. Funny," I smile. I look up and see Josh across the table, his eyes on my hands.

"Josh?" I say, still rolling.

He looks up and I see that his cheeks are full, his jaws chewing slowly. His eyes are bleary, glazed.

"You okay, honey?"

"Uh-huh."

At last the stuffer is sheathed and ready to go.

"Now tie off the end so your meat can't escape," Chef Harvey tells me. "Charlene, start pumping."

I hold the limp gut in my hand, feel it swell and fill with meat. "Is it supposed to be this hard?" I ask, bringing a fresh round of laughter from the class. I twist the individual links awkwardly at first, then settle down to produce a regiment of perfect sausages, each one linked to the next.

I catch Josh's eye again, look down and see the erection pressing out from his pants. How long has it been since I've seen that? How long since I could make him hard from across the room? He sees me looking and turns to leave the room, but I call out "Josh. Stay." His eyes lock back onto my hands, and I tease him, fondling the links, pulling on them, encircling them with my fingers.

Out of the corner of my eye, I see hands begin to move over Charlene's body, male and female. I feel a hand on my ass, another moving around to my tits, but I shrug them off. "No. Not you," I tell them, staring into Josh's eyes.

When the last link is filled, the stuffing chamber empty, I surrender. I feel his arms around me, lifting and carrying me across the room. He opens my mouth with his fingers, fills it with sausage.

When the last link is filled, the stuffing chamber empty, I surrender. Josh opens my mouth with his fingers and fills it with meat. I chew, chew, swallow, and reach out for him.

He is as excited as the first time we made love, as skillful as the last time, the urge of youth and the finesse won by experience merged together. "Bratwurst," he whispers in my ear, then sweeps his tongue, thick and hot, around the whorls, down my neck. His hands pull off my T-shirt, release my bra. I whimper a little, embarrassed, but he presses a finger to my lips. "Pepperoni," he tells me firmly, unsnapping my jeans. He kneels to pull down my panties, then holds them aloft, showing everyone the soaked crotch. He lifts me, spreads my limbs on the cold, hard table, and, in a moment, I feel my husband's naked body surround me, loving and warming me.

His cock is impossibly thick, impossibly long, but my pussy knows him well and I stretch and gasp and take him in, rocking with him, our hips locked, lips banging together as we thrust. "Merguez!" he calls out. "Wienerwurst!" I scream, my orgasm building, growing inside me. "Boudin! Kielbasa!" He is mine and I am his and we are one, coming and coming. Spent, I lie next to him and let the smells take me over, fennel seed and hot pepper flakes, searing pork, rich liver, spunk and pussy and sweat.

Chef Harvey calls out "Everyone! This is the best part! Let's eat what we've made!" Kim and Charlene come around the table on either side. Kim offers me a slice of salami, but I shake my head, smiling. This time, I know how good it is, but I'm content to lie back and hold Josh's hand. Kim extends the rolled slice to Charlene. Her lips open to take it, then pull back, teasing. In a moment, they are locked in a kiss, the salami pressed between four hungry lips. I watch Omar lift a whole garlic wurst from a tray, then unzip his pants. He rubs it rhythmically on his cock, thrusting and chafing. Approaching Jenny from behind, he reaches between the two women, letting each rub her crotch on one end of the double-headed sausage as he presses his own garlic-scented meat against Jenny's ass.

I drop Josh's hand and reach my arms out, ready to join the odd frenzy that has begun. Strange nipples brush my lips, mouths suction to my breasts. My outstretched fingers probe new, wet openings as a cock pushes between my toes until it spurts, come running over my instep. I watch a woman strap on a sausage dildo and bend Chef Harvey over the stove, rubbing butter into his ass until it shines.

People smile, condiments flow. What are we all but meat, fat and water, stuffed into our skins? Everyone has everything they need.

We walk out, holding hands. In our matching backpacks, we carry quart containers stuffed with fresh sausage, folders of recipes, a course catalog.

Anything for You

by Odysseus Eleftherios

B utch?" she said.

We were lying in bed, recovering. We had made love three times, which is about my limit, without at least a couple of hours' recuperation. I don't think Camilla has any limit. If she does, I've never reached it, before hands, tongue, and pecker give out.

"Yes?" I answered. Her palm rested on my tuckered pumper, as if she wanted to be sure it wasn't going anyplace without her.

"You know how you say you'll do anything for me?"

"That's true," I said. "Absolutely true."

"Anything to get me excited?"

Well, I'd indulged Camilla in every imaginable foreplay, in tickling and tonguing, in biting and sucking, in nibbling and gnawing, in feathers and whips, in toe suckings and bottom lickings, in spankings and sprinklings, in showing videos and making videos, in the car, in the kitchen, in the park, in the alley, sitting, standing, sliding, and sledding, on the beach, on the porch, on the freeway, on the golf course, in the laundromat, on vacation, at work, at play, at ease, at attention, at rest, at the movies, at our parents' houses, in the theater, in the restaurant, in the bathroom—of the theater, of McDonald's, of the plane, of friends' houses—hiking, fishing, swimming, bird-watching, hot-tubbing, night-clubbing, in taxis, in buses, *in flagrante*, intrepidly, insouciantly, impulsively, and indefatigably.

"Anything," I said, "your sweet depraved heart can think of." Camilla gets turned on when I jokingly call her "depraved," "perverted," "twisted," and so on.

"You're sure?" She squeezed my languid lunger, as if to impress her question on me. Or on it.

"I'm sure."

"You won't get upset?"

"Nothing that excites you could upset me, my little insatiable sex maniac."

"Well," she said, tugging my convalescing cudgel this way and that, "I've been thinking, what would really excite me, what would really turn me on . . ."

"Yes?" I imagined she would say, lessons in tantric yoga, or one of those nude weekend workshops, or—

". . . would be to watch you with a man."

"Watch me with a man?"

"You know. The two of us in bed with a man, a nice man, and I'd watch you suck his cock."

"I'm not queer."

"Of course you're not. That's why it would excite me."

"I've never been attracted to men."

"You've had dreams."

"They were just dreams."

"They were your subconscious telling you you'd really like it."

"What about you and a woman? To excite *me*?" I thought I might be able to turn the conversation in a different direction.

"Of course."

"Really?"

"After I watch you with a man."

"I don't know, sweetie."

"You said you'd do anything for me."

"What say I skydive? Bungee jump? Walk naked down the street?"

"Watching your lips close around a really handsome penis,

and watching it get hard in your mouth, and watching your head move up and down, and I pressing my fingers into my pussy, and he getting harder and more excited, until finally—"

"But who? I'm not going to just wander into some gay bar and pick up a guy."

"Lorraine's boyfriend, Tim. He's good-looking, he has a great body, and he's a regular guy."

"But he's her boyfriend."

"He's bi. He's also clean. He's easygoing, he's relaxed, he won't pressure you or anything."

"I don't know . . ."

"When you're between my legs, eating me, I imagine that I'm a man and you're sucking my cock. I come quicker that way." She squeezed my slack squirter, emphasizing her point.

"But to suck off a guy," I said, "it's like I'm subservient to him."

She put her lips around the head of my awakening penis. "Do you feel I'm subservient?" she mumbled. Her tongue flicked back and forth. "I'm in command." A breathy suction drew my tired thruster further into moist warmth, into hot compression. "You're at my mercy." Her teeth lightly nibbled my stiffening spumer.

"You would do it like this," she instructed. I began to involuntarily move my hips forward and back. "He would not be able to control himself." My pulsating pusher rubbed the roof of her mouth, the top of her tongue, the ridge of her careful teeth.

"You'll love the sensation," she cooed, coming up for air. She waggled my ruddy rod, wet and shiny and suddenly cool. "You'll feel him grow in your mouth, and you'll feel such power. You'll have control. You'll be in charge." She licked her lovable lollipop. "He'll be dependent on you for his hardness, for his pleasure, for his ecstasy." She kissed the hopeful head. "You'll be the boss." She tongued the little opening, enticing it mercilessly.

We had dinner at a fancy restaurant. Camilla wanted us to meet in a neutral place, so I would feel no pressure. She said we would simply see how it went. She said if I didn't want it to go further, that was fine. She said my comfort was the most important thing.

Actually Tim and I hit it off right away. He was casual but assured, friendly but not presumptuous, an easy talker and an attentive listener. He was about my age but looked a little younger. His blond hair flopped over his forehead. When he brushed it aside, his gesture had a touching innocence to it.

He kissed Camilla when he came in. He shook my hand, firmly but not aggressively. Lorraine kissed me. Her auburn hair hung in ringlets, and her saucy breasts peeked from her low-cut blouse. We always kissed when we met, but this time her tongue was in my mouth, and her green eyes sparkled mischievously.

Lorraine and Tim sat on opposite sides, as did Camilla and I. As we drank our cocktails, Lorraine's hand found itself in my lap, under my napkin. Tim's hand was out of sight also. I couldn't tell where it was, not until Camilla gave a little jerk and almost spilled her manhattan. She was wearing a miniskirt and no panties. She glanced at me. Her eyes were bright with excitement. I had an inkling the evening might not be about only Tim and me.

As we munched the appetizer, Lorraine's foot rubbed my ankle.

During the salad Tim occasionally touched my arm to emphasize some point he was making, or to agree with some point I was making.

During the entrée Tim's hand rested now and then on my knee. Lorraine's hand rubbed my thigh. Camilla seemed distracted. Tim's other hand was moving—somewhere.

Eating dessert, Lorraine's fingers insinuated themselves under my napkin, unzipped my pants, and found their way to my daring darter, while with her other hand she ate her crème brûlée. Camilla's free hand seemed to be elsewhere as well, as she spooned her raspberry sorbet, and as Tim smiled in some enigmatic pleasure. Then Tim, never pausing over his chocolate mousse, let his fingers join Lorraine's under my napkin, which was jumping up and down, causing a passing waiter to pause, then hurry on, while Tim's and Lorraine's fingers played a little duet on my pliable piccolo.

My napkin pointed like a tent, and Lorraine's hand working in and out under her miniskirt, and Tim's hand in Camilla's lap, and Camilla's foot in Tim's lap rubbing his bulge, I proposed we take our after-dinner cognacs and liqueurs at our house, right away.

We departed the restaurant in a state of charged anticipation. I was no longer worried about my manhood. I was not in doubt about my gender identification. Hadn't Kinsey said that we are all bisexual? Wasn't friendship and pleasure more important than society's narrow prejudices?

Once at home, we put off our postprandial imbibings and headed straight for our large circular bed. There was a moment's hesitation, as we stood looking a little awkwardly at one another, but then Camilla unbuttoned her blouse, and Lorraine dropped her skirt, and soon we were all staring at one another's glorious nakedness—at Lorraine's sassy breasts and impudent pink nipples and at her neatly trimmed reddish pubic hair, at Camilla's larger, freckled, upstanding breasts with their perky nipples and her provocative triangle of bushy muff—and, yes, at Tim's unembarrassed penis, hanging enticingly at ease, of an inviting length and alluring girth, not so large as to be frightening but large enough to take notice of.

Tim's gaze took in my penis. He seemed satisfied. Lorraine seemed approving. We crawled onto the cool soft sheet and lay back. We admired our four bodies in the mirror on the ceiling. Lorraine and Tim lay on either side of me. They turned on their sides to face me. Camilla knelt at our feet, taking us all in. I felt utterly relaxed, comfortable . . . and horny.

Lorraine gathered my balls in her hand.

I squeezed her breast.

Tim wrapped his fingers lightly around my stirring schtuper.

Camilla ran her hands up and down my legs, Lorraine's legs, Tim's legs.

Lorraine closed her lips around my sanguine spouter. Her head bobbed up and down. Tim's hand scooped up my balls. Camilla crawled between Tim's legs. She flipped his penis back and forth, flopped it against her lips, nibbled its head. Tim cupped her breasts. She straddled his hips and lowered her nipple into his open mouth. His hand slipped down her belly and onto her bush.

Lorraine left me, high and wet, to crawl behind Camilla and rub her buttocks. Camilla stuck her bottom higher into the air. Lorraine held Camilla's buttocks open, lowered her head, and inserted her tongue. Camilla squealed with pleasure, as I knew she would. Lorraine tongued her until her tongue was tired, then lay back, arms out, legs spread, surrendering to whatever might come her way.

Camilla climbed over me—giving my tantalized torquer a squeeze and a tug on the way—to hover over Lorraine, Camilla's mouth poised over Lorraine's moist muff, Camilla's piquant pussy descending above Lorraine's receptive mouth.

I looked at Tim, lying on his back on my other side. His eyes were closed. His penis lay alluringly on one thigh.

I twisted about—close quarters!—trying not to disturb Lorraine and Camilla, who, arms wrapped around each other's bottoms, breasts flattened against each other's stomach, were quietly licking and lapping—well, not so quietly, as slurps and sips broke the charged silence—and, resting on my elbow, looked down at Tim's penis a few inches from my mouth.

I no longer had doubts. I no longer had inhibitions.

I held his prime pumper in my hand. How soft! How smooth! How tempting!

His eyes were still closed, but a hint of a smile quivered on his lips.

I opened my mouth. I felt the spongy spumer between my lips. I lowered my head. His plump plunger glided over my tongue. I slid my tongue back and forth across its underside. I felt it grow . . . longer . . . thicker . . . firmer . . .

I examined it, moist and sturdy. I licked the head, the way Camilla liked to lick mine. Tim quivered with excitement. I let the head rest between my lips. I sucked. He grew harder. He began to thrust. It was as Camilla had said. I was in control. I was in charge. I was having as much pleasure as he.

I was getting excited, too. Without anyone touching my impulsive intriguer, it was straightening, it was raising its impish periscope, it was sending urgent messages to my nervous system. The more my mouth made his slick sprayer hard, the firmer mine became. The more his hips quivered, the more mine trembled.

The bed bounced. Camilla and Lorraine had abandoned their mutual libation—or had they come already, quietly and secretly?—or loudly and thrillingly, and I had been too absorbed by Tim's lusty lunger to notice? Camilla kneeled behind my head. She brought her face close to watch. Having her so close, knowing she was watching—my God! That was even more thrilling!

Now he was pumping. He couldn't help himself. That turned me on even more, his cock plunging to the back of throat, then almost escaping my lips, my lips plucking at the rim of his circumcised head. He whimpered involuntarily.

Lorraine kneeled behind his buttocks so she could watch too. Her eyes danced with delight. Her lips were wet with Camilla's juices. She leaned closer, her face next to Camilla's, next to mine. I could smell the love juices on each of them. That aroused me still more.

Lorraine kissed my cheek. She kissed Tim's hip. She kissed Camilla. I watched their tongues plunge into one another's mouth, their tongues tasting their own juices.

Tim's poker pushed faster. His whimpers became moans. Camilla and Lorraine broke off their hungry osculation. They came closer. They watched.

I pulled teasingly away. His rigid rocket quivered in the air.

He thrust frantically. He searched madly for my mouth.

I held his buttock. I let his penis poke at my cheek, my nose, my chin. His moans grew frenzied.

Finally I closed my lips around his frenetic pulsing.

"You're turning me on," Camilla breathed, "you're turning me on like never before."

My tongue welcomed his trembling girth.

"Suck it," Camilla whimpered.

Tim's cock pumped faster.

"Suck it till he comes in your mouth," Lorraine urged.

I would have replied, but my mouth was busy.

"Fuck his mouth," Camilla said.

Tim's lunges took on a new insistence.

"Fuck him hard," Lorraine said.

His cock pressed the sides and roof of my mouth, rubbed back and forth, seeking new sensations.

"Suck him, Butch!" Camilla cried.

My teeth grazed his cock as it stabbed in and out. It drove him even wilder.

"Grab his balls," Lorraine said.

I squeezed Tim's balls.

His cock plunged deep into my mouth.

Camilla and Lorraine's hands squished and splashed into their perfumed secretions.

I grabbed Tim's buttock. My fingers slipped into his crack.

"He loves that," Lorraine moaned, her cunt rocking against Camilla's hand. She plunged my hand into her sopping pussy. I slipped my slippery finger into his ass.

Tim's cock made a final thrust into my mouth. My finger glided deeper into his pink pucker.

Camilla cried, "I'm coming!"

Tim's cock jerked against the roof of my mouth.

A hot thick spurt hit the back of my throat.

I swallowed. Sweet, salty, tangy, silky.

Lorraine eased his cock from my mouth. She wrapped her lips around it. She sucked out what was left.

Camilla's tongue searched my mouth, licking, tasting.

I suctioned her tongue. I tasted her, I tasted Lorraine, I tasted Tim.

We fell back, exhausted. My jaw ached, but I didn't mind.

After a few moments, Camilla kneeled beside me. "Now," she announced, "it's time for your reward."

"I get a reward?"

"Of course, silly. After all you've done for me?" She wiggled my penis. She pointed it toward Tim's mouth.

Tim's lips closed around my penis.

Camilla's hand rested in the crevice of my butt.

Lorraine licked one side of my penis while Tim licked the other.

Camilla's wet finger wriggled into my anus.

Lorraine sucked my balls.

Camilla's agile tongue slithered up my anus.

My plucky pumper plunged deeper into Tim's gulping mouth. He sucked and tongued my pecker until it was iron stiff.

Camilla rolled me from my side to my back. My cock never left Tim's mouth. His head bobbed up and down as he kneeled over me. My cock drove even deeper.

Camilla kneeled over my face. Lorraine joined her. They were belly to belly. They were muff to muff. They lowered themselves. Their pussies dripped onto my face. Their labia brushed my nose. They rocked back and forth. My tongue licked first one, then the other, back and forth, labias, clitorises. Their sweet, lovely juices filled my mouth.

Tim's mouth was hot and wet like a woman's pussy, like Camilla's pussy.

I exploded.

Tim gulped, Tim swallowed, Tim vacuumed my jerking rod.

I was still squirting as Lorraine plunged my cock into her mouth and sucked out more.

Then, as if sharing a luscious lollipop, or an ice cream cone that's going to melt soon, Lorraine popped my yummy spumer into Camilla's mouth, and Camilla sucked out a few spurts, sucked so hard it felt like she was pulling my soul itself out of my balls, out of the pucker of my anus, out of the depths of my bowels, and Camilla milked my trickling tickler, and kissed it, until it was floppy and droopy and, well, too durned pooped to pop.

"Thank you, darling," she murmured to my stalwart shooter, "for doing anything for me."

Under the Bridge in Warsaw

by Jason Rubis

The tall blond guy—Kevin thought his name was Jeff—pointed at the table, whooping. "There! That's *it*, honey, that's my perfect man, right there!"

Everyone laughed. "Shows where *your* mind's at," Carolyn said, and the laughter became deafening.

"Got to keep a sense of proportion about these things," Dr. Alan ventured, to modest chuckles. Everyone called him Dr. Alan. Apparently he really was a doctor; he had an office on Connecticut Avenue. He and his wife—whom everyone just called Barbara—had matching silver hair and very white smiles.

Carolyn had scattered several dozen Polaroids in a wide arc across the top of her kitchen table. She would select one, give it a slow, considering smile, then either discard it or add it to the vaguely X-shaped arrangement forming in the table's center. Her guests had watched this little show with rapt attention. Only Kevin seemed less than fascinated. Carolyn used to do shit like this in college all the time. He was over it.

Each Polaroid in the X showed a different male body part: a beefy, hairy chest; some guy's shaven head, his face twisted up in a cartoonish grimace; muscular, tattooed arms and legs. In the center Carolyn had placed a shot of what in reality was probably a very modest-sized cock, but which, against the rest of her assembly, was a gargantuan, ropy-veined monster.

"What do you think of that?" Dr. Alan asked Jana, nudging closer to her. "They have anything like that back in Budapest?"

"Alan, she's from Prague."

"Prague, right. Czechoslovakia. I know, Barbara."

Jana gave him an absent smile, which she then shifted back to the Polaroids. That was pretty much all Jana did: smile demurely and hang close by Carolyn, shyly stroking her shoulder now and then. She had long black hair and dusky skin, and a brief black cocktail dress that managed to look like a piece of lingerie.

"Where'd you get all these pictures, anyway?" Jeff wanted to know. "Are you really like the slut of the century or do you just buy them on eBay or something?"

"God, don't tell him!" his friend Don cried. "I have a hard enough time getting on the computer at night, he's always on the boy-sites!"

"No, I'm glad he brought it up," Carolyn said in businesslike tones. "Anyone who comes in here, I have to take a picture of their best part. House rules. And I get to choose which part is the best," she added—rather needlessly, Kevin thought.

"So you've got pictures of girls too?" he asked, and promptly wilted under five pairs of eyes. Jana looked calmly at her fingernails.

"Hey, you got 'em, I wouldn't mind seeing 'em," Dr. Alan laughed.

"Forget *that*!" Jeff said, tugging off his shirt. "I want to be a star. Here, Carolyn, get your camera!"

"Oh, Jesus," Don moaned.

"Nobody's taking any pictures of *me*," Barbara said loudly.

A flurry of activity erupted, much laughter and shouting as Jeff stripped. Kevin turned his back on it and wandered into the living room. Five more minutes. He could slip out easily enough, in the middle of the picture-taking, and trust it would be another eight years before he ran into Carolyn again and got invited to one of her shindigs. Might be interesting to see what she'd be into then.

Thinking all this, he was startled when someone behind him said, "You want to see?"

"I'm sorry?" Jana was standing behind him, arms flat at her sides, smiling her sphinxlike smile. She looked like a doll. Kevin had a crazy impulse to go over and lift her arms, bend them into some ridiculous pose. He felt sure that she would let him do that, and then hold the pose for him, smiling all the while.

"Girls. Like you said." Jana padded over to the bookshelf next to the window. There was a small box of polished wood on one of the shelves. She took it and handed it to him.

Inside was a neat stack of Polaroids. The one on top showed a fat, rosy-nippled tit. Kevin shuffled through those underneath. The palm of someone's hand, turned white by the camera's flash; another tit; a face in such extreme close-up that it was little more than a pale blur with a mouth in it; a round, brown-skinned ass with two maroon-nailed hands spreading its cheeks.

"These are all friends of yours?" Kevin asked politely. "Yours and Carolyn's?"

The question didn't seem to mean much to Jana. She nodded. "You like them?"

Out in the kitchen, light flashed. "My God, *look* at him!" Barbara's voice shrieked.

"I . . . sure. Yeah, I like them. Do you?"

"Sexy," Jana said, tilting her head slightly, looking closely at him.

"Are any of these of you?" Jana raised an eyebrow. Kevin pointed at the pictures, then at her. "You?"

"Oh." She took the box and, after some digging, plucked out three of the Polaroids. One showed a smooth, dusky-skinned belly. Light played over its contours, making it look like part of a sculpture that had nothing to do with the human body. Another picture was a full crotch shot: a hemisphere of black, wet-looking hair, surrounding a pink slash. The third showed a pair of bare soles, resting on a pillow. The toes were clenched, showing red nails. Jana took that one from him, looking embarrassed.

"Ugly," she murmured.

"No, they're pretty. You've got pretty feet." It seemed a stupid thing to say, but it came out anyway.

Jana wrinkled her nose. She said "Ugly" again, but she looked pleased.

"So what are you children up to?"

Kevin looked up and saw Dr. Alan coming at them, a full glass of wine in his hand. His eyes were locked on them, grinning.

"Fucking," Jana told him.

Dr. Alan pulled up short. He looked as surprised as Kevin felt, but he said, gamely, "Oh. They fuck with their clothes on in Czechoslovakia?"

"I'm fucking him," Jana said insistently. She hooked an arm around Kevin's shoulder and licked his ear. He gasped, his legs feeling like they were going to collapse. Dr. Alan nodded, smiled tightly, and retreated.

Jana gnashed her teeth in Kevin's ear, making a weird gurgling noise: "Ahn-gnagh-umum*um*!" Then she took his hand and pulled him back to the kitchen, laughing. He dropped the pictures and they fell all over the floor, dozens of them.

Barbara had her blouse and bra off and was standing with her hands on her hips. She was blushing furiously, but her eyes were bright, her nipples proudly erect as Carolyn aimed the camera. Jeff and Don, both in their briefs, hooted and pumped their fists. Dr. Alan was at the counter helping himself to more wine, shaking his head.

"Okay," Carolyn said, taking the fresh picture from the camera and giving it a quick jiggle before laying it on the table. "Your turn now, Alan. And then you, Kevin."

"Not me."

"I'll pass, thanks."

"Hey. House rules, remember?"

"Let's all go down to the Ambrosia!" Jeff cried suddenly, jumping up and whirling. "And da-ance the night away!"

"I like the Ambrosia," Barbara said.

Carolyn looked displeased. "On a Saturday night? It'll be *packed*."

"I know a game," Jana said. She spoke so softly that Kevin thought he was the only one who heard her. But Carolyn clapped her hands loudly. "Okay! Everybody! Jana knows a *game*!"

"Got to, uhhh," Jana said, making vague gestures, "the clothes. Naked. Everybody."

"Naked?" Barbara asked, eyes wide. "*Completely* naked, you mean?"

"For Christ's sake, Barbara, you just showed your tits to everybody in the room!"

"What's this game like?" Don asked.

Jana explained. When she finished, there was a sudden confusion of clothes being shed and a new burst of excited laughter. Dr. Alan spun his trousers over his head.

"I'd better be going, actually," Kevin said quickly. "Thanks for the invite, Carolyn. Nice to meet all of you."

In the midst of a general protest, Jana reached for his belt and began unbuckling it. In no time at all she had it hanging limp around his hips. Then she got started on his zipper. When Kevin tried to stop her, he got his hands slapped.

"Looks like you're staying," Don told him.

Kevin thought, I don't believe I'm doing this.

The game was called "Under the Bridge in Warsaw." Everyone sat around a table. One person got underneath and tried to make another of the players react—shout, cry, laugh, whatever. If they succeeded, the victim took their place under the table and it started all over again. It would have seemed pretty pointless, if not for the no-clothes rule.

As it was, there was no shortage of volunteers for the position of first one under the bridge, but it was Jana's game, Carolyn told everyone, so she got to pick. No one seemed surprised when she picked Kevin.

So there he was, sitting naked with his head down, his balls cooling on Carolyn's linoleum. He was surrounded by bare feet and legs and people's private parts. There was a low murmur of voices all around him.

"Bet he goes for Jana," someone giggled.

"Shhh!"

"Jealous, Carolyn?"

"Eat me."

"If *I* get under there, you might just get your wish."

Laughter.

Kevin watched Barbara's foot creep out, prodding casually around the floor with its red-painted toes. He let it find his thigh, then work its way up to his dick. Once it reached its destination, it seemed to relax. The ball of her foot felt smooth and dry stroking him, and he surprised himself by getting mildly hard. Barbara got his cockhead between her toes and pulled gently, in a way that suggested she had done this kind of thing at least once before.

Looking idly around, Kevin saw Dr. Alan's brown, hairy legs sitting stock still, his own penis regally unaroused. Carolyn's legs were plumper than he would have thought. They spread every now and then, flashing him a glimpse of very brown, very plentiful bush. Don and Jeff were both playing with Jeff's cock. Jana pushed her feet out, not searching for him as Barbara had, but wriggling her toes invitingly.

"He's being awfully quiet down there."

"He's shy."

"I could cure *that*."

"He's a nice guy, shut up."

"*You* shut up."

"*Now* who's jealous?"

A voice Kevin recognized as Barbara's purred, "He's nice, alright."

Kevin reached down and gently tickled her sole. Barbara squeaked, and her foot jerked up off him.

"What?"

"Did he get you, Barbara? Is that an admission of defeat?"

"No. I'm fine." Her foot came back. Amused, Kevin allowed it to reposition itself on his cock, then tickled again. Barbara's foot wriggled wildly, but it stubbornly kept stroking. He found a place on her arch that really drove her crazy. He let himself recline, keeping one finger on the spot while Barbara tried to keep her foot steady.

"So Barbara. While we're waiting. I understand you're a lawyer."

"I. Uhm. Yeah. I . . . I *am*!"

"What's wrong, Barbara?"

"N-nothing . . ."

"Look at that smile on her face!"

"Hey Barbara, is something tickling your fancy down there?"

Lying back put Kevin's head next to Jana's feet. One lifted and waved over his face, perfuming the air with a warm, fleshy smell he didn't find terribly unpleasant. He blew on her sole. The toes quivered, as though this were a prearranged signal, now received. She lowered her arch onto his mouth. Soft and warm, just a bit on the damp side; a foot only recently freed of its shoe. Kevin found himself licking it. He felt strange doing it, but what Barbara's foot was doing to his cock made it unavoidable—the pleasure in his groin translated to an odd need to do something with his mouth. He imagined the foot was actually Jana's pussy; that made it seem, if no less strange, then a bit more acceptable. He began nibbling.

"Ohh-hh!"

"Jana?"

"Oohh! Oh my *God*! It's . . . it's *orgasm*!" Jana's voice was louder than it had been all evening.

"Shit, look at her *face*!"

"That's it! Come on up, Kevin, you've won this round! Jana . . ."

Don grinned and saluted him as he took his place at the table. "Welcome back, Cap'n. You gave a brave account o' yerself in the battle, sir!"

Kevin had to laugh at that. He returned the salute and Don poured him a glass of wine.

Jana made a lot of noise getting under the table. Once she was there, though, there was another long silence.

"The anticipation is driving me cra-zy," Jeff droned.

"I know someone else who's good at driving people crazy," Barbara said. She was seated next to Kevin, staring at him and pointedly licking the rim of her glass.

"Ooh, tell us *all*!" Jeff cried.

"When you're a little older, sweetie."

"Better watch those two, Dr. Alan!"

Dr. Alan only grunted. He was busy settling himself as low as possible in his chair, trying to be inconspicuous about it. His feet slapped audibly on the floor as he spread his legs.

"Oh yeah?" Don laughed. "Seems to me Jana was the one who was up here screaming 'Orgasm' when Kevin got her. I still say it's Carolyn who . . ."

"Don. Shush."

Kevin sat and sipped his wine, not really listening. He was waiting for Jana to do whatever she was going to do. When he felt the first kiss on his cockhead, it was so gentle that he almost dropped the glass. It was like a butterfly had lit there. A very little butterfly, one with gently quivering, soaking wet wings. He had been only slightly hard up to now; now he was rigid.

"So Barbara? I know this guy who could use a lawyer. See he went into business with this other guy . . . this online thing . . ."

Jana was taking her time. Kevin could feel her head nestling between his thighs. If he looked down, he could see her black hair, a glimpse of her forehead. She kissed his head again and touched the tips of her fingers to his balls. She dragged her nails down his thigh.

"He's like in love with the guy? But *I* think he's getting reamed."

Kevin's erection felt heavy, impossibly long and thick. Jana bumped it to one side with her nose, lavishing kisses on it. Then, with a little sigh, she took it in her mouth. Kevin slid down slightly in his seat, fumbled for the table's edge and gripped it hard.

"Honey, if your friend doesn't want to take action there's nothing *I* can do. Anyway, we're not real big on . . . oh my God!"

Everyone saw him now. Everyone was looking at him.

"Oh my God is right! Kevin, what is she *doing* to you?"

"Didn't waste any time, did she?"

Jeff jumped up, pouting. "Well, this is fucked! Now Kevin's going to have to go under the table again and he's just gonna eat Jana's pussy again or *whatever*!"

Barbara moved closer to Kevin. Her bare breasts nestled warmly against his shoulder. "Look at that," she whispered, staring down at Jana's bobbing head. "*Look* at her! Jesus, that is *so* hot!"

Don said, "I hope you're not saying *you* wanted Jana to suck your dick! I really *hope* that, Jeff."

"No, I'm saying *I'm* going to the Ambrosia! Anyone wants to come with me . . ."

"We'll go," Dr. Alan said, rising from the table and grabbing his shirt up off the floor. His movements were quick and decisive, his face twisted up in a frown. "Barbara . . . ?"

Kevin felt like he should say something, officially admit defeat. But Jana wouldn't stop. She sucked with a warm insistence, pulling at him with her lips, occasionally mumbling. All he could do was gasp. Carolyn made no move to persuade her guests to stay. She leaned across the table and took Kevin's hand, squeezing it, keeping her eyes fixed on him. Barbara sat buzzing liquid syllables in his ear. When Dr. Alan called her a second time, she deposited a surprisingly gentle kiss on Kevin's cheek, letting her lips linger there for a long while before she got up and let her husband dress her.

Don patted Kevin's shoulder as the four of them made their

good-byes. Jana waited until the door closed before she
released him.

He shut his eyes. He was still hard, pulsing, itching inside.
He wanted to get up too, but he couldn't find the energy. He
hadn't come yet, but he felt drained. Carolyn opened his hand
in hers and ran a finger down his palm. "You liked that?"

"Yeah." It was all he could say.

She smiled at him. "Good. Just sit there a minute. Relax."

She got up and moved around behind him. Jana got out
from under the table and joined her. Kevin was aware of them
kissing and touching just behind his head. Their mouths made
soft sucking noises. For no good reason, that irritated him. He
got up, blushing and glaring.

Carolyn, still entwined in Jana's arms, stared at him.
"What's wrong? I mean, she *picked* you, why are you pissed?"

Kevin, looking for his shoes, said nothing.

"I thought she'd go for Jeff, you want the truth. Normally
she likes gay guys. Sort of like a challenge."

"No," Jana giggled. "No. Not Jeff. Too . . ." she shook her
hands. "Too funny."

"Whatever. What about Dr. Alan? He's kind of hot. I guess."

"No, no." Jana laughed loudly. "Oh, no!"

Kevin had the feeling that he was slipping out of the conversation. In a moment, it would be like he wasn't even there.
"Well, thanks. Thanks very much."

He didn't know why he was so angry—jealousy must have
figured into it, but what part could jealousy play in an evening
like this? None. He supposed that was the whole point. The
thought made him feel ashamed, like he was throwing a four-
star tantrum for nothing. Jana broke away from Carolyn and
grabbed at him as he shook out his empty jeans.

"You're going? Don't! Your . . . this . . . still hard!" Before he
could turn away, she ran a hand over his cock. The idea that he
might leave without coming seemed to disturb her, as though
he were leaving a dinner party without dessert, and she was
the world's most conscientious hostess.

Carolyn brushed her hair back. "Yeah, come on, Kevin, don't be a poop." Her voice got softer. "I haven't seen you in forever. You're looking pretty good, you know."

Kevin shuddered. His balls, resting in Jana's palm, ached. "Oh yeah?" He wanted to sound arch, dry, uncaring. He knew very well he sounded anything but.

"Yeah. Why the hell do you think I invited you tonight?" Then Carolyn was kissing him, putting her arms around his naked shoulders and pulling him close, biting at his lips and sucking at them. It struck him that he had never, in all the years he had known Carolyn, actually fantasized about her. Not even about kissing her. She was a hell of a kisser, though—fervent and noisy.

He was caught. He had waited too long. Stepping away, telling Carolyn to stop . . . none of these was an option now. Jana slipped behind him, molding herself around his back. Fingers and tongues crept over him, soft laughter was snuffed out against his skin. Eventually he was pulled to the floor.

Carolyn said, "Go, if you want to. But . . . what the fuck. You know?" Kevin was vaguely aware that she had her camera again, and was looking at him through the viewfinder. It gave her a robot's steely, mechanical face. He found he didn't mind. As the flash went off, his hips twitched. Carolyn wrapped her fingers around him and his back arched. When Jana bent her beautiful face over his and whispered in an eager but tentative voice that she was going get condoms now, and was that okay, Kevin only whispered, Hurry back. Please.

More Sunscreen, Please

An Erotic Adventure Story

by Julia Rebecca

My husband and I live on an island in the Caribbean. We own a forty-five-foot trawler that has two cabins and two heads down below and lots of flat deck space topside. She has a large raised, partially shaded sundeck amidships that is covered by a comfortable cushion. We stretch out on this cushion and read, sun ourselves, enjoy the view of the islands and, at night, watch for shooting stars.

As with most boats, ours has a name on her transom for the public to see and a private name known only to her owners and special guests. Our boat's private name is Erotic Adventure and this is one of her stories.

The tourists had gone home. Most of the anchorages were deserted and the beaches were quiet. The sun was shining and there was just enough wind to keep us from getting too hot but not enough to roughen the sea. Perfect conditions for a long, off-season weekend. Our destination was a little cove on the south side of St. John. The plan was to go in behind the reef, pick up a mooring ball. and stay a couple of nights.

Our friends Jason and Charlotte were joining us. We had met when they first arrived on the island a little over two years ago. The decade difference in our ages wasn't an issue;

we had instantly become good friends.

We met at the dock around 7:00 A.M., and began stowing provisions. We teased each other about all the stuff we were loading, remarking that we always looked like we were headed out for weeks, no matter how we tried to pare down what we took.

"I plan to be comfortable this weekend," Charlotte said in defense of her bulging duffle bag. "I also plan to read, drink a little, and have lots of sex."

"I think I can live with that." Bill put his arm around Charlotte and pulled her close. Gazing into her wide lagoon-green eyes he asked, "Weekend rules apply, right?"

"Absolutely," Charlotte replied. She pressed her breasts against Bill's chest while she ran her hands over his broad shoulders. Glancing at me she said, "Sara, your husband is so hot!"

"Weekend rules" are simple—what happens on the boat stays on the boat. The four of us are very close. Some of the attraction is physical, as both of them are a pleasure to look at. Jason is tall and fair with broad shoulders and good-looking, open features. Charlotte is his perfect complement. She is sultry, with dark brown hair that just sweeps her shoulders.

Charlotte likes to flirt with my husband and run her fingers through his thick, prematurely silvered hair. Bill has warm brown eyes, a strong handsome face, and soft lips Charlotte enjoys kissing. He appreciates her generous mouth and hourglass figure. Bill is more than a match for her flirting, as he is not as easily embarrassed in public as Jason.

Jason and I are drawn to each other, as well. His gentle strength, boyish charm, and embarrassed patience with my teasing are very appealing. He seems to appreciate my uninhibited behavior, which he cautiously encourages Charlotte to emulate, especially when it comes to nude sunbathing.

We have emotional ties to each other, too, forged by seeing each other through some adversity since we met. What is also unique about our relationship is that Charlotte and I are attracted to each other. Perhaps this affinity has grown from the pleasure we find in each other's company and our feeling that we are soul sisters.

These multilevel mutual attractions have led us to indulge in sexual banter, kissing and a few adolescent-type caresses when we have been away on our weekend trips or visiting each others' homes. We have confined this light sex play to private time on weekends. Hence the term, "weekend rules."

Turning to Jason, who was watching Charlotte and Bill as well as trying to see if anyone else could see us, I smiled up at him. While Charlotte had the advantage of being almost as tall as Bill, I was not so fortunate with Jason. I put my hand on his cheek and drew him down to me until our blue eyes met. "Do weekend rules work for you?" I asked before gently kissing him on the mouth.

Lightly returning my kiss, he replied, "I'm for anything that makes you women happy. Let's get the last of this junk on board and shove off."

"Don't I get a 'Good Morning' kiss, too?" Charlotte asked me as she moved away from Bill.

"Of course. How thoughtless of me," I replied. I kissed her firmly on the lips and then turned to hand the last bag of ice to Bill. Our eyes met and he grinned.

Turning to Jason, Bill remarked, "Sara and Charlotte are already at it. I think this is going to be an interesting weekend." His words proved to be more accurate that he could have imagined.

We quickly finished loading the boat, cast the lines off the dock and headed out of the harbor. Once out of the mooring field, Bill pushed the throttle forward and we picked up a bit of speed. Charlotte and I headed for the foredeck seating, which faced aft, intending to enjoy the beauty of the Caribbean morning. We intended to provide our men, who were at the mid-ships steering stations, with a different sort of view.

"Well," Charlotte asked after we were seated, "are you going to take off your shirt?"

"I certainly am." I matched the words with the deed, tossing my shirt down an open hatch. "Are you?"

"Absolutely." Charlotte pulled off her tank top and tossed it
after mine. She had beautiful breasts; they were large and full
and, because she had done very little topless sunbathing, pale
enough for their delicate blue veins to make them appear as if
they were made of a rare, warm marble. We both settled back,
wearing just our bathing suit bottoms and sunglasses, and let
the rising sun caress our bodies.

"Is that all that's coming off?" Bill called up to us.

"That's it for now," Charlotte replied.

Jason had a hopeful look on his face as he asked, "Do you
girls need some sunscreen?"

"Sorry. I put some on before I left. Charlotte, what about
you?"

"Nope," she called back to the guys. "I've got some on,
too."

"Well, you two are no fun," Bill complained. "What are we
supposed to do?"

"Just enjoy the view and drive," Charlotte said. "Maybe
we'll need some later."

We cruised at a comfortable fifteen knots. At that leisurely
pace, we reached our island destination in just over an hour.
The place was deserted, as we had hoped, and we slowly
motored in to pick up a mooring. The small bay was protected
by two reefs, which resulted in calm, clear water and a beautiful white-sand beach.

After I picked up the mooring line and secured it around
the forward cleat Bill shut down the engine. All we could hear
was the sound of the sea and the birds. Turtles we startled into
diving when we entered the cove resurfaced and the big old
barracuda that lives there glided through the turquoise water to
hide in the shade provided by our boat. The breeze blew the
heady scent of island flowers from the shore where it mingled
with the scent of the sea to create a unique perfume. I never
tired of this scent nor of the feel of the warm breeze on my skin.

I stretched and let the soft wind caress my body while Jason and Charlotte looked around, delighted smiles on both their faces. They had never before been to this hideaway and I could tell they were very pleased we had chosen that secluded spot. "The land here belongs to the park service," I explained. "That's why there's no development. Plus, it's a two-mile hike to the road, which is why there are no people on the beach. It's like having our own private bay!"

"I'm hot. Who's for a swim?" Jason called out. He loved to snorkel and I could see from the slight bulge in the front of his swim trunks that he needed to cool off in more ways than one.

Bill decided to go in the water, but only to check on the new props and scrape some of the growth off the hull. He was most happy when he was tinkering with the boat.

Charlotte decided to stay on board for a while. "You and Sara go ahead. I'm way too lazy to do anything right now but read. I had a stressful week and just need to chill."

Jason and I got our snorkel gear, I loosened my hair, and we slipped over the side, hoping not to startle the turtles and other creatures any more than we already had. Since I had explored this cove before, I took the lead and swam slowly away from the boat.

Though a big man, Jason moved with ease and grace through the water. I couldn't help but see him as an attractive man instead of a friend. The beauty of our surroundings, coupled with walking around barely clothed, heightened my sensual awareness. The warm sun on my skin juxtaposed with the cool seawater was a delicious feeling. My long hair, moved by the sea's gentle currents, alternately touched then moved away from my body; sometimes touching my back, other times curling around to graze my breasts. It felt as if an invisible lover was delicately touching me. *No harm in looking*, I thought. *I know he was looking at me on the trip over here.*

When I forced myself to focus on my surroundings, I spotted an Eagle Ray a short distance off. I waved to Jason and, when he turned to follow, kicked off toward more open water.

We slowly approached the ray, which was circling the sand bottom in search of food. We tried to keep above and to one side of him, backing and turning in the current to keep him in sight and not scare him off or kick each other.

While trying to stay with the ray, I suddenly realized I was too close to Jason and out of control. I waved him off but, mistaking my gesture, he came closer. I crashed into him, mashing my breasts against him. We maneuvered upright, each spitting out our snorkels and asking if the other was okay.

"I thought you spotted something and were waving me over," Jason explained.

"No, I was out of control and trying to wave you off so I wouldn't hit you. Sorry."

"No harm done. The blow was pretty well cushioned." He smiled and dropped his eyes to my chest. "You're not hurt, are you?"

I laughed. "No, your arm is not that hard. I'm getting hungry. Let's head back to the boat by way of the grass beds and see if we can spot a turtle on the way." I replaced my snorkel and let Jason lead the way back. He watched for a turtle; I watched him.

We climbed aboard and rinsed off using the freshwater shower on the swim platform. Bill and Charlotte had obviously gotten hungry, too, as they were setting out fruit, cheese, and crackers as we dried off.

Jason regarded Charlotte with feigned hurt. "Were you going to eat without us?"

"We thought about waiting, but it looked like you were having a little too much fun out there, so we decided to hell with it." Giving Jason an arch look she asked, "What game were you two playing without us?"

I laughed. "Klutz that I am, I ran right into Jason while we were watching a ray." I glanced sideways at Jason and added, "He didn't seem to mind being smacked with my nipples, though."

Jason cleared his throat and asked if I would like a drink.

"Iced tea, thanks." Turning to Charlotte I said, "I think I embarrassed your husband. Again."

"Don't worry. He should be used to it by now. Anyway, I think he likes it."

Picking up some cheese and crackers, I settled on the sun deck and turned to my husband, who was listening to our silliness from his captain's chair. "And what were the two of you up to while we were out in the water observing nature?"

"Wild sex," he nonchalantly replied. "You know, the usual."

Jason handed my drink to me and sat down near the food. Turning to Bill, he smugly informed him, "I'll have you know that there is nothing 'usual' about sex with my wife."

"Thank you, honey," Charlotte said. "Hand me some grapes, will you?"

We settled down to eat, read, and quietly enjoy our secluded surroundings and each other's company. I washed the dishes and decided to clean up the boat a little. When I went down below I discovered that Bill had made up our bed and neatly stowed our gear. I gave him a big hug and kiss when I came back up on deck.

"That was nice. Was it for anything in particular?"

"Yes, it was a 'thank you' for making the bed and putting away our stuff. I appreciate not having to wrestle with the sheets."

"The only thing you're going to wrestle in that bed is me." He put his hand up to cop a feel as he spoke.

Charlotte stood. "Okay, you two, that's enough. The kissing and sex talk has gotten me hot. I'm ready for the water."

"Didn't your mother ever tell you not to swim after eating?" Jason teased.

"I'm not going to swim, I'm going to float around on a noodle and have a drink. Who's going to join me?"

Jason and Bill got the noodles, brightly colored Styrofoam cylinders we use when we want to be lazy and float around behind the boat, while Charlotte and I made the drinks. Jason slowly went down the aft ladder while Bill jumped in all at once.

I handed noodles down, then put on my sunglasses and slipped into the water, which the sun had warmed to a perfect eighty-four degrees. I asked Charlotte to hand my drink to me, then Bill wanted his hat and Jason decided he needed his sunglasses. After getting all this, she stared down at us, hands on her hips.

"Is everyone happy now?" she asked with mock sarcasm. "I can't believe it. This was my idea and I'm the last one in the water. Someone at least take my drink, so I don't have to try and reach it from the water."

She knelt down on the aft platform and leaned down to hand her drink to Bill. As he reached up to take her cup, he grinned at her. "Lean down a little more, doll, and I can reach something else."

Charlotte leaned back out of his reach and shook her breasts at him. "Oh no you don't. If you wanted to touch my boobs, you shouldn't have left me up here alone," she teased. "Eat your heart out, and move away from the ladder so I can get in the water. If you behave, maybe you can feel me up later."

Jason had moved a few feet from the boat, and was looking down at something, but his head came up when he heard that. "Do I have anything to say about that?"

I kicked closer to him. "I know you like to watch; you've said so before. Besides, Charlotte plays fair. If she gets Bill I get you."

Jason cleared his throat and in his usual, subtle way of changing the subject, asked if I'd seen the squid hanging out by the stern of the boat. My answer was to laugh and splash water at him.

Charlotte entered the water, claimed her drink, and grabbed a noodle. There was the usual teasing about which of us had the biggest noodle, that Jason's was purple and so forth. We floated in the warm water, chatted, and sipped our drinks. After a long while, I started getting waterlogged.

"I've had enough; I'm getting out." I headed for the swim

ladder, putting my noodle and drink on deck before I climbed out. The others followed me to the boat and I found myself in Charlotte's earlier position, bending over to get everyone's drinks and noodles out of the water before they joined me on deck.

"Look, she's really cold." I heard Charlotte say teasingly. I glanced down to see that she was referring to my nipples, which had hardened as the breeze dried my wet skin. Or maybe they had reacted to the appreciative looks I was getting from Bill and Jason as I leaned over the two of them.

It was early afternoon by then, so Charlotte and I retrieved our books and settled on the cushioned sundeck under the awning. She propped up some cushions so she could face aft; I lay on my stomach facing the same way. Bill had claimed his captain's chair and was reading the latest spy thriller, and we could see Jason securing the toys and cleaning up.

After a few minutes, Charlotte looked over at me. "Sara, I think my sunscreen washed off while we were in the water. Would you put more on me?"

"Sure." I got to my knees and reached up to the storage bag that held the sunscreen, and knee-walked over to her side of the cushion, where she still reclined. "Back or front?" I teased.

"Front, of course, since I'm lying on my back. I certainly don't want burned nipples."

"Okay," I said. "Just checking."

I approached slowly, giving her a chance to laugh or say she was just kidding. She had put down her book and was watching me, perhaps waiting for me to back down; this was a first for both of us. As I squirted the thick lotion out and rubbed it onto both my hands, I was peripherally aware of our men's reactions.

Other than to slowly lower his book in order to get a better view, Bill had not moved. Although I couldn't see Jason, I could tell by the lack of sound behind me that he had ceased his cleaning. My guess was that he was frozen in place, just as Bill was. As I moved close enough to Charlotte to touch her, I

heard Jason move around to my right, then stop. I assumed he
had positioned himself for a better view of what was to come.

Whatever that was. This was a new experience for me. Sure,
I'd put sunscreen on my girlfriends before, but always on their
backs. I had never deliberately touched another woman's
breasts. Maintaining eye contact as well as I could while wearing sunglasses, I reached out and lightly ran my hands from her
breasts to her neck, leaving a light trail of lotion. Other than to
draw a deep breath and lean her head back a bit, she did not
move. I decided to continue.

When I again touched her, I cupped my hands under her
breasts, surprised at the weight and warmth of them. I had not
expected them to feel so heavy. As for the warmth, well, maybe
the sun had warmed her and maybe my hands had gone a bit
cold. I gently massaged the cream into her skin, running my
thumbs over her nipples. She inhaled sharply, but did not pull
away. I moved my hands to the tops of her breasts and then
gently stroked her upper chest and neck, making sure the sunscreen was evenly distributed.

Because I was fascinated with the feel of her, I continued
my upward strokes, moving my hands lower at the beginning
of each stroke. She must have been enjoying the sensations as
much as I was because she arched her back as my thumbs again
approached her nipples. By now there was no question about
what we were doing. I was no longer applying sunscreen, I was
touching my beautiful friend and getting turned on. I had no
idea what Bill and Jason were doing; I was totally focused on
Charlotte's soft sighs of pleasure.

I changed my touch, caressing her breasts more firmly and
rolling her nipples between my thumb and forefinger. "Oh,
that's good," she said in a low voice. My hands wandered
below her breasts, spreading the lotion across her abdomen
and down to the top of her bathing suit.

"You'll lose those tan lines faster if you slide off your
bathing suit bottoms." I heard myself say it, but I don't know
where it came from. I had no thoughts at all other than how

good it felt to touch her and how much I enjoyed pleasing her.

She slid down to lay flat, lifted her hips, and pushed at her bikini bottoms. I helped her get them past her knees, at which point she was able to kick them off while I reached for more lotion. I never heard the suit land, because Bill's harsh gasp nearly drowned out Jason's tentative, "Uh, Charlotte?" Jason must have remembered he had joked more than once that Charlotte and I could have sex with each other anytime we wanted to—as long as they got to watch—because he didn't say anything else.

Charlotte smiled at me. "Do you think we're driving them crazy?" she asked, as my lotioned hands came to rest at her waist.

"Oh, yes." *And you're driving me crazy, too.* Still kneeling beside her, I continued to spread the gooey cream on her body, moving my hands lower a little at a time. Down her stomach I stroked in small circles, until I reached her thighs. The whitest part of her was covered with curly, auburn-colored hair, which she had trimmed very closely. Softly brushing my hand over her mound, I said, "This is the worst place to get burned. Would you like some sunscreen here, too?"

"Yes, please." She spread her legs just enough for me to fit between them instead of staying by her side. I caught just a glimpse of her lower lips and vaginal opening. I was transfixed at the sight of her, having seen this view only in porn movies or my husband's "girlie" magazines. Granting her request, I quickly squirted more sunscreen into my hands and moved to kneel between her legs.

As I reached down to her, I heard my husband shift in his chair and mutter, "Holy shit."

Jason's choked comment was "Oh. My. God."

Frankly, I had forgotten they were there. My attention was totally focused on Charlotte and the sensations I was producing as well as feeling. The thinking part of my brain had shut down; I was lost in pleasure and growing desire.

I placed my hands at the tops of her thighs and moved

them in small circles. Still rubbing lotion into her skin, I moved my left hand to her lower abdomen and with my right hand stroked lotion down over that soft, red-brown hair. A low moan of pleasure from her encouraged me to become bolder in my touch. I continued to stroke down, finding her hooded clitoris with my thumb. I massaged her there with gentle up and down strokes, feeling the small hard knob beneath the skin.

"That's just perfect." Charlotte moaned and spread her legs a bit wider. She was very beautiful in her arousal, her pink inner lips resembling the petals of the island hibiscus flower. There was a hint of moisture on those petals and I wondered if I could bring forth more. Removing my left hand from her abdomen, I reached down and put my first and second fingers between her inner and outer lips. I slid my fingers in long strokes up and down that delicate flesh as I slightly increased the pressure of my thumb.

I must have been doing something right, because Charlotte was gasping for breath at that point. Her hips had begun to move against rhythmically, and her own wetness was beginning to replace the sunscreen. She bent her knees and opened her legs a little more, giving me an amazing view of her swollen flesh. Did we all look that beautiful when aroused? All I wanted to do was keep pleasing her. I pressed harder with my thumb and, unable to resist, slipped my left index finger inside her. She cried out and reached back to grasp the railing her pillows had been resting against.

The heat inside her was incredible. I suddenly had a better understanding of a man's overwhelming desire to put his extremely sensitive penis inside a woman. I wiggled my finger as I slid it in and out of her and I could feel her muscles grab at it. Startled by her reaction, I must have broken the rhythm of what I was doing. She bucked her hips and whimpered a bit. I hastily resumed my activities, slipping a second finger inside her and increasing the pressure of my thumb on her clit.

"Shhh," I said. "I won't leave you like this." I ignored my own growing arousal and concentrated on Charlotte. My strongest desire was to bring her to orgasm. I continued to touch her with slow, even strokes and heard myself making crooning noises to her. She allowed me to continue to masturbate her, body trembling, until suddenly her back arched, her vaginal muscles spasmed around my fingers, and the liquid result of her orgasm filled my hand.

I left my fingers unmoving inside her until she settled a bit. When she had calmed, I carefully withdrew my hands from between her legs and moved over her body, putting my hands on either side of her head so I could look at her. Her beautiful face was flushed with pleasure and her eyes, when she opened them, were filled with wonder. "Wow," was all she could say. As I kissed her, touching her tongue with mine, her hands came up to cup my breasts.

"I think you need sunscreen, too." Groping for and finding the bottle, she put sunscreen in her hands and then massaged the lotion onto my breasts, paying careful attention to my hardened nipples. Her hands felt wonderful, and I became even more aroused than I had been. I enjoyed her attentions for a few minutes, then sat back so she could sit up.

Charlotte ran her eyes down my body. "You're still wearing your bathing suit bottoms!"

I glanced down at myself. "I was a little too busy to take them off."

From her sitting position, she urged me up on my knees. She placed her hands on my hips, grasped the sides of my suit and looked up into my eyes. "Let me help you out of that."

Jason's interruption made us pause in our game. "What about me, I mean, us? You girls have been having all the fun and we've been left on the sidelines."

"Yeah," Bill said, "don't we get to join in?"

Charlotte and I looked at them, briefly considered, and then shook our heads. They had been hinting around for something like this for a long time. Now that they had what they wanted, they wanted us to hurry up. I didn't think so.

"You guys can wait your turn. You've been panting for girl

sex and now you've got it, so just be patient until Charlotte and
I invite you to join us."

I turned back to Charlotte, whose hands had stayed on my
hips. I met her eyes and nodded. Slowly, she slipped the fabric
down my legs, leaning forward to ease it beneath my knees and
off my feet. She fingered the drenched fabric with a knowing
smile, then deliberately tossed it behind her to where Bill was
sitting. He aim was perfect; it hit him right in the face, then fell
to his lap. I laughed at the look on his face, but sobered quickly when I felt Charlotte's hands on my thighs. I looked down
into her eyes; anticipation and desire had brightened their hue
to emerald.

"Spread your legs," she whispered, "and I'll show you some
things I learned in my all-girls high school."

"I knew you had to be sandbagging; you spent too much
time teasing me. Why didn't you tell me you'd done this
before?"

"Isn't it more fun to find out like this?" she said, as she
moved her hands to my knees and urged them apart. "Spread
your legs," she repeated firmly.

I obeyed and reached up to take hold of the radar arch. I
felt her palms move to the inside of my thighs and slowly make
their way upward. I was so aroused that I thought I might have
an orgasm before those hands reached their destination. As her
fingers made their way up my legs, I heard a low moan from
Jason.

I raised my head and turned to meet his eyes. He quickly
lowered his gaze. "Jason," I said softly, "it's all right to watch."
He raised his eyes to mine, nodded, then focused on
Charlotte's hands. I closed my eyes and let my head fall back.

Slowly Charlotte's hands continued to move up my thighs.
As her hands moved, she extended her thumbs to slip them
inside me and leaned forward to flick my clit with her tongue.
My body jerked with immediate, intense orgasm, throughout
which Charlotte continued to move her thumbs around inside
me and work her tongue. Knowing that Bill and Jason were

watching us made my orgasm even more intense than usual. I dangled from the radar arch as waves of pleasure flowed through me. Finally, I begged her to stop; I couldn't take any more direct stimulation.

She quit touching and licking me, and urged me down next to her. We sat there with our arms around each other and caught our breath.

Bill's plaintive request interrupted us. "Now can we join you?"

"Yeah," Jason chimed in, "when is it our turn?"

Charlotte and I broke our embrace and reached out to our men. We most definitely wanted them to join us. "It's your turn when you're naked and hard as rocks," Charlotte answered.

Two pairs of men's swim trunks hit the deck and we were shown proof that they were both ready to join us; they were painfully, and pleasingly, hard. I didn't know about Charlotte, but I was ready. All I needed from Bill was a kiss or two, then for him to slide his hard dick inside me and fuck me for as long as he could.

I held my arms out to my husband. "Care to come play with me?" His answer was to step over the coolers and walk onto the sundeck. I glanced over toward Charlotte and saw that Jason had already moved to her side and was kissing her while moving his hands over her body. Watching my adored friends make love was a powerfully erotic experience.

I embraced my husband and kissed him, feeling his hardness between us. Putting my mouth to his ear, I whispered, "If I get on my hands and knees, will you fuck me from behind?"

He kissed me, turned me around so I faced aft and eased me onto my hands and knees. "I thought you'd never ask," he said as he slid inside me. His penis was rock hard and hotter than I had ever felt it.

By accident or design, though I was no longer putting anything past Charlotte, she and Jason had assumed the same position, but faced the opposite way, which was toward the front of the boat. Our shoulders were about even and, if I ducked my head a bit, I had a clear view of Jason moving in and out of Charlotte. Feeling a hard dick slide in and out of me while watching one slide in and out of her was such a sensory overload that I had another intense orgasm. I closed my eyes while waves of pleasure washed though my body.

When I opened my eyes, the scene in front of me gave me a mischievous idea. As all barriers between us seemed to be down, I decided to act on my impulse. I thought that if I leaned down and braced myself on my elbow I might be able to reach far enough to put my hand between Charlotte's legs. While Bill pushed in and out of me at a steady pace that guaranteed he would last a while and that we both would experience a soul-rocking orgasm at our finish, I tested my naughty theory.

Once in position, I reached out and put my hand on Charlotte's stomach. I inched my hand toward her crotch; I wanted her to anticipate the moment my fingers would reach their goal. "Oh, please," she began to moan. While I fingered her to another orgasm, I could feel Jason's penis move inside her. I often reached back to feel my husband fuck me and I loved the sensation of hard against soft. Feeling my friends was mind-blowing.

Jason groaned as I increased the pressure of my fingers on his dick; apparently he enjoyed my touch. To feel Jason slide in and out of Charlotte while Bill was inside me was overwhelmingly sensual. Charlotte's body shook with another orgasm, as did mine. Turnabout was fair play in Charlotte's book and I felt her fingers giving us the same attention I gave to them. She brought me to another quivering climax.

Still caressing them both, I felt the change as Jason approached orgasm. His movements became a bit more urgent and as I masturbated Charlotte to a final orgasm he thrust himself hard into her. I stretched my hand as far as I could and touched Jason's balls while his penis spurted inside her. I looked up in time to see an expression of ecstasy on his handsome face.

Their mutual orgasm triggered our release. Charlotte kept

her hand in place, her fingers urging me to a final orgasm, while Bill performed those last, hard thrusts that put us both over the top.

We collapsed on the cushions and lay facing each other. I noticed the scent on my hand. It was the familiar smell of sex mingled with the unfamiliar essence of our two friends. As one, Charlotte and I reached our sticky hands across the cushion and lightly clasped them. Silent reassurance, perhaps, that all was well?

The four of us lay there listening to the susurration of the sea mingle with the sound of our breathing slowing to normal. I knew that we had moved, in one giant step, very far away from sexual banter and a few kisses. Would anyone be ashamed or sorry it happened? I wondered if our precious friendship had been damaged or enhanced. Maybe all of us quietly pondered the same questions, afraid that any movement or sound would shatter the magic of what we had just shared.

Finally, I dared to look over at my friends. Charlotte's eyes met mine. "I just love boating," she sighed.

We both started to laugh. The spell was broken, but our friendship was not. I pushed off the sundeck. "I'm all hot and sticky. I'm going for another swim. Last one off the boat has to hand down the drinks."

Charlotte, Bill, and I all hit the water about the same time, leaving Jason on the sundeck looking somewhat bemused. Modestly wrapping a towel around his waist, which made Charlotte and I share another giggle, he prepared our drinks and handed them, along with our noodles, down to us before he dropped his towel and dove in.

"You okay?" I asked him when floated near me.

"Never better, Sara," he replied with a smile. "Never better."

As we drifted and sipped our drinks I knew we would be fine. Later we would talk about what happened and figure out a way to redefine our friendship to include this experience. Would it happen again? Maybe. Did I want to explore more fully the sexual aspects of our friendship? Probably, but I would decide that later. All I knew right then was that I was with my husband, whom I loved, and my friends, whom I also loved, and that we had shared a binding encounter that was a truly erotic adventure.

Group Sex, Once Removed

Or, Leading a Swinging Lifestyle Without Having to Involve Yourself with All Those Other People

by Chris Bridges

So, you two have been kicking around the "swingers" idea again, have you? Been looking fondly at passersby? Letting the flirtations at work creep up to the next level, the one just below "actionable"? Wondering if Russian mail-order brides have a "try before you buy" program? Or perhaps the two of you have just been enjoying the same meal, metaphorically speaking, for so long that it's becoming predictable, unappetizing, and easy to skip?

When your lover becomes less of a banquet and more like greasy leftovers, it's time to change something.

First of all, be honest with each other about it. Sneaking around on your lover is rude, and, worse, it's getting harder to get away with. In times past you just had to watch for mysterious lipstick stains, odd-colored strands of hair, bodily marks that weren't there before your "business trip," and the occasional accidental public meeting and subsequent judicial decision. Now, what with current technology carelessly bounding along, it's entirely possible that the coat you got for Christmas contains a hidden GPS homing beacon or that your secret evening rendezvous in the park was caught on somebody's webcam and broadcast live, worldwide, with zooming options.

Couples can make a go of the open marriage thing if they *both* have some action on the side, since by unspoken agreement all probing questions (like "Where were you last month?" and "When did this get pierced?") are to be avoided at all costs for fear of mutual disclosure. But unless you are both extremely well-adjusted (and really attractive), these kinds of arrangements tend to self-destruct. There is no situation more dangerous than an open marriage where only one spouse is successfully getting laid. And scheduling becomes a major undertaking, especially if you only have the one car.

One option is to try a threesome. At some point in your sexual career the idea will come up of safely introducing another player into your previously closed set, usually when the man starts having dangerous thoughts about twin sisters and best friends and harems and things, or when the woman starts wondering what it might be like to meet someone who's at least heard of a clitoris. Then you have the benefit of new nookie without the fear of discovery, unless your lover sleeps really soundly.

But whom to choose? Another man, or a woman? Or another couple? How do you go about finding them? Ask a friend? Advertise? Should you swap partners, or just go at it concurrently, as it were? Should everyone be in the same room? What if (I/my lover) like(s) him/her/them better than (my lover/me)? What if they're perverts? What if they think we're perverts? What if they're from Vice? What if they're secretly recording us for blackmail, or to sell online? What if word gets out? What if we're not any good? What if the kids walk in? Oh dear god, what about diseases?

It's a big step in any relationship, especially one like yours, and you should be careful to consider all the ramifications:

Pro: There's always a hand or mouth free when you need one. Con: Simultaneous orgasms are even trickier to pull off.

Pro: Someone can go for beer without interrupting things. Con: Tougher for three people to decide on pizza toppings.

Pro: You get to watch your best friends making love. Con: You get to find out what kind of really sick things your friends like.

Pro: Simultaneously enjoying intercourse and oral sex has to be experienced to be believed. Con: Trying to find safe places to put your elbows.

Pro: You can safely check yourself for any homosexual tendencies without necessarily doing anything about it. Con: You might discover homosexual tendencies you didn't suspect or want.

Pro: Enough people to play gin rummy if things don't work out. Con: You have the option of wrecking twice the normal number of relationships.

Pro: Three-person kisses are fantastic. Con: Now there are two wet spots to avoid.

Pro: It can get really weird. Con: It can get really weird.

If adding one new and potentially diseased and/or psychopathic bedmate isn't enough, there's always group sex. The concept is extremely appealing: multitudes of friends or intimate strangers, touching and loving and kissing and biting and thrusting and . . . well, you get the picture. A panorama of unqualified love and acceptance, a vista of exploration and discovery.

But not for me. I have nothing but admiration for those souls who enjoy broadening their horizons in this manner, but I doubt seriously you'll see me in the punchbowl line at the next All-County gathering. Just a few of the reasons why:

Never enough places to rest a drink.

That awkward moment at the beginning, when no one's quite sure how to start and the guys start making half-assed references to strip poker.

I'd always want to be on the bottom so I can see what's coming at me. I mean, jeez.

My embarrassing habit of vomiting at climax.

A crippling fear of running out of bean dip.

You know how, whenever you go to an orgy, there's always some guy with the hanging paunch and spindly legs, and you turn the corner and see him crouching and just pounding away at some poor woman, and all you can see is gray hairy skin and swinging balls and you wish you had never gazed upon such a horrifying, mood-killing sight? I'd be that guy.

I'd be afraid that the group would begin assembling some strange geometrical shape, and I'm shitty at math.

I'm pretty sure I could only completely satisfy eight, maybe nine women in an evening, and I'd hate to slight anybody.

The awkward moment in the middle, when you're in between turns and everyone else is still going, and you start wondering what's on TV.

My fondness for screaming my orgasmic cries in an Elmer Fudd voice.

Seduction lines don't work when everyone in the room already heard you the first time.

My secret fetish of sneaking up behind copulating people and screaming AAAAAAAAAAAAAAGGGGGHHHHH!

Did you know that when semen from different guys pools together, it makes weird little designs that keep endlessly mixing and swirling, like oil on water? I get distracted easily.

Indecision, combined with the sure knowledge that few women wish to be chosen for erotic bliss via "eeny meeny miny moe."

The uncontrollable urge I would feel to mix up all the clothes and then yell, "Run! The cops!"

The suspicion that if someone came up behind me and smacked me sharply and playfully on the buttocks with a leather paddle, I would turn and deck the bastard. You have no idea how embarrassing that is, or how legally expensive.

The indescribable feeling you get when you suddenly realize that the woman with the amazing tattoo that you've just bent over a coffee table is your child's second grade teacher.

I just know I would want to get everyone going in a spontaneous and synchronized rhythm to a snappy beat, like in Hollywood musicals.

Navel lint. A roomful.

The way I feel after I'm sent out for more drinks and pizza, for the fifth time.

I can't get everyone to shut up during *The Simpsons*.

Never enough towels.

The ordeal of trying to find a bathroom that you can actually use as a bathroom. Alone. Off-camera.

The fear of getting voted out of the room.

If I really please my boss's wife, will he be happy? Or pissed?

I don't think I would fully trust any food I didn't watch prepared, especially white sauces or dip or any vegetables that are longer than they are wide.

The obsessive need to know where all the pets in the house are at any given time. Don't like surprises.

Pool filters won't handle as much as you'd think.

My weakness for practical jokes. "That guy over there? Loves Mountain Dew enemas, surprise ones. No, really, take this and . . ."

The awkward feeling at the end when everyone's done and gone except for one couple who are apparently out to break some heroic record and they're too far gone to hear your subtle nudging.

The stuff that comes up in the vacuum the next morning.

I'm not saying that all these problems will arise (although they probably will), or that they can't be overcome if they do (dream on), but there are plenty of ways to pump up your sex life with that swinging thrill without having to clean up the living room, and I don't mean just dressing the wife up as a tart.

Dressing the Wife up as a Tart

It is a place to begin, however. Just because you're committed to one person doesn't mean you have to keep sleeping with the same one over and over, does it? It's said that every person contains many personalities, so why sleep with only one of them? Dressing up in costumes is one way to go about it, although there does need to be some role-playing involved.

Only an enema bag full of ice water could be more chilling than hearing, "Right, so I'm a nun. Let's get this over with, this thing is itchier than a burlap thong."

Even simple makeup and different clothes can work wonders. Hit the clearance aisles and pick up marked-down eye shadow and bizarre lipsticks, grab some elderly suits and ball gowns from the local Goodwill, and don't neglect Halloween sales. A three-foot-high Marge Simpson wig has done wonders for my own sex life, and sometimes my wife will even wear it.

Pretending to be other people can be a harmless way of siphoning off some of that urge-to-swing pressure, and you're virtually guaranteed to discover something about your bed-mate that you never suspected before, even if it's only of the "He should be prohibited by federal law from ever wearing tights again" variety. You can even take it out in public, arranging to meet each other in bars and such, although it would probably be a good idea to agree on matching costumes beforehand. Unless of course you get really turned on by the thought of, say, Martin Luther picking up Cinderella in a sports pub and taking her in a back alley for a quick stand-up.

Come to think of it, that doesn't sound too bad…

Lovers by Proxy (or Sex by Mail)

You don't necessarily need a new person in the room, you just need some new viewpoints. Try a few of these handy tips:

Pop in a porn tape, turn the volume up, and turn the set toward the wall. Now you can pretend you've been invited to a massive orgy and the two of you just ducked into a side room for some privacy.

Pop in a porn tape and join in. Do what they do, when they do it, for as long as they do it. Try to avoid picking tapes that feature stars capable of things you could never do even with vitamins and a fence puller, and be sure to alternate purchases so she doesn't buy four *Bend Over Boyfriend* tapes in a row. Unless you want to, of course.

Pick a famous couple and act out what you think their sex

life must be like. No fair picking anyone from the Royal Family or a Kennedy—they're too well documented. Or you could pick two famous people that you think really should have sex (here I'm thinking Madonna and Dr. Watson). Alternately you can pick your own friends or acquaintances and act out what you think *their* sex life is like. Make sure you don't get too interested in your lover's masterful rendition of Miss Jenkins from Accounting, however. Anything you say can and will be used against you later on. You should definitely avoid such exclamations as "Oh, Margaret, this is exactly how I imagined it!," or "I thought you'd be thinner."

If you really want to challenge your emotional stability, have sex as each other. Dress up in your lover's clothes, use his or her favorite seduction techniques, if any, and live life from the other side for once. Try to avoid sarcasm or obvious parodies, and make sure that any firearms in the house have locked trigger guards.

Pick up some good written smut and act out the sex scenes. Simple test for good smut books—pick it up and open it three times at random. If you hit a sex scene twice, buy it. Fortunately this works in almost any book published in the last twenty years that doesn't actually involve Harry Potter.

Play the stock market. Not the boring way, with money and everything, but in bed. Take an assortment of stocks, write them out and assign a different sex act to each one. At the close of trading each day, check the returns and map out your evening playtime from the results. This also gives you the extra anticipation from watching the stock market throughout the day. "C'mon, Amalgamated! Two more points and it's blowjob city! Go baby, go! I need this bad!" Don't worry about your coworkers talking about you—all investors talk like this.

Bringing in a Whole Other Person
If you're really having difficulties changing your perspective, you can get some outside help without compromising your fidelity or having to share your towels.

Invite a friend to provide choreography. Whether by e-mail, prewritten suggestion, or even a whispered comment before you leave work, your friend can provide a game plan that you might not have considered. Even a passed note at lunch that says "Apply lubricant with a whitewash brush and bucket" can add a new depth to your evening activities. You could even trade notes every day, get a sort of one-upmanship competition thing going. "Okay, I did him in the rectory like you said, now tonight you have to let him strap you to the ice cream truck." Bringing it up with your friend in the first place is your problem.

If you need on-the-spot advice, dial up a phone-sex number and let her (or them) talk you both through. Think of it like calling up a sex hotline, where operators are lying by. You can call a friend for the same purpose but by that point you may not be capable of explaining yourself and people tend to hang up on late-night breathers. Call a pro.

Get online and join a chat room, then let everyone decide by consensus what should happen next.

— Dude! Grab her titties!
— No no kiss her first
— Are there any hot ladeez here?? Im what you need!!!
— Get her on top and get her to lean back til shes laying back on your knees, that's always really good an she'll like it
— Radiohead Rules!!

Spend some time investigating chat rooms before you do this—you don't want to discover that your sex life is being directed by a group of eleven-year-old quilting enthusiasts.

If you're bold enough, you can invite a friend over to call out suggestions from the next room. It can be an incredible rush knowing someone else is so intimately involved with what you're doing, it's oddly relaxing not having to decide what to do, and extremely thrilling wondering what your friend will think up next. To get past the inevitable embarrassment, a glass or two of wine for everyone can be invaluable. You might even let them bring a date, in case they feel more comfortable that way. Or you can invite a small group of friends over to get a more varied collection of suggestions. Yes, I think that would be the best way. A roomful of your buddies, roaring drunk, screaming sexual advice at your bedroom door. What could be more romantic?

You can involve friends and still remain private. Invite a trusted friend to videotape you and your lover at play, but blindfold them to maintain decorum. They can follow the noises for the most part. If focus is really a problem or if you tend to move around a lot, have them creep up slowly until their toes touch flesh, then stop and just aim the camera down. Or you can work out a modified version of the water game "Marco Polo."

Wouldn't it be nice to visit Mom? Just stop by as a surprise, maybe bring some dinner. She'll be so pleased she won't even notice the two of you taking so long to visit the bathroom and you'll be able to relive some of the teenage excitement you haven't really experienced since you moved out and finally lost your paranoid habit of listening for slippers coming down the hall.

Go Cruising Together

If you really have the three-way bug, take her out to a public place where attractive people of questionable morals congregate, like a bar or a strip club or a courtroom, and start picking out which stranger you'd most like to boink. Argue over relative merits and unfortunate shortcomings, and build up your fantasies about what you'd all do to each other. Then you can go home and tell them to each other as you work yourselves into an uncontrollable frenzy of lust and unbridled sensuality. Watch an adult movie together and imagine the stars climbing out of the television to seduce the two of you. Pick a friend you can both agree on and include him or her in your fantasy life (although you must be careful to keep it private, lest they wonder why you're smiling at them that way in the elevator). Or you can get into a raging fight over whom to pick and get divorced, and than you'll have the freedom to go back and find the Hooters girl you were looking at. Either way, it's new sex.

There are many fun and exciting ways of improving your sex life while still keeping it in the family (the two-person family, I meant—leave her sister alone). Sleeping with someone else just because your current sex life is boring is like giving up on your favorite team during a losing streak. Just like with your team, try encouragement and different plays for a few seasons before you trade them for someone younger with faster hands.

Meet Maureen

by Florence Hoard

Dean Martin crooned "You're nobody till somebody loves you" so loudly that Gerard didn't hear the women come in. Audrey's leather walking coat brushed his arm and jarred him away from his *Rolling Stone*. He looked up to see her walking by the couch, followed by a chestnut-haired woman with a fabulous ass.

He stared after them, wondering what was up. Who was that woman? Audrey had said she'd stop by after she went shopping that morning and he understood she'd be alone. She often just let herself in with her key, so he didn't mind that, but why had she just walked by him now without saying hello or introducing her friend?

He returned to his magazine, unable to focus, curious about what they were doing in the kitchen. After reading the same paragraph four times without absorbing a single word, he muted Dean a bit and wandered into his kitchen. Audrey and the woman stood near the stove, waiting for the teakettle to whistle, laughing in that way women have that makes you feel like they've just been discussing the last time you couldn't get it up.

"Hey, Gerard," Audrey finally acknowledged him. "This is Maureen. I met her in Bucktown when we were fighting over the same belt." They laughed, he smiled. Maureen's big dark eyes assessed him thoroughly and he felt every moment of her inspection.

"We thought we'd have to wear it at the same time," Maureen said to him without looking at him. Her rich brown hair, only a few shades lighter than her suede coat, hung thick and touchable around her shoulders. She was just slightly taller than Audrey, maybe 5'3". He wanted her to look at him.

"Nice to meet you," he said, extending his hand to her. She took it, finally shifting her gaze to meet his. Gorgeous eyes.

The teapot screamed and they all jumped. Audrey set about pouring the boiling water into two mugs. "Did you want any tea, babe?" she asked, knowing he never drank it.

"No, thanks. I guess I'll leave you two alone. Nice to meet you," he directed to Maureen, who nodded and grinned sweetly.

He returned to the couch, irritable and still curious. Suddenly, whatever they were talking about held more interest than Dean did. He lowered the volume yet again, straining to hear their conversation as he pretended to read. Their talk grew more hushed, the laughter less frequent, until finally he heard nothing at all.

Audrey appeared at the doorway, cocking her head in that way that usually prefaced a request. "Gerard?"

"Yeah?"

"Are you very busy?"

He held up his magazine, sparing no exasperation, to demonstrate his obvious leisure. Audrey turned behind her to Maureen and nodded. They both walked in, Audrey looking sly and Maureen blushing.

"We were just talking in the kitchen," Audrey began, "about how to please a man."

"Really." His pulse raced but he'd be damned if he'd let either of them see him turned on. "I don't think I can help you. I've never pleased one."

"No, but you've *been* pleased," Audrey continued, running her fingers through his hair as she sat beside him on the couch. "Haven't you?"

"What the hell are you up to?" He didn't want to waste a hard-on on something that was going nowhere.

"Just a little education. Maureen says she doesn't think she gives good blowjobs." Maureen hovered uncertainly by his leg.

"What am I supposed to do? Call her boyfriends to find out?"

The more flippant he was, the calmer Audrey became. "No . . ." She looked up at Maureen and winked. "I'd like to give her instruction. On you."

Maureen knelt, tossing her beautiful hair to one side, her nearly black eyes imploring and seducing. She was no longer blushing.

"I don't believe this. You're fucking with me," he laughed, more nervously than he intended.

Maureen leaned into his lap, heading for his belt buckle. As she slipped the leather through the buckle, Audrey spoke.

"I just want to give her a few tips. It won't take long."

He wanted to tell his girlfriend she'd lost her mind, but suddenly he realized that she was giving him his fantasy, the one they'd often discussed. As her gaze penetrated his, he understood this and relaxed. Audrey smiled with relief. Maureen unzipped his fly.

"Take your cock out for Maureen," Audrey instructed.

He obeyed eagerly but with some trepidation. Who was this woman, really? Could she be trusted? As her hot breath spread over his erection, his worries subsided.

"Start slowly," Audrey said quietly. "Run your tongue up his shaft and avoid the head at first."

Maureen licked him with one long, slow, upward motion, catching the very edge of his swollen head as she ended her stroke. She repeated her movements several times before Audrey continued.

"Everybody thinks they should only go up and down on a guy's meat, but it's fun to gum it a little from the side. Go ahead, like a dog holds a stick in its mouth to carry it somewhere."

The willing student wrapped her voluptuous lips around his shaft and sucked while she licked. She glanced at Audrey for approval.

"Yeah, that's good. Isn't that good, Gerard?"

"She's doing fine," he replied, hoarse.

"Play with his balls, too. You can use your hands, if you want, but I like to suck one ball in my mouth at a time and then pop it out, really gently. Suck his balls, Maureen."

She'd definitely sucked balls before. As she dipped downward, she took hold of his cock and massaged gently but confidently. Meanwhile, her full lips parted to accommodate the circumference of half his sac. His right ball disappeared into her mouth and while she held it inside, her tongue circled it, over and over. He groaned.

"Mmmm, he likes that. Suck the other one," she said as Maureen was already moving to do so. Moments later, with her face buried in his crotch, his entire ball sac undulated under her busy tongue, filling her hot mouth. He watched, fascinated by how she could accommodate all of him.

"Oh, Maureen, you look so hot with Gerard's balls in your mouth. Look, Gerard, her whole mouth is stuffed with you."

He was looking, all right. In fact, he was growing tired of looking. His cockknob needed some attention. Soon.

"Hear him breathing heavy? Now's the time to stick his cock down your throat." Maureen ejected his now tight sac from her steamy mouth. "But first, flick your tongue around the head. Catch some of that pre-cum."

Maureen's tongue flicked like a rattlesnake's across his cum hole. She licked until she'd lapped up every trace of his early ejaculate. He couldn't take his eyes off her, wildly tracing the edges of his knob, paying special attention to the smooth spot that was most sensitive. Audrey pointed it out to her. He wasn't used to having two women so focused on his dick, but decided he could get used to it.

"Suck just the head. Not too hard. Pretend your mouth is a cunt. Coat his head with the same kind of pressure that your pussy would give it. Fuck the head like it was inside you."

Her mouth became the twat Audrey described. It pulled with wet insistence, encasing him like a glove. He felt the churning in his balls and knew he wouldn't last much longer.

"I'm gonna come," he said breathlessly, wincing at his own pleasure.

"Let him go," Audrey announced to his horror. Maureen stopped sucking immediately and looked to her new friend for guidance.

"Why did you do that?" Gerard demanded.

"Because I want to show you what I bought today while I was shopping." She dug into her purse.

His jaw dropped. When he noticed Maureen's grin, however, he squelched his own anger and decided to wait and see what was in store for him next.

"So, you think Maureen learned all she needed to?" he wondered aloud, hoping for a negative answer.

Audrey stood and was already halfway out of her clothes before he knew what was happening. Maureen stroked his leg absently, focused more on Audrey's movements than on his raging hard-on.

Wearing only a black lace bra and matching thong, Audrey removed a dildo and harness from her purse. Maureen started to strip, obviously excited. As Audrey strapped on her big, purple dildo, Maureen lay back naked on the carpet and spread her legs so that he could see her deep pink folds. They shone with slippery welcome, thanks to her Brazilian wax. Her tits were smaller than Audrey's, but nicely shaped with perky nipples. He held onto his dick to keep from pushing it into her.

Audrey, looking armed and dangerous with the purple cock swaying from her abdomen, positioned herself before the trembling Maureen.

"You want me to fuck you, Maureen?"

"Yes. Yes, put your fat dildo up my cunt."

Audrey fingered her first, frigging the woman so that he could hear her juices whipping to a froth. Maureen squirmed and spread her legs wider.

"There, you're nice and wet now," Audrey said, holding the dildo in her hand like a man about to masturbate. She exuded

an aura he'd never noted before, but he couldn't place it.
Whatever it was, his cock was wild about it. He watched the
expression on Audrey's face change from self-conscious and
haughty to self-confident and in control.

"Tell Gerard how much you want my thick cock in your
hole."

Maureen turned to Gerard and tweaked one of her nipples
as she spoke. "Please tell her to fuck me."

"Is your pussy dripping for it?" He jumped on the opportunity to play, too.

Maureen nodded, whimpering.

"Then you better open nice and wide so I can see your
cream. Prove to me that you're ready."

He slowly fucked his pulsing, rock-hard cock in his hand as
she showed him her deep pink twat. Taut and trim, Audrey
knelt poised over the woman, wagging the purple dildo men-
acingly at her target.

Audrey parted Maureen's slit with the silicone head and
slipped inside. Maureen called out in unintelligible sounds
before she gasped "yes" several times.

Audrey pumped, fast and furious. Her tits jiggled as she
rammed the woman, whose owns breasts bounced with each
thrust. Audrey diddled Maureen's clit with her thumb as she
fucked her.

He imagined himself the purple dildo, sliding in and out of
Maureen's juicy cunt, feeling the wet walls squeeze and massage him. He beat his meat in time to Audrey's movements, so
mesmerized he couldn't speak. The veins on Maureen's neck
stood out and she bit her lip as her hands clenched.

He'd never had such a vantage point to a woman's orgasm.
Never seen one that he wasn't responsible for (not counting
porno flicks, where he didn't believe the orgasms were real,
anyway). Having Audrey act in his place took away his control
as it heightened his excitement.

Power. That's what Audrey exuded as she stuffed the dildo
into the writhing Maureen. He hadn't been sure until this

moment, but now he knew. His girlfriend's strength and power turned him on as much as the sight of Maureen's fields being plowed.

Maureen arched her back and yelled, pushing her fists into the floor. Audrey rammed harder and faster at her lover's climax, then slowed in tandem with her denouement. She gyrated her hips against Maureen's spasming cunt, moving the dildo in circular motions inside her. Audrey leaned forward to squeeze Maureen's breasts affectionately before she kissed her belly, leaving a lipstick smear behind.

"You two don't think you're done, do you?" He suddenly found his voice.

Audrey turned to him, arousal steaming off her body, her eyes dark pools of seduction. "What did you have in mind?"

"It's time for you to get fucked, young lady. Maureen, strap that dildo on."

The chestnut-haired beauty shot a glance at Audrey, who was suddenly in a position of granting permission. She shrugged her assent and Maureen forced herself into a vertical posture. Audrey fiddled with the straps of the harness and freed the contraption from her hips, not bothering to remove the dildo.

"Get on your hands and knees, Audrey," he commanded, looking forward to directing the rest of this little floor show. He liked watching his girlfriend move—her fitness regimen had produced one of the finest bodies he'd ever known. Her legs, now bent and poised to take thrusts from behind, held her sturdy with muscles flexed and ready.

Maureen positioned herself behind Audrey and ran her palms over the woman's shapely ass and thighs. As she bent to kiss Audrey's smooth derriere, she slipped a hand between the toned brunette's legs. Audrey raised her bottom as if to push it in her lover's face. Remarkably, Dean launched into "When the moon hits your eye like a big pizza pie, that's *amore*."

"What are you doing? I told you to fuck her."

"I can't kiss her?"

"When I tell you."

"So, what do you want me to do now?"

"Fuck me!" Audrey hissed impatiently over her shoulder.

Maureen withdrew her hand from Audrey's dripping pussy.

"Give me your hand," he said to Maureen. "Let me taste her cunt off your fingers."

Maureen extended her arm to wave her hand before him. He leaned toward her and sucked one manicured finger at a time, relishing Audrey's familiar scent and taste. When he'd licked the woman's fingers clean, he told her to insert the dildo into the nearest cunt.

"Spread her ass cheeks for me so I can see everything you do. I want to see her take that cock all the way up her pussy."

Maureen obeyed, displaying Audrey's asshole and labia, now drenched with juice.

"Push your cock into her hole. Push it deep. She likes it that way. But go slow. It drives her crazy." He spit into his palm and started to fuck it.

The purple dildo disappeared gradually into Audrey. With all of it buried in her twat, he told Maureen to start pumping her.

"Ram her hard. Make her big titties shake. Yeah, that's it. Stuff her cunt with cock."

Maureen held Audrey's hips for support and did as she was told. Not only did Audrey's titties bounce, Maureen's jiggled provocatively as she threw her weight into her thrusts. She made sure that every insertion was total, that Audrey felt the tip of the dildo deep inside her vagina over and over again. Audrey absorbed every thrust with a yelp, which told him the dildo surged as deeply as he normally did. She fucked the dildo back, pushing herself onto it as it plunged into her.

He stopped spanking his monkey long enough to take off his clothes and crawl over to the women. As Maureen screwed Audrey, he knelt beside his girlfriend and took a nipple in one hand and her clit in the other. He rubbed and kneaded both of them until he felt them harden.

"Come for us, baby. Don't you like having your clit rubbed while you get fucked? Fuck her pussy, Maureen. *Fuck her!*"

Maureen grew breathless with exertion but continued to do as he instructed. He could watch this spectacle indefinitely, he thought, as she thrust her hips forward like a man, sticking her dick into a hot, wet cunt.

Audrey threw her head back and yowled. Her ass cheeks clenched and she lowered her head to the floor, where the carpet helped to muffle her screams. He moved his hand from her clit to Maureen's pubic hair.

"Slow up. Then pull out slowly," he said.

When the dildo finally popped out of Audrey, he couldn't resist stooping to lick it clean. He loved the taste of her so much that he'd even lick something that resembled a cock, he laughed to himself. He then moved his face to her cunt, where he kissed her hot, pulsating lips, smearing her juice over his chin, nose, and cheeks.

Grabbing the dildo, he pulled Maureen closer to him as he ate Audrey's pussy. When she was close enough, he turned his head to sample a bit of her twat, too. He pulled the women toward his face so that all he had to do was turn his head in either direction and he had a mouthful of dripping cunt. He ate until his cock ached, which wasn't long.

He sat up straight, still on his knees.

"Take off the dildo, Maureen."

She did and handed it to him with question in her eyes. He strapped the thing onto his hips, bemused by the sight of two hard cocks in his lap.

He spread Audrey's juice from her cunt to her asshole with his fingers. He needed more lubrication on the dildo.

"Come here and ride the dildo for me, Maureen."

Dutifully, she straddled him as he knelt there on the floor. She lowered herself onto the purple cock. With her arms around his neck, she bounced beautifully on him. He was unable to resist rimming her asshole as she bobbed up and down on the fake dick. She dripped so much juice that even her asshole was moist. When he thought the dildo had enough pussy juice, he lifted her off it.

"Now, go slide yourself under Audrey and suck her big tits for me."

He gently nudged the dildo into Audrey's little bunghole, being careful to wait for each muscle to relax before feeding her more of it. When most of it was in, he stuffed his own needy member into her other hole.

Audrey trembled as both her orifices were filled to capacity with pumping cocks. Maureen's long legs were all he could see of her as she busily tongued Audrey's sensitive nipples. Audrey, twisting and nearly delirious, called out with sounds he'd never heard her make before. Her pussy clutched at his cock, signaling that she would be coming any second.

He knew it wouldn't be long before he'd have to shoot his load. With no time to consider where to put it, he spewed into Audrey's hot cunt, unable to stop fucking her even as his cum oozed out of her. Through his own dazed consciousness, he vaguely heard her moans.

Maureen got out from under her new friend and left the room. Gerard slowly withdrew both his cocks from Audrey's raw holes and caressed her ass. Exhausted, she fell to one side, limp and satiated.

He curled up next to her on the floor, spooning her from behind, stroking her dark hair affectionately. Maureen, now dressed, reappeared and stepped over their legs as she snuck out of the apartment. He thought he heard her whisper goodbye, but couldn't be sure.

"You okay?" He said softly into Audrey's ear.

"Oh, yes. You?"

"I don't think it would be possible to be better. Thank you for what you did today."

"Mmmmm," she said before they both dozed off.

The Arbitrageur

by Bill Noble

I'm a dealmaker. Disregard the Ivy League elegance, the law degrees, the carefully appointed, hushed offices I maintained on Montgomery Street for twenty years; I get in the middle of things, wanted or not. Sometimes with honey, sometimes with a hammer. I make money, anywhere in the world; a decade ago I was forty-five, with a net worth that teetered somewhere below nine figures. My wife, Emily, ten years my junior, would have loved for us to spend several more months each year in Europe. But, for me, the amusements of money and power were too sweet to abandon.

This story, though, is mostly about another matter than money. An adventure, if you will, and one I chose not to communicate to Emily, for reasons that were obscure to me. A private adventure, into unfamiliar territory.

It began nine years ago in the fall, at a private reception celebrating a new exhibit at the De Young Museum, in San Francisco. After several glasses of an excellent Napa chardonnay, I wandered off alone into the galleries.

I was admiring an enormous bronze temple bell when two young women came into the room. They appeared to be in their mid-twenties, educated, self-possessed, and with an edge of chardonnay-induced mischief.

They joined me in silence around the bell. One of them, blond and willowy, raised her face to me. "You must be Professor Mallory."

"I'm flattered." I bowed with a self-mocking smile. "But I'm merely one of the many patrons of the arts."

"A most distinguished patron," the one with the fashionably bobbed dark hair smiled back, looking me up and down.

No man of my age could have ignored such an opening. "Merely one with a great appreciation of beauty," I said, letting my gaze linger on the portion of bosom blossoming above her evening dress.

The corner of her mouth tilted up. "The appreciation that age brings, I imagine."

A riposte was on the tip of my tongue when the blond woman gestured around the room. "Perhaps he only meant the art, Caillie."

"At his age, maybe," the dark one said.

"I assure you, my appreciation is fully intact," I replied, "for beauty of all sorts. Perhaps the young have an incomplete understanding of the skill and range that maturity can confer. The worth of age."

"What worth is that?" Her eyes locked with mine. I felt a wave of heat sweep over me.

I laughed. "More, I'm afraid, than youth could afford."

"Is that so?" The space between us crackled.

"It is."

"What's your asking price?"

I had never been challenged like this by a woman. It wasn't calculation that produced my answer; it was testosterone. I spoke with a casualness I did not feel. "For you? A special deal: say three thousand dollars."

The blond was watching us both. "Caillie . . ."

"What would that buy us?"

"Us?"

"The two of us. Would it buy us the night, this 'special' of yours?" Her words went right to my sex.

"It would buy you whatever you wanted. Including the night." This was happening too fast, but I was damned if I'd pull back.

The blond put her hand on the other's arm. "Caillie . . ." The dark one shook it off, eyes still locked with mine. Her purse made an audible *snap* as she opened it. She had not the trace of a grin now.

She fished out a gold money clip. One by one, thirty hundred-dollar bills sailed to the floor at my feet. She counted as she dropped them. "If you're man enough," she said. "For a special."

She closed the purse. "And, of course, not too old."

I heard an accusatory tone in Emily's voice on the outgoing voicemail message. Of course I imagined it. Emily and I were forthcoming about any little adventures; we both had lovers from time to time in California, and we both traveled. We enjoyed sharing stories afterward—and often beforehand, in naughty anticipation. This time, though, whatever was about to happen seemed too open-ended and odd to confess until it was over, or at least that's what I told myself; it had an edge that was both silly and slightly humiliating. Or perhaps it was just that my heart was beating too fast to leave a longer message.

I spoke into the phone. "Darling. My meetings in L.A. have been moved earlier tomorrow, so I've decided to fly down tonight. The De Young was delightful. See you tomorrow evening."

Nob Hill had a Wednesday-evening quiet as I gave the valet my car. The lobby of the Mark Hopkins was unusually empty, and I was thankful. My disquiet grew.

Room 427 was close to the elevator. I took a deep, slightly shaky breath before I knocked. The door opened to Caillie's wry smile. I stepped inside. The door clicked behind me.

Caillie was wearing a smoke-colored, near-transparent gown and gold sandals. The blond woman was already in the big double bed, covers half pulled up, looking fresh out of the shower. I opened my mouth to say something, but Caillie put her fingers to my lips. "'Whatever we wanted,' you said. Then our first request is that you not speak. We won't be requiring conversation." She slipped the gown over her head, kicked the sandals aside, and slipped into the bed. "By the way, this is Bren." The blond woman curled against Caillie's breast looked at me.

"First," Caillie said, "you're still dressed for the museum. Take off your clothes."

A blush spread over my face. Whatever I had been fantasizing, the evening appeared to be taking its own course.

"Now."

I unknotted my tie and laid it over the arm of a chair. My shirt followed, then shoes and socks, pants and briefs. The two women looked me up and down.

The blond, Bren, murmured, "He's not bad."

"Not for his age. But if he was twenty, he'd be erect by now." Instead of fading, I could feel the blush extending over my chest. "What do you think, Bren? Wouldn't he be more amusing hard?" Bren's hand moved to cup Caillie's breast.

Caillie's eyes were unwavering. "Stroke yourself."

I reached awkwardly, after a moment, to touch myself. Caillie twined her tongue languidly with Bren's.

This was unique for me, to stand naked in front of two strange, young and beautiful women, ordered to arouse myself. Despite the erotic intensity of the situation it took me a disturbingly long time to become erect. My conflicted feelings mirrored themselves perfectly in the indecision of my body.

When I was finally fully hard—I credit them for choosing not to embarrass me—Caillie called me to the bed. I stood there, the pulse knocking in my erection, but well aware of its precariousness. Caillie's hand snaked out from under the covers and gripped me. My hips gave an involuntary jerk. "What do you think we want now?" Her eyebrows rose, mocking. "Perhaps you'd like to service Bren? She's very wet. Aren't you, Bren?" She turned and tongue-kissed her again, smiling through the kiss as she felt me swell further.

"But I don't think so. I know you'd like to fuck *me*." She laughed as my cock leapt. "Male dominance, isn't it? Though you're clearly finding it a turn-on to be naked, mute and powerless, you also find it terrifying. And you're not at all used to powerlessness, poor man."

She released my cock and her brow drew down. "Kneel."

In for a penny, in for a pound. I knelt at the side of the bed. She threw off the covers and leaned back in Bren's arms. Her silken legs hooked over my shoulders. "Lick me. And do it well, my *man of mature skills*."

As I moved between her thighs, the scent of moisture, of heat and sex, overwhelmed me. I began to tremble. She grabbed my hair and pulled my face into her.

Alas, it's not the evening's sex that this story is about. Let me say only that it was a long time before I rose from my knees, and hours longer before I fell into a hazy, unfulfilled, erotically charged sleep on the carpet, at the foot of their bed.

I found myself unable to tell Emily what had happened. Perhaps I feared her disapproval. Or worse, her ridicule. The emotions were more complicated than that, though: My powerlessness that night was a shameful, dirty secret, and I treasured it.

A month later, my cell phone rang as I headed down 280 to Menlo Park. Caillie's voice cut instantly to my core.

I stuttered, "How . . . how did you get this number?"

"From your phone, while you were asleep. I'm afraid we used you very hard—for someone of your age. I want you for another evening. What's your price?"

"Another evening? What sort of evening?"

The line went instantly dead. I found I had an erection.

Two weeks later she called again, in the middle of a business meeting. She didn't bother to say hello. "Give me your price. You have two seconds; otherwise I'll never bother to call again."

"Two," I blurted out. "No, three." I had kept the first money hidden, folded in my dresser under the socks, a talisman for something I couldn't quite name; day by day I was less inclined to share it or my story with my wife.

"Good. The same room at the Mark, eight tomorrow night. A different woman. She will be submissive. She expects the sex to be safe."

"I have an engagement tomorrow evening. Is there another . . ." She had disconnected.

At 7:58 the next evening I knocked again at the door of Room 427 in the Mark Hopkins. I had put Emily off with an ineptly improvised story about a sudden Asian client, and left her to explain to our guests. Unlatched, the door swung inward at my touch.

A muscular woman with long, curling chestnut hair, perhaps forty years old, lay over the writing desk, which had been pulled into the center of the room. Her hands and feet were bound to the legs of the desk, leaving her buttocks and genitals exposed. She was blindfolded and breathing hard, but she was clearly there because she wanted to be: I caught the thick gleam of moisture between her spread legs. Her mouth gulped my cock when I thrust it at her blind face, as if it had been hungry a long time.

Again, the details of what I did are incidental to this story, though I found my ego much repaired. I had served the woman—and myself—well. Hours later she was tucked snugly into bed, still blindfolded. A pile of bills lay on the bedside table. Many of them were twenties, worn and creased: It was clear to me that she had been saving for a night like this for a long time. I shoved the double handful of them deep into my suit coat pocket. I knew as I left that I would keep them secret from Emily, too.

Caillie's next call was in the spring, nearly three months later. "Tomorrow night at the Mark. This time *you* will bring three thousand dollars. You will have the money in your right-hand pants pocket"

"Caillie . . ." I began, but the line was dead. Emily looked up from her Forsyth novel and cocked an eyebrow. "Who's 'Caillie'?" she asked. I opened my mouth, but no words found their way out. After a long appraising look, she went back to her reading.

The next night I pushed open the door to Room 427 for the third time. It was impenetrably dark. Slender hands pulled me in and closed the door. Two women extracted the roll of bills from my pocket and undressed me, lingeringly, in the darkness. One of the women who I thought for a moment might be Caillie reached up and kissed me as I had never been kissed before, a languorous, modulated, musical kiss, a Mendelssohn kiss, a Brahms kiss. Her fingers played over my face as if she had known my features all her life. The other woman moved behind me, to press her furred mound and nippled breasts against me, to breathe, open-mouthed, into my ear.

For the next three hours I was made love to as though my pleasure was the sole object of Creation. I was nurtured and teased—mouths, nipples, fingers, toes—until I was delirious, and then I was invited, wordlessly, to master two pliant, entwined bodies. I thrust and gripped and called out as I had not done since my twenties.

But, again, that night's coupling is not really what this story is about. As I lay spent, the bedside light came on. The tall woman was African, Nilotic perhaps, sculptural and serene. Her companion was Asian, a temple goddess, delicate, high-breasted and cream-skinned. They kissed me goodnight, and departed. After they left I heard a rustle of silk. I turned to discover Caillie sitting on the other side of the room.

I understood without being told that I was to remain silent. She came to the bed and took me with great gentleness in her hands to bring me to a third, or fourth, climax, one at the utter limits of my physical capabilities.

She stroked a long semen-slippery finger over my lips. Her enigmatic smile told me . . . nothing . . . but left me haunted and uncertain for days after. She retrieved the roll of bills from the bedside table, threw a brocaded wrap round her shoulders, and went out the door.

My fourth assignation was announced a month later, in a voice-mail. Caillie's cool, measured orders: "Tomorrow night. Eight o'clock." It was easy to arrange this time. My calendar was clear, and Emily had mentioned that she would be gone all afternoon and evening. I would not be forced to lie, though by this time I was so inured to deceit that it hardly mattered.

The door to Room 427 swung open at my touch. A television and VCR sat on the desk. Drinks were laid out on a side table along with an extravagant bouquet of roses, lubricants, and a bowl of condoms. The bedclothes lay in a tangled heap at the foot of the bed.

I stepped into the room, breathless. The door swung shut. Emily stood smiling behind it. My wife.

She was wearing nothing but a long rose-pink scarf that swirled around her thighs as she moved toward me. "My dear," she said. "You're perfectly on time." She put her arms over my shoulders and bussed me on each cheek. "You've always been so punctual."

"You know Caillie, I'm sure." Caillie emerged from the kitchenette in her smoky gown. She joined Emily, and the two of them undressed me. I began to explain to Emily, but she shushed me.

"I know as much as you do, my dear. More. Caillie called several weeks ago when you were in the shower, and we've had a whole series of delightful talks." She raised her eyebrows. "But perhaps I should have told you all this before? Do you think?"

She smiled. "You know, of course: You won't be expected to talk tonight."

From the sink counter, she produced an odd-looking apparatus, which she fastened to the frame above the bathroom door. It had dangling chains and oiled leather straps.

"Come here, dear, won't you?" Her cheeks held high color

and her eyes glowed. She raised my hands above my head and strapped them together. The chain clattered as she pulled it taut, securing me. My cock began to swell. So did my apprehension.

"Emily," I began.

She walked to the dresser. From her purse, a thick wad of folded bills appeared—the money from my dresser! She riffled the bills, then came and kissed me. "Surely you don't think we can really keep secrets, after all these years?" She grinned and kissed me. "Three thousand dollars. What an impressive amount of money! But first . . ."

At a gesture, Caillie slipped a cassette into the VCR. An eerie green-and-white image filled the screen—interwoven, moving human forms. With a jolt, I realized it was myself and the two courtesans, illuminated somehow in utter darkness. It was superbly edited, hours compressed onto a single tape, its erotic intensity magnified and focused. We watched in silence, arousal and terror fighting in me. Caillie stroked her breast. Emily smiled a hooded smile that kept my breathing shallow. In the last segment of the tape we watched as the lights came up; Caillie appeared and, ultimately, took her money and departed.

"Emily," I tried again.

A brusque knock came at the door. Caillie opened it.

A broad, thick man in a pearl gray suit stood there. His face was a rich red-brown, his cheekbones impossibly high and prominent. He had a Mayan nose and sensual, pouting lips. Shining black hair fell past his waist. He set a thin calfskin case on the table, bowed to the two women, and then to me. His suit, given his extraordinary build, was a miracle of tailoring. His shoes had the sheen of some exotic leather, shaped for his feet alone. I looked up into his eyes. They were black, impenetrable, eyes that would reveal nothing unless he willed it. And I suspected he would be rarely inclined toward self-revelation.

Emily handed him the sheaf of bills. He put it in the calfskin case.

"Emily . . ."

He began to disrobe.

"My dear, this is Domingo. He has flown here from London. Caillie arranged it—isn't she a wonder?" Domingo's eyes flicked over me, naked in the doorway.

As Domingo stepped out of his pants, his cock began to rise. I'm sure I gasped. It was common enough in length, but grotesquely thick. Massive blood-charged cylinders, side by side, swelled it to the width of a man's fist. Beneath, a ridge of flesh the size of an ordinary man's phallus sheathed the urethra. The head shone with the dense, moist gloss of liver.

Domingo's body, in contrast to his astonishing cock, was preternaturally smooth, shaved, and oiled till it gleamed. Thick, corded muscle stretched his skin. His black nipples stood out like a woman's, ornamenting his barreled chest. A double gold chain hung around his neck, each link inset with winking garnets.

Emily took him to the bed. Her scarf fell away and she flung one leg over his hips. She braced a delicate hand on his chest and took his cock in the other. She levered it up between her legs. As she lowered onto him, I watched the tendons of her inner thighs begin to vibrate. When he was half-embedded, a bull-like rush of air escaped him, and Emily made an abrupt guttural sound I had never heard from her in all our years together. Caillie perched next to them and brushed Emily's hair from her forehead.

Emily raised her eyes to me. They were, in that moment, as unreadable as Domingo's. "Isn't he magnificent?" she whispered. Her voice was unsteady, husky.

I glanced at Caillie, who was coolly stroking the two of them where they merged. Emily giggled and caught her breath. "Oh, my dear! You think he's for Caillie and me? Oh, no. No, Caillie and I have been together all afternoon. We're quite satisfied with one another."

Emily's smile, always dazzling, broadened and broadened. Sweat sheened her face and chest. She sank deeper onto

Domingo. I hung in the bathroom doorway, helpless, as Emily held my gaze. "Oh, no, my dear. He's for *us*. For me and for *you*. Oh, and well, well worth the expense, don't you agree?" Another guttural groan forced up from her gut. Domingo began to thrust. She dissolved into his embrace, crying out.

Caillie's hand cradled Domingo's full, dark sac, tugging it, caressing; her fingertips teased Emily's lips. I swung in the doorway, my arms aching.

Caillie's eyes sought me, large and dark. I could not tell if she was smiling.

So that's my story. Emily and I are older now. We leave Provence no more than half a dozen times a year, sometimes together, sometimes not. I occasionally find myself back in San Francisco, where we maintain an apartment. I still cut deals, these days mostly in cyberspace. I still have my bite. And these days Emily has taken to hinting we should have a *third* home, in Bora Bora or Tonga, or Queensland. Caillie, for good or ill, seems to have concluded her business and has never betrayed any further need to contact us. As far as I know, I say to Emily, probing, but she only smiles.

After that last evening at the Mark Hopkins, I let go of secrets. After Domingo, it was hard to imagine anything could ever again seem so intimate or so embarrassing as to invite concealment. But my nakedness that night—my nakedness of soul and psyche as much as my ravaged body—gave an edge to disclosure, a deliciousness to confession that I had never known.

Last year, I dallied with a French woman during a week in Deauville, a business partner's wife. When I told Emily, she said, "Perhaps I should punish you." And when my responding arousal betrayed me, we burst into laughter. "Now I see why you never try to do deals with me," she said. And then we made love, as I whispered in her eager ear the long and intricate story of my pleasure.

Jessie's Girl

by Jayden Blake

The lake wasn't crowded that day, even though the temperature hovered around ninety. And it was humid—a steamy, dripping scorcher of a day, when the only thing that mattered was keeping cool.

There were small knots of people scattered around the lakefront. They lay unmoving in the sun as if immobilized by her rays, but the three of us opted for the semi-shade of a scrubby ash tree. We too were motionless, feeling the sweat trickle down our bodies.

I felt a tickling as a bead of perspiration slipped from under my bikini top and trailed down my torso. Jessie reached over and caught it, then lifted his index finger to his tongue.

"You taste great even when you're well-done, Jen."

I turned my head to face him, laughing at his mischievous expression. Jessie grinned, brushed a lock of his shaggy hair out of his blue eyes, and spread his hand over my stomach.

Lang rolled up on his elbow. He watched Jessie's hand traverse the moist hills and valleys of my body and his face twisted into a mask of resentment. "I wish Crystal was here," he said. It was at least the twentieth time he'd expressed this sentiment.

I felt sorry for him. We'd been planning this picnic for weeks, then Crystal had called and cancelled at the last minute. Lang's disappointment was palpable, so Jessie insisted he come along with us anyway. He had, but he'd been brooding all day.

"I'm sure she's just as bummed out as you are," I assured him, rolling to face him, "and she can't be having much fun—spending a day like this sick in bed."

I stopped talking, because I saw he wasn't listening. Instead, he was staring at my chest. I glanced down and saw that the strap of my bikini top had slipped down over my shoulder, allowing one breast to nearly pop free of its narrow confines.

Lang's eyes were popping in a similar manner. "Anyhow," I continued, adjusting my strap, "maybe we could plan another picnic for next week, when Crystal's feeling better."

"Maybe," Lang agreed, but his eyes were still on my body. The undisguised lust in them made me a little uncomfortable but, in truth, I didn't really mind him looking at me that way.

I'd always found Lang exceedingly hot, with his curly dark hair, olive skin, and solid, muscular body, and I knew he was attracted to me, as well. Lang had a weakness for tall, willowy blonds and I was just his flavor, a fact that he transmitted by an occasional smoky flash of his dark eyes. He'd complain how Jessie had always gotten the best girls and teased us both, singing that Rick Springfield song from the '80s, "Jessie's Girl." "Where can I find . . . a woman like that?" he'd chant and I could tell Jessie got off on the fact that his buddy found me so attractive, but I sometimes wondered if he realized how deep that admiration ran.

But Jessie had no reason to worry, not really. No matter how hot Lang and I found each other we'd never act on it, because Jessie was too important to both of us. Lang and Jessie had been roommates since college and close friends since childhood. They were different as night and day—if Lang was dark and mysterious as the night, then Jessie was the bright gold of day, with his long blond hair, quick smile, and lean swimmer's build. Each was intensely sexy in his own way, but it was Jessie I loved. We'd been a couple for two very happy years and I knew he was the one I'd be spending the rest of my life with.

Much as I adored Jessie, though, I couldn't resist indulging in the occasional naughty fantasy about Lang. Some nights when Jessie and I made love, the mere thought that Lang was in the next room was enough to send me spinning into a potent, savage orgasm.

The way Lang was looking at me now made me wonder if he'd heard me on some of those occasions. His dark eyes seemed to lap me up and I flushed, shifting back against the solidness of Jessie's body. Despite the heat he readily spooned around me and I felt his crotch fit snugly into the hollow beneath my buttocks.

Jessie reached for the strap of my bikini top. "Leave it," he commanded, drawing it back down over my shoulder. "It looks good that way. Doesn't it, Lang-o?"

"It does," Lang agreed, his eyes once again on my partially exposed breast.

Jessie kissed my shoulder, his hand moving around my body. As Lang watched, Jessie's fingers surrounded the soft circumference of my breast and gave it a firm, deliberate squeeze.

Lang's eyes widened and I was shocked speechless. Before I could recover, Lang scrambled to his feet. "I'm going in for a dip," he said abruptly, heading for the water.

Jessie laughed softly and nuzzled my ear. Normally this melted me, but this time I pulled away and glared at him. "What was all that about?"

His blue eyes were wide and innocent. "What?"

"You *know* what!" I snapped, yanking the strap of my bikini back into place. "Why are you groping me right in front of Lang?"

He chuckled again and sneaked another quick feel. "I'm sorry, Jen. I just couldn't resist. He's got such a hard-on for you he can hardly look at you."

"He does not," I insisted, but I felt the flesh twitch between my legs.

"Oh, yes he does," Jessie maintained, his fingers stroking the underside of my breast. "Didn't you notice he was pitching a tent?"

As a matter of fact I had, and I could see that Jessie sported a similarly stiff rod. "Lang is your best friend," I reminded him. "Doesn't it bother you, to have him check me out that way?"

"No," he assured me. "It doesn't. I can hardly blame him. I mean, look at you, babe."

His hand slipped lower and burrowed between my legs. I cast an uneasy glance over my shoulder. "Jessie, somebody might see . . ."

"No one's close enough," he whispered, his hand coaxing my thighs apart.

But one person was. Lang was no more than twenty-five feet away, standing in waist-deep water. His eyes were on us as he sank to his knees, the water rising to his chin.

"You know what he's doing, don't you?" Jessie asked softly. "He's jerking off, wishing it was *him* with his hand on your pussy . . ."

I could feel my vagina loosening, becoming slick. Jessie kissed me then, slipping his tongue into my mouth as his finger slipped around the edge of my bikini bottoms.

"You want to fuck him, don't you?" he whispered against my mouth.

My eyes widened and I shook my head, but Jessie pressed closer. "Tell me the truth," he urged. "You've thought about it, haven't you? Taking his big cock, sucking it," he continued, as his fingers probed the slippery crevice between my legs. "Fucking it . . ."

I couldn't lie, because he could feel how hot his words were making me. "Maybe I have," I confessed, "but I love *you*, Jessie. I would never . . ."

"But what if I said it was okay?" he said, stroking my swollen nether lips. "What if I said you could fuck him . . . if I could watch?"

I'm not sure if it was outrage or arousal that caused my sudden shortness of breath. "I couldn't do that," I said. "Jessie, I just couldn't! And what makes you think Lang would want to, anyway?"

"Because Crystal's holding out on him," Jessie confided, his index finger gently nudging my clit. "He told me. He hasn't gotten any in three months, not since he started dating her, and he's ready to explode."

I couldn't answer, suddenly suffused with the vision of myself naked in bed with Lang as Jessie stood over our intermingled bodies. I'd never done anything like that—ever. A spark of desire flared in my stomach and plunged downward, making me tremble as it ignited between my legs.

My excitement must have shown, because Jessie's eyes took on an incandescent glow. "You just leave it to me, babe," he whispered as Lang came splashing out of the water.

Then I was merely a prop, an observer who watched, fascinated, as my boyfriend seduced his best friend. He used my body to do it: drizzling suntan oil over my torso; massaging it into my flesh with long, sensual strokes; running his fingers over the small scraps of fabric covering my most private parts; making my nipples harden right through the cloth.

Lang made a pretense of ignoring us until Jessie pushed my bikini top aside, far enough to entirely bare one breast. The angle of Jessie's body kept me shielded from the eyes of other beachcombers, but did nothing to conceal his actions from Lang, who couldn't tear his eyes off my erect nipple.

It was getting late in the day, and the sun had begun to creep down in the sky, her rays peeping beneath the cover of our tree. Jessie drizzled more oil over me. "Don't want my girl getting burned," he remarked, grinning at Lang. "Want to help me out here, buddy?"

Lang didn't need to be asked twice. He took over kneading the oil into my breast and Jessie's hand slipped into my bottoms. Jessie teased my clit as Lang took possession of my nipple, pinching and rolling it between his oiled fingers, his breath coming in short, hard gasps.

I moaned softly as Jessie took his hand from between my legs. He shifted closer, slipping his thumb into the waistband of his shorts. He drew it down, just far enough to free his cock, and I felt its silky head gliding over my stomach, lubing itself on my oil-drenched flesh.

Lang let go of my nipple and gripped his own crotch with urgency. He was visibly trembling. "God, you're killing me," he groaned, fumbling at the front of his bathing trunks. "I gotta . . . man, lemme . . ." He tugged and his dick sprang out, stone hard and oozing clear juice.

They pressed against me, one on either side, and as I closed my hands over their cocks I felt the differences between them. Jessie's shaft was an elegant wand—long, sleek, and graceful. Lang's was shorter but twice as thick, a solid, sinewy piston. They slid between my hands and buttery flesh and I let them nudge each other. I heard Jessie's swift intake of breath and that was when I realized my man didn't just want to watch Lang fuck me. He wanted to fuck Lang himself.

When Jessie suggested relocating to a more private place, Lang didn't answer, just jumped to his feet to gather up the picnic gear. We carried it to the truck and Jessie stowed it in the back as I got into the cab. Lang was beside me in a second and he kissed me for the first time, his mouth tasting of beer and passion.

Jessie got into the driver's seat and kissed the back of my neck as Lang was kissing my mouth. I could feel Jessie's fingers untie my top. It fell away and Jessie was cradling my oiled breasts, lifting and offering them up for Lang's mouth.

"Such beautiful tits . . ." Lang's voice was hoarse. "Gimme those big, beautiful tits . . ."

Lang buried his face between my breasts, squeezing them together so he could suckle both at once. Jessie tugged at my bikini bottoms, so I raised my ass and he peeled them down to my knees, then pushed my thighs apart. My cunt yawned open, glistening wet and quivering, and Lang plunged his hand between my legs, to grope and squeeze greedily.

"When we get home," Jessie told him, "I'm going to watch you fuck my girl, buddy. That okay with you?"

"Yeah," Lang breathed. "Just hurry, man. I can't wait to fuck this." He slid a finger inside me, then two. "Christ, this pussy is wet . . . wet and ready . . . shit, man, *hurry*!"

It took about twenty minutes to reach their apartment and Lang fingered my wet cleft the whole way. I squirmed, my naked ass wriggling against the vinyl seat as his busy fingers teased and fondled my clit. Jessie concentrated on driving, a small smile on his face, but I could see that his dick was so hard it seemed about to rupture his shorts.

By the time we pulled into the driveway, I had come twice; short, sharp bursts that I knew only hinted at the delights to come. Jessie didn't give me a chance to put my bikini back on, just grabbed the beach blanket and swathed it around my near-naked body then hurried me inside, calling for Lang to bring in the beer cooler.

As soon as we got through the door, Jessie tossed the blanket aside and lifted me onto the kitchen table. "Did you get a good look at his cock, babe?" he whispered, kissing me deeply as his hands stripped away the scraps of my bikini. "Are you hot for it, that stiff, thick cock?"

I moaned my assent as he pushed me back and lifted my legs high. "You look so beautiful, spread wide and ready to be fucked . . ." he murmured, burying his face between my legs. I shivered when his lips wrapped around my clit, sucking it like a warm, wet vacuum.

And that's how Lang found us when he came inside a moment later: me stark naked with my heels pointed at the ceiling, Jessie's hands cradling my ass while he devoured my pussy. Lang stopped dead and dropped the cooler with a clatter.

"Holy fuck," he sighed, bracing himself against the table with one hand and gripping his crotch with the other. "Shit, that's hot. That's so fuckin' hot . . ."

Lang reached out but before he could touch me, Jessie wrenched his mouth away and pulled me to my feet. "The bedroom," he urged, his voice syrupy with desire.

A minute later I lay across the bed, groping for a condom while Lang ripped off his shorts. Jessie slipped one into my hand as Lang crawled on top of me. He grabbed my legs and hooked them over his shoulders, humping impatiently as I unrolled the condom over his rigid cock.

When he was sheathed, I pointed him into my hot, wet cunt. "Fuck me, Lang," I begged.

"Yes, fuck her," Jessie urged and when I looked up at him I saw that he too was naked, his hand wrapped around his own stiff pole. "Give Jen what she wants, buddy."

Without further preamble, Lang's thick cock plunged into me, impaling me up to the hilt with one jab. He fucked me with short, hard strokes and it was good . . . so damn good I was catapulted into an immediate orgasm, heaving and moaning from the powerful waves of pleasure coursing through my body.

"Fuckin' hot pussy," Lang puffed, "This is some sweet, hot pussy." He inched my legs up around his neck and my back bowed as his hands lifted my ass even higher.

"Do it harder," Jessie encouraged, and I saw that he was stroking himself in time with Lang's thrusts. "She likes it fast and deep . . . so fuck her hard, buddy." The movement of Lang's hips accelerated, his cock pistoning like a jackhammer, and I could feel his balls slapping my ass he rammed into me.

I squeezed my eyes shut as I began to come again, moaning and sobbing with the intensity of it. I rode the crest of my orgasm and, as I wound down, felt a silken touch on my cheek.

I opened my eyes. Jessie was kneeling over us, his cock hovering near my face. "Suck me, babe," he urged. "Suck my cock while Lang fucks you."

I arched my head back, opened my mouth wide, and took Jessie's long cock down my throat. Lang was still pumping, obediently fucking my pussy while Jessie fucked my face. Watching me suck Jessie's cock seemed to turn him on even more and he voiced his approval while he fucked me: "Yeah, baby—suck that cock. Take it all, Jen, swallow it down . . ."

Jessie slid his cock nearly all the way out of my mouth and

paused, lingering just on the tip of my lips. I was well-attuned to what he liked and so I gave it to him, my lips sucking and nibbling the so-sensitive spot just below the dome of his penis. Lang fucked me in a slow and steady rhythm, and one particularly firm thrust caused me to lose my lip lock on Jessie's cock. It reared up, striking Lang's face and he recoiled, but Jessie groaned out loud and I realized then what my man wanted most.

I took hold of Jessie's cock, suckled gently, then slipped it from between my lips and switched my attention to Lang. I kissed him deeply, sensuously, then turned back to Jessie's cock. I nuzzled it, sucked it, and kissed Lang again.

I kept it up, alternately kissing and sucking, and I could hear Jessie moaning, felt his cock throbbing in my grip. This time when I drew Lang close for another long, passionate kiss, the tip of Jessie's cock was still in my mouth.

Lang's body stiffened in surprise, but I writhed beneath him, my tongue darting back and forth between his mouth and Jessie's cock. I swirled my tongue faster and faster, caressing Jessie's hard prick and Lang's soft lips at the same time.

I was on fire, my hips rearing up against Lang's cock with utter abandon while my mouth gobbled Jessie's cock. "Come on my face, baby," I pleaded. "Come on my face while Lang comes in my pussy. I want it so bad, Jessie. Please . . . Lang, come on . . . help me . . ."

Then Lang's mouth opened and we were sharing Jessie's cock. It glided between our mouths, our tongues mingling around it, and I could see wonder in Lang's eyes, and heat.

Jessie's hand gripped the back of Lang's neck and he was groaning, animal sounds that told me he was going to come. I saw his balls tighten, retract, and jets of heat exploded across my face. One . . . two . . . three spurts, his thick cream streaming over my mouth and chin.

"Shit!" Lang shouted. "Shit, me too, man! Me too . . ." He arched his back and heaved against me, his body spasming with the power of his orgasm.

For a moment, all of us were motionless: me with my legs locked around Lang's back and Jessie's cock against my face; Jessie poised on his knees above us, leaning against Lang's shoulder; Lang with his cock buried deep within me, his eyes wide with surprise.

Jessie reached down, scooped a bit of milky cream onto his finger, then fed it to me. I lapped it up dutifully, murmuring. With his other hand, he stroked the back of Lang's neck. "Everybody okay?" he asked.

Lang was watching me lick the cream off Jessie's fingers. "Oh yeah," he whispered, and kissed me, his tongue reaching into my mouth for a taste of Jessie.

We lay side by side in the darkening bedroom. The temperature had dropped along with the sun and a soft breeze wafted through the open window, fresh and cool against our damp bodies. We didn't speak, each lost in our own thoughts of what had passed between us.

Lang was in the middle, so quiet that I wondered if he was asleep. I heard Jessie stir and, when I looked over, saw that he was stroking Lang, exploring his body with the gentle fingers I knew so well. Lang remained still, his eyes squeezed shut.

Jessie touched his nipples, caressed them, and my own hands moved to canvass the dense area between Lang's legs. Lang's breath tightened, proving that he was awake after all, and, when Jessie put his mouth to a nipple, I saw Lang's cock twitch.

I reached for it as Jessie's head descended. His mouth left a wet trail as he followed the thin line of hair that tapered down Lang's abdomen. Lang's cock was lengthening, stiffening in my hand. I offered it to Jessie and, when he took it in his mouth, he wore a rapt expression. I watched his lips surround the velvety head, watched him take it deep in his throat, so deep that his nose nudged Lang's public hair.

Lang opened his eyes then, saw who it was that was sucking his cock with such reverence. "Dude, I don't know about this," he said, although his hips were moving back and forth, responding to the ministrations of Jessie's talented mouth. "Jess, I don't know . . ."

Jessie lifted his head. "Relax, buddy," he whispered. I took Lang's throbbing cock in my own mouth while Jessie moved to his balls. He kissed and fondled them, his finger tracing a slow, sensuous path over and behind the twin sacs. I couldn't quite see what Jessie was doing back there but, judging from the volume of Lang's moans, it was something extra special.

When Lang's cock reared up hard enough to make me gag, I pulled my mouth away and moved for a better look of what Jessie was up to. I saw that he was caressing Lang's anus, stroking and gently prodding the tight ring of flesh.

Jessie slipped a finger inside his ass and Lang moaned, spreading his legs wide. Jessie's finger burrowed deep, his tongue tracing the same trail his finger had blazed. When Jessie's tongue snaked into Lang's ass alongside his finger Lang went crazy, thrusting and rearing and moaning out loud. "Shit, that feels good . . . so damn good . . . nobody's ever done that to me . . ."

Jessie gave him a gentle push and Lang rolled onto his stomach, his ass rising high in the air. I had to touch myself as I watched Jessie tongue-fuck Lang, had to caress my pussy as Jessie's mouth caressed Lang's anus. Lang humped his ass against Jessie's mouth and I could see that he was completely under Jessie's spell, ready to submit utterly to whatever he wanted.

Jessie reached between my legs, lubed his hand on my juices, then slipped first one slick finger, then two, into Lang's asshole. He held out his other hand and I gave him what I knew he wanted—a condom.

When Jessie withdrew his fingers to slip on the condom, I saw that Lang's anus had opened—flowered—and was quivering with need. Jessie pressed the head of his sheathed cock against Lang's ass, raising his eyes to me. "It's your turn to watch, babe," he said as he began to work his penis into Lang's wet hole.

And I did watch, mesmerized. Jessie took him slowly, little by little, fondling Lang's genitals as he penetrated his ass. Lang was grimacing, clutching the bedclothes with white-knuckled hands. "Shit, that hurts," he grunted. "Dude, it hurts . . ."

"It will stop hurting," Jessie whispered. "Just relax. Don't fight it." He stroked Lang's cock as he pressed deeper into his ass, and didn't stop until he was fully submerged, his own balls flush against Lang's.

They seemed suspended, poised on the edge of something. Lang's body was rigid, clenched, his face twisted in a rictus of pain. It seemed they were soldered together, then the something gave and I watched Lang's body relax and sink back against Jessie.

Jessie began pulsing his hips back and forth. Lang emitted a long sigh and Jessie lengthened his strokes, releasing Lang's cock to grip his hips. Lang's body began to move in tandem with Jessie's, and Jessie increased the power and depth of his thrusts.

Jessie's head was thrown back, his eyes closed and his mouth wide open, contorted with profound pleasure. Lang's face was buried in his arms, but the murmurs coming from his throat were unmistakable sounds of ecstasy. Between his legs, dipping and bobbing freely, was the hardest cock I'd ever seen. It seemed ready to burst: skin stretched tight and shiny, its tip leaking gobs of clear juice. I had to touch it, suck it, lap up those drops of slippery pre-come.

I reached for it, but before I could get there Lang flung his head back. "Oh shit!" he shouted. "Oh fuck! *Fuck* . . ."

His cock exploded and he came, ropes of semen shooting across the bed clothes. Jessie tightened his grip on Lang's hips, plunging ferociously, and when he came, it was with a short, sharp cry and a final thrust of such force that Lang was propelled forward, his face disappearing into the pillow.

They rested together, Lang's face hidden, Jessie's still twisted in ecstasy. As his breathing slowed Jessie withdrew, removed the condom and tied it off, then dropped it to the floor beside

the bed. He ran his hand over Lang's back—a luxuriant stroke
that began at Lang's shoulder and slid down his spine to linger
briefly between his buttocks—then Jessie rolled over on his
back and stretched out between us, mindless of the semen
spattered on the blankets.

Lang lifted his head, contemplating Jessie with a peculiar
expression. Jessie met his eyes steadily, holding his gaze for an
endless moment. Finally Jessie smiled, then rose up on his
elbow. Lang stayed very still as Jessie kissed him, the lightest,
gentlest brush of lips against lips.

Lang sighed then, his body relaxing and sinking down in
the bed until his head rested against Jessie's chest. It seemed
an incredibly intimate action, far more than anything that had
come before, and, watching them, I felt a sudden stab of cold
in the pit of my stomach. For the first time, a nameless fear
took hold of my heart.

I must have withdrawn physically, because suddenly Jessie
was gripping my arm, pulling me toward him. He drew me
against his side and smiled down at me.

"I love you, Jen," he told me. "I love you so much." And he
kissed me, with the same passion and adoration I'd always
known from him. I melted against him, reassured, and felt
Lang touch my face.

When I looked at him, he was regarding me with a similar
tenderness. "I love you, too, Jessie's girl," he whispered. Then
Lang kissed me, as well, with a new affection and warmth.

Jessie curled his arms around our shoulders, hugging us to
him. As I snuggled against his body I reached for Lang's hand,
happy to find that there was ample room for both of us there,
on Jessie's strong chest.

Agua

by Jennifer Maer

azatlan, Sinaloa, Mexico is a city with a lot in its favor. It's coastal, it's warm, and, unlike Cancun or Ixtapa, it has a reason for existing outside tourism. Shrimp boats comb the shoreline, while the Pacifico brewery puts summer in a bottle, sending it north for the rest of us to enjoy. The city does not, however, offer much in the way of lesbian nightlife. Mazatlan's only gay bar, Pepe Toro, is as male focused as they come. Aside from the occasional dyke tourist, hardly any women enter the carefully guarded doors.

It was the next to last day of the year. My partner Lori and I were at Pepe Toro to suss out its New Year's Eve party potential. Holidays in the sun are certainly the way to go, but when the ball drops, you'd better be somewhere safe to kiss. Pepe Toro seemed just the spot. With a deliberate pat on Lori's ass, I showed the bouncer that yes, we knew it was a gay bar. And no, we weren't just fag-hags or cruise boat ladies slumming it for the night.

The two of us stepped up to the bar and had a look around. The place felt familiar, but small-town gay bars are a singular constant in the universe. They're all the same. Which leads to a certain level of comfort, really. Like ordering fries at McDonald's after weeks of eating strange, unidentifiable foreign foods. It may not excite your palate, but at least you know what you're going to get.

Pepe Toro had a dance floor, a small stage for drag per-
formances, and a raised seating area from which to sip your
drinks and view the proceedings. And, of course, it was decorated with creepy, black-and-white, happy-sad theatrical masks.
"They must sell them in bulk at the International Gay Bar
Outlet," Lori remarked. The speakers churned out a predictable but undeniably danceable mix of vocal house, with the
occasional Latin beat. The place was perfect.

Malibu and pineapple were the order of the day, perfect for
warm Mazatlan nights and pounding holiday hangovers. Lori
headed to the bar for another round. That's when I first saw
Maricarmen.

She was out on the dance floor, a lone woman amidst a
swarm of men, taking hearty slugs off a Corona. She looked
nineteen or twenty at best. Short, slender, and girlish. And she
was staring right at me. I turned around to check behind my
back. Yes, I confirmed. Me.

Lori came back, drinks in hand. "Check it out," I said. "That
girl keeps looking over here."

Lori assessed the situation. "That's weird," she said, checking behind us, just as I did. "She's looking, all right."

We watched the girl for a few more minutes, and the girl
watched us.

"She's cute," Lori concluded. "But she looks like she's in
high school."

As if on cue, the girl started toward us, parting the crowd
as she advanced.

"*Buenas noches*," she said, and then launched into a
Spanish monologue—none of which I could understand—
peppered with frequent attempts to touch my hair or take my
hand. I cursed myself for choosing French over Spanish in high
school. It had seemed the more romantic choice at the time. All
crêpes, café au lait, and French *Vogue*. A fat lot of good it was
doing me now. I had forgotten everything anyway.

I looked to Lori for help, but we were both stumped—useless monolingual Americans. "*Lo siento*," I said, mustering all

the Spanish I could. *"No hablo español."* But the girl kept talking a mile a minute.

"She's a little tipsy," Lori whispered.

"Gee, ya think?"

And still, the girl continued. Through frantic gestures and
a few familiar words screamed over a pounding bass, we found
out the basics. Her name was Maricarmen. She was twenty fingers old. She loved me—"I loooove you" she repeated, over
and over, becoming a cartoon version of herself—and she
wanted my phone number.

The pantomime became ridiculous. How do you act out
"I'm in a committed relationship, but I think you're very sexy
and I wish you the best of luck getting laid in this old-world
culture?" Somehow, I managed to get across "We're together"
and "You're very pretty." It was a combination that did nothing
to dissuade Maricarmen. In fact, she seemed encouraged.

"Ahhhhhh!" she said. And Lori and I went "ahhhhhh" with
her. But she continued, saying something in Spanish that
included the word *"dos,"* while wildly pointing back and forth
between Lori and me, smiling like a kid on Christmas day.

"Shit!" Lori said. "She thinks we're going to have a three-
way!"

This was not a good thing. Not at the time. Lori and I were
in the middle of trying to heal our relationship. A few months
before, I had let an office flirtation go one step too far, and the
betrayal, however unintentional, had torn at our seams. Lori's
trust was fragile, and allowing a third party into our bed was
no way to cement it. We had come to Mexico, after all, to be
alone.

"No, no, no," I explained to Maricarmen. *"No es possible.
No."* But Maricarmen was not to be put off, convinced she'd
soon be hopping in bed with two experienced American
women.

I held my index finger up in the international gesture of
"Gimme a minute." Maricarmen nodded her agreement, stepping back a few feet into the fringe of the dance floor, but

never taking her eyes off us. Lori and I huddled together.

"What do we do?" I asked.

She laughed at me.

"I'm serious, Lori. I don't want to hurt her feelings. Do you know how hard it would be to meet women down here?"

"And she's cute," Lori added.

I couldn't keep from smiling. "Well, there's that."

Lori thought for a moment. "You know, if we were fags, this wouldn't be a problem. We'd head to the bathroom, suck each other's dicks and be done with it."

"But we're not fags," I said. "And I left our dick at the hotel."

"Let's just buy her a drink and say '*No, gracias.*'" Lori said.

I leaned around Lori's shoulder to look at Maricarmen. She was still trying to work a vampy stare, but the effect was more endearing than seductive. I shot her a sheepish grin, and her face exploded into a smile reserved for imminent booty. "Okay," I said. "I'll get her a drink."

When I returned from the bar with another Corona, Maricarmen was dancing with Lori. I handed her the beer. She seemed delighted and took a long, thirsty pull. She motioned for me to come near, and took me by the hand. I leaned in to hear what she had to say.

Her breath was warm on my face. "*Gracias,*" she said, punctuating the thanks with a tongue in my ear. I felt a sudden loss of altitude.

"Whoa, whoa, whoa there. No, no. No tongue." Subtleties were impossible. The music was deafening, the language barrier nearly insurmountable. There was no way to discuss the gray area between desire and promises. Instead, I stepped away and shook my head "no."

Maricarmen's smile disappeared. She looked rejected for the first time. Her eyes were cast toward the floor, and I read embarrassment in the way she held her shoulders, now curling them forward as if to hide. I felt horrible, like I'd kicked a puppy. She raised her beer as a farewell gesture and headed back out to the dance floor.

"Great," I said to Lori. "I feel like Queen of the Asshole People."

Now it was Lori's turn to look hurt. "So you didn't get to bang the Mickey Mouse Club. You still get to go home with me, you know."

I had managed to fuck up in two languages.

Somehow we salvaged the evening. Maybe it was the Malibu. Maybe it was even Maricarmen. Despite Lori's jealousy, she was every bit as turned on by our sexy Mexican baby dyke's advances. I think the girl made us both feel a little less thirty.

We caught occasional glimpses of Maricarmen at the bar, always with a fresh beer, always with a "no harm done" smile for us. And at last call, when we headed for the door, she was still there.

Lori looked at me and read my thoughts. "Oh, come on," she said. "Let's go say good-bye."

Maricarmen's eyes were heavy. She was swaying back and forth on her seat, threatening to topple over at any moment.

"Hey there, Maricarmen," I said, realizing she probably didn't understand me. "You okay?"

She didn't answer.

I tried again. "Do you have some way to get home? Maricarmen?" I looked around for help, but all the men were hurrying off in pairs.

"We can't leave her here," Lori said. "This isn't the best part of town to be drunk and alone at night."

"Are you suggesting we take her back to the hotel with us?" I asked, incredulous.

"We have to do something."

So it was decided. Lori and I got on either side of Maricarmen and hoisted her to her feet. We managed to get her out of the bar and onto the street, hailing one of the open-air golf cart cabs that dart through the city at all hours of the day and night. Twenty pesos got us home, and ten more said "Thank you for not giving us a hard time about the girl passed out in the back of your cab, señor."

Up the elevator and into our air-conditioned room we went, flopping Maricarmen unceremoniously onto one of the two queen-sized beds in our suite.

"She looks like a little angel," said Lori. "A passed-out, horny little angel."

"Should we take off her clothes and put her in bed?" I asked, quickly adding, "That's what they always do in the movies."

"She's fine where she is," Lori said, stepping toward me and unbuttoning her shirt. "She's out like a light."

Aroused by our sleeping guest, we started to kiss. "You don't think she'll wake up?" I asked.

"Nah. She's down for the count."

Lori led me to the other bed and began stripping us both. I watched her reveal her tan lines, Day-Glo white against golden brown in the dim evening light. I vowed to trace every inch of the border with my tongue. We tumbled into each other and began to make love with an abandon that is particular to vacations. Not-at-home sex. Someone-else's-bed sex. Loud, sweaty, tropical-holiday sex.

"Where's the cock?" Lori asked, panting. "I want you to suck it for me before I fuck you."

I hopped to it, never needing to be asked twice. I handed her the dildo and harness. I turned to look at Maricarmen as Lori stepped into the apparatus (a procedure that's really best not to see, for the mood's sake). Maricarmen was lying on her side, mouth open, oblivious. Suddenly, I felt extraordinarily sleazy, and in a very, very good way. I dropped off the side of the bed and onto my knees. Lori stood before me, ever hard and urgent. I opened my mouth to take her in.

Sight and sound are key when you're blowing a silicone dick. The pleasure is in your mind first, then your groin. Lori looked down, watching me, and I made a good show of it, taking her in and out of my mouth, groaning as I did so, my eyes closed in rapture. If anyone had told me ten years ago that some day I'd enjoy sucking a cock-shaped, lavender rod of plastic, I'd have called them insane. My oral fixation, however, is a mighty one. Combine it with the anticipation of a spit-slicked fuck, and I'm ready to go.

Lori put her hands on the back of my head, taking fistfuls of hair, and I reeled from the feeling of submission. Both of us were lost in the moment. Perhaps a little too lost.

When I finally opened my eyes, Maricarmen was watching us intently. I jerked back with a start.

"Oh, you're not done yet, you little cocksucker," said Lori, totally unaware, and staying in the scene. My head was held firmly in place. I was frozen in position with a mouth full of dick and my eyes wide on the girl.

"MMMMMM MMM," I choked, unable to speak.

Lori opened her eyes and saw me looking not at her, but over the bed toward the door. She followed my gaze and saw what was there. We were caught like thieves in a blind alley.

"*Agua?*" Maricarmen said, making a drinking motion with her hand.

We were too shocked to speak.

"*Agua?*" she asked again.

"Water!" announced Lori, freeing my head and pulling out of my mouth. The situation was too absurd for attempts at propriety. Lori walked, bobbing dildo in place, to the kitchenette to fetch a bottle of cold water.

Maricarmen accepted it gratefully, unscrewed the cap and took a greedy gulp. "*Continuan, por favor,*" she instructed, making herself comfortable on the bed.

Lori and I looked at each other. It was a moment so awkward, so completely unlike us, that continuing seemed like the only the thing to do. But the tenor of the situation had changed: we had an audience. Now we wanted to watch her watch us.

We started up again, keeping our eyes on Maricarmen. She watched us hungrily, licking her lips after every sip of water. It became a game. What would Maricarmen like to see? If we weren't going to sleep with her, at least we could show her a good time.

Maricarmen seemed to be enjoying herself. Without hesitation, she began unbuttoning her shirt, stripping slowly for our pleasure as well as her own. Her body was a gorgeous shade of brown, almost red in the darkness, and more curvy than I'd expected. She unzipped her jeans with one hand, keeping the other hand on the water bottle, taking sips that made me jealous of the plastic.

Maricarmen drained the bottle and stood up to shed her remaining clothes. She walked naked to the refrigerator and opened it. A sliver of light illuminated her body. Lori and I stopped what we were doing and stared at her perfection. She closed the refrigerator door and faced us.

"*Agua*," she said again, with a confident swagger this time. She opened the second bottle and took a drink, then held it close to her body and let it tip. Water spilled over her breasts, dripping down her body and onto the tile floor. She took another sip. "*Está buena.*" It was our turn for a show.

Maricarmen poured more water onto herself, smoothing it around as if soaping up in the shower. She trickled the water over her breasts, making thin, sparkling ribbons that trailed downward, then poured the water in a stream that started at her belly button and ran to the dark triangle of hair between her legs, a river's delta in reverse.

"Damn," Lori whispered in appreciation. She let the word roll around in the back of her throat, as if the sound of her voice could reach out and take a lazy stroll down the length of Maricarmen's body.

Standing before us, Maricarmen began to touch herself. She didn't look like a stripper, mimicking pleasure with exaggerated, theatrical motion. No, she looked like a woman at home, touching herself the way she would if she were alone, with nothing but an aching cunt and an hour to spare. When the pleasure became too intense to remain upright, she bent over the foot of the bed, her feet on the floor, chest on the mattress, hand on her pussy. Though her face was turned toward us, her eyes were squeezed shut tight. She was in her own world, chasing down a powerful climax.

Maricarmen yelled out as she came, screaming into the mattress, then crawled up on the bed, panting.

Lori and I turned to each other once again. The throb in my pussy demanded attention. We refocused on our own pleasure, touching each other's familiar bodies, finding all the right places with all the right pressure. We were slippery as newborns, lubricated with sweat and hours-old sunblock, smelling like a day in August. We were waiting and waiting. Pushing and pulling back. We straddled the line that divides tension and release, then finally tripped the wire to blow the whole thing sky-high. We came at the same time, which is rare for us, even with such intimate knowledge. Collapsing into a heap of limbs, we laid tangled together, catching our breath. Finally, I looked up.

"Maricarmen?"

No answer. We sat up and looked around.

The girl was gone.

"She couldn't have made it out the door without us hearing her, could she?" Lori asked.

"I wasn't exactly paying attention."

We looked around the room again. We checked in the bathroom. There was no sign of Maricarmen, save two empty water bottles on the bed. I picked one up, and saw the bright red lipstick smudge on the mouth of the bottle.

"Damn it," I said. "We're out of water."

Sharing What I Borrow and Coveting What Is Mine

by Stacy Reed

Like many women who reject Freudian theory as fundamentally sexist, I'd never admit I first learned about possession from my father. Regardless, as *his* daughter, I was obligated to please him. I made straight A's, and this made him proud. I had a psychotically possessive older boyfriend, and this did not. David came to assume more control in my life than my father, and Daddy hated him for that.

I had never questioned my dad's control over me, and I didn't question David's. I'd always been assured that I'd been punished or spied on or otherwise coerced out of love, and I wasn't ready to start questioning. I took it for granted that Dave needed both a blow-up doll and a whipping boy; he happily fucked me, then called me a slut for putting out. Even though David demanded I fuck, he felt compelled to first purify me by denouncing my very willingness. That I'd fucked boys before I met him was especially reprehensible. David wanted to mold me into that elusive will-o'-the-wisp: the well-trained and experienced innocent, the perpetual virgin who can rise, phoenixlike, to offer herself anew over and over. I saw the logic. Dave reinforced Father's lesson: When a man says he loves me, what he means is he wants to control me. He wants to control who I am with him, but he also wants to control who

I am when he's away, who I will become, and who I was in the past. Especially the past. Dave wanted to reinvent my history such that everything was foreplay for the debut of the star I'd long been waiting for. Dave punished me for allowing any man to take center stage before his majestic entrance, for to have given it up to anyone but him proved me a whore.

Once David left for the University of Missouri I divided my time between studying for the SAT, which my father approved of, and running up outrageous phone bills, which he did not. David's absence relieved Dad of the grating suspicion that Dave might be doing more than holding my hand, but this new distance undermined Dave's confidence that he was the *only* one doing more. And so we fought. I don't care to recall how many times I agreed to hang up and call David back in the middle of some argument he'd started because he could no longer afford to talk. Still, I was willing to foot the bill; better to be broke than unloved, and to be loved was to grant control. If my boyfriend insisted we fight, how could I argue?

Well into his sophomore year I talked David into having what liberal eighteen-year-olds of the late eighties called an "open relationship." In today's parlance this would mean that David and I were each other's primary partners, but we were free to fuck secondary partners; we could swing. This negotiation was my first venture beyond the confines of strict monogamy. It was a few years before AIDS started to scare heterosexual suburban kids whose realm of drug use extended to pot, so we didn't discuss rules for safety. Instead we set up boundaries to control who could kiss whom where, drew up rules to govern oral sex, and debated to what degree of distance the secondary partner be removed from our inner posse. It was all about ownership, even after I had talked David into sharing his possession. The equation was still brutally simple: his love in return for my submission.

I strategically negotiated this change from "closed" to "open" relationship upon my acceptance to UT Austin. I'd soon be free from my father's control and the thought of continuing to cater to David's will began to disgust me. Though I had redefined David's standing, he couldn't resist calling every half hour starting at nine each evening to make sure I was sequestered in my dorm room. Whenever I left to study at the library—no matter where I actually went, the library, which was open twenty-four hours, was my alibi—I'd return to an answering machine overflowing with alarming messages that ranged from anxious questions to raving accusations. Often David would fill the entire cassette. If I defied him by ignoring these speculations and condemnations, one of his friends would call with the disconcerting but predictable news that Dave had locked himself in the bathroom and might swallow the contents of the medicine cabinet if I didn't call. So I'd call, and of course try to end it. But trying to dump a guy is not dumping him. I was too young to understand that hanging on the phone for hours trying to close a relationship was in fact perpetuating it. I didn't see that explaining why I no longer wanted to speak with him *was* speaking with him. Over and again I surrendered in exhaustion. *Alright, alright. I'll be your bitch if I can just go to sleep.*

After a few months at college I wised up and refused to swallow the nightly interrogations. What David called love at last bored me, and at any rate I'd grown too tired to argue. I couldn't summon the interest or energy to once again delineate the boundaries of our relationship, especially if that effort could be spent on a boy who was actually around, someone I could talk to whether or not the long distance rates had dropped. I finally learned to ignore David's increasingly hysterical messages and his melodramatic friends' suicide warnings.

Despite cultivating this measure of control over my present circumstances, I still believed what Dave had taught me: My past, as he'd dramatically referred to a handful of partners, was a disgrace. I felt ethically obligated to reveal my shameful secret to every man I dated so he would be aware of what a slut he was seducing before he sullied himself by fucking me. It was the beginning of my first summer away from home, and I was dutifully confessing to a prospective boyfriend every sexual liaison I had foolishly indulged in. *If only I had waited for you!* After I'd finished, Guy just laughed and said, "That's funny; you and I have slept with the same number of people." My elaborate admission meant nothing to him. That one sentence saved my life.

The flip side to my liberation was—unbeknownst to me—my obligation to forego control over Guy. This responsibility saved my life too, though fulfilling it was not nearly so easy as accepting Guy's cavalier absolution. Despite my relief, I resisted having an open relationship with Guy. During college I danced topless on weekends, and I knew monogamy was a tall request from someone who made her money in the most socially approved arena for cheating monogamy: a men's club, a space that allowed me to be overtly sexual with dozens of strange men every night while maintaining the status of Faithful Girlfriend. Topless dance clubs form an institution where swinging is sanctioned by people who would otherwise insist on their partner's monogamy: The dancer's boyfriend tolerates the dancing because it's only for money; after twenty years of marital turmoil the client's wife doesn't care what her husband does as long as the neighbors don't know; the client assures himself watching naked girls younger than his daughter is not cheating because he's paid; the dancer thinks taking her clothes off in front of hundreds of men a night is just her job. The dynamics of a men's club allow for a tame, low-grade third-party sex—for both the men and the women involved—that would otherwise be off limits. Not only do they express themselves sexually outside of an exclusive relationship, groupings change: two or three dancers stripping for one guy; a group of men watching one dancer together. It did not escape either me or Guy that I, someone who cashed in on this shady yet thriving economy, had precious little room to judge. Still, I refused to consider having an open relationship.

That didn't stop us from having one. This time I wasn't the

one in the luxurious position of violating the order; I soon learned that during the short time Guy and I had been "exclusive" he'd fucked a couple of dozen girls. I knew my discovery of his habit wasn't going to change it. Though in fact my only choice was between Guy with sidekicks and no Guy at all, I reluctantly "agreed" to share him. Implicit in this supposed concession was the premise that he was mine to share.

Though I continued to think of Guy as mine, the switch from alleged exclusivity to openness left me feeling less and less his. Though his entanglements continued to bring out my jealousies and insecurities, before long I began to pursue men as energetically as he pursued women; if I had to endure the indignities of this new agreement I might as well exploit the perks. Soon I understood that I could be fantastically turned on by the art student across the street and remain in love with Guy. I could swing and my love for him remained unscathed. If I never stopped loving Guy, then just maybe his affairs didn't cheapen our romance.

Maybe. I learned—for the first time but certainly not the last—accepting something logically is a separate matter from embracing it emotionally. I still winced when Guy told me about what I couldn't help think of as yet another "indiscretion," what he no doubt thought of as an "adventure." I no longer, however, *acted* on my desire to possess him, and after a while my sense of entitlement faded. An angry black bruise lightened to a rosy sunrise.

My new sexual ethics jibed nicely with my politics. In the early nineties, being a feminist in my circle demanded a critical take on the traditional (read monogamous, heterosexual) relationship. A woman could hardly claim admission to the clan if she had a problem with "her" boyfriend fucking around. It was all about female solidarity, and competition among women for men was seen as an obstacle. No man should ever come between us girls! Passing a guy around like a joint eliminated infighting. Any woman who set up a rivalry by hoarding a stash wasn't down with the program. Besides, men were just for

kicks; it was what went on among grrrls that counted. Fucking
women was optional, but if a nineties feminist wanted dick she
should at least never lose focus on how replaceable and incon-
sequential it is. My self-concept as a girl-allied, progressively
permissive, heterosexual-yet-open-to-suggestion uber-feminist
gelled.

So depending on the light, I saw men as either so desirable
it was downright immoral to keep one all to myself or so
insignificant it was wasteful to pay them any mind. It was then
easy to bring myself to share what didn't matter, simple to
forego possessing the worthless. Before long these competing
sensibilities allowed me the ability to acknowledge a given man
as a valuable jewel, and to take in his beauty and brilliance
became satisfaction enough; I no longer needed to own the
treasure.

Until this change of attitude, my life offered little variety
between compulsive studying and the stress of either
monogamy or imposed freedom—whether I was forcing it on
David or Guy was forcing it on me. Given the space, opportunities presented themselves that didn't fall within the confines
of either Boyfriend Solo or Boyfriend à la Person Boyfriend
Allows Me to Fuck Behind His Back. I found chances to explore
my curiosity on the bus, at the gym, in the park, on the way to
class, and at work. After Guy and I parted the very closest of
friends, within weeks I stumbled onto the kinkiest grouping I'd
encountered during my burgeoning desire for group sex.
Priscilla and Veronica and Sarah, strippers I danced with at the
Yellow Rose, invited me out after our shift. When our cab
pulled up in front of the Hilton, I assumed we were getting a
drink. But instead of heading for the bar, they led me to the
elevator. I had a reputation as a control freak, so I resisted asking any questions. The doors opened at the eleventh floor and
they marched me to the end of the hall, where Priscilla let us
into an enormous suite overlooking Town Lake. The view so
impressed me it was several seconds before I noticed a middle-
aged man with a bushy gray mustache lying on the king-sized

bed. I was soon to learn this was Craig, the psychologist they all lived with and gave their entire earnings to in exchange for therapy. After I watched them count out all of their money and give it to him, Craig called room service for four bottles of cabernet and fresh towels. He tipped the bellboy extravagantly with his girlfriends' money when the wine and linens arrived. I looked on in amazement as he proceeded to methodically uncork the impressive selection, pour everyone a bit from each bottle to taste, and then toss the remaining wine down the sink.

It was the bottles themselves Craig wanted. He ordered us to lie facedown across the bed. I still hadn't been introduced to this man, and that is no doubt why I was willing to do as he said. He didn't know me. I had no identity to him so I was invisible; I had nothing at stake. I lay down beside the other girls. Craig pulled down each of our panties in turn and gently worked the neck of one bottle after another snugly up our assholes. I imagine we looked like a late-twentieth-century take on one particularly riveting detail from the central panel of Hieronymus Bosch's triptych *The Garden of Earthly Delights*: a nude rendered blissfully passive by a bouquet of flowers up her butt. Though Craig's instruments were hardly pastoral, the wine bottles proved as restrictive as the most complicated bondage equipment; none of us were going anywhere until Craig had his way. This certainty made me nervous and hot, but not scared; the other girls were giggling too much for me to think there might be something to worry about. I watched as Craig worked his hand under the narrow hips of Veronica, the girl to my left. I could tell from her expression and her breathing that he had learned from practice exactly what she liked best. Her rapture didn't make me forget I was next. I felt a warm trickle of cream slip from between my labia and slide over my aching clit.

After she came, Craig took his hand away and ran his fingers, slick with her juices, up the inside of my right thigh to my pussy. He avoided my clit and spent long minutes just stroking my labia and swiftly darting a finger or two into my vagina. When he at last honed in on my clitoris, he gingerly squeezed it between his thumb and forefinger. I lost all composure under this gentle pressure and reflexively pressed my pelvis into his hand. Immediately he retreated to the wet folds of my labia. No one was going to come until Craig allowed it, and the less I resisted his will the sooner I'd get my way. Though I'd never been in bed with more than one person, I knew the rules to this game by heart. I'd long understood the exchange of power between the sovereign and the subject, and I knew that despite appearance and rhetoric the underling often assumes control. As soon as I bowed to Craig's will I could make him do what I wanted.

So I acquiesced. I obediently relaxed my body and when I felt Craig's fingers return to my throbbing clit I forced my muscles to remain still. I kept my breathing quiet and shallow. I willed my vagina not to clench around his agile fingers as they dipped inside me to further wet my swollen clitoris. I had entered into a bizarre competition in which winning meant resisting orgasm under the condition of expert stimulation. I wanted nothing more than defeat. As I felt the pressure in my cunt build I willed my body to remain slack. Still, there was no way I could will myself to ignore the masterful fingers persistently exciting my clit, and I groaned shamelessly as my entire body bucked into Craig's hand. I fell into a shallow sleep listening to Priscilla and then Sarah moan.

After I finished my degree I thought dancing a waste, so I left Austin and never saw Craig's harem again. I moved to Houston and took a job as a technical writer at Enron. (No, I never bought stock.) Stripping was better; I cried in the ladies' room on my coffee breaks. To ease the boredom of writing manuals for pipeline construction, I wrote erotic short stories whenever my supervisor left the office. At the end of the first two weeks I took home $1,500 and my first manuscript. Though I thought I'd grown up to be a technical writer, and my supposed aspiration was to become a journalist, the smut I'd cranked out on someone else's time turned out to be my true calling; I've been publishing porn ever since.

In that sense, I was never truly monogamous again. I was always reaching into someone's sexuality with my stories. On one level that lay far from my waking life, I had laid my fantasies before anyone who cared to notice. There I lay my imagination open for anyone to fuck. Anyone interested could have me. Go ahead. It's been paid for. I became forever engaged in sex with people outside my recognized romantic relationships.

I kept my exploration of the soft, pale underbelly of fiction a secret and presented myself as a "professional." This posture led me into the more rarefied circles of Houstonians between eighteen and twenty-three. Within months I was engaged to a promising young architect studying at Rice. Eric was presumptuous enough to tell me he was indeed the best, and when he won a preceptorship at the prestigious Renzo Piano firm in Paris I believed him. I felt simultaneously proud and diminished, and started to lie about various fascinating responsibilities of my Enron job; I grew desperate to impress Eric in the face of his latest success. When a good review of my writing ran in a trade magazine I finally told him my pen name. He said he was proud, but he always pushed me to write something "serious." I sat in Les Deux Magots that summer outlining a novel I never wrote. Paris was damp and hostile.

We'd both taken French from sixth grade through college, but our shaky grasp of the language didn't make us popular with the neighbors any more than our ambitions could change the circumstances. Despite our best intentions, Eric and I separated within six months and divorced a year later. Problems abounded, but the marriage did not fail for lack of devotion. Perhaps an affair or two might have saved us from suffocating each other.

Now I'm working on my second marriage to a man who has suffered two already. Early on Marty and I agreed that the only rule was discussion. We reached this agreement long before there was anything to discuss. Then I met Drew, and she presented the impetus to set our potential energy into motion.

Drew was the first prostitute I got to know. We met while I was vacationing in San Francisco, visiting some old friends who'd moved west. Drew roomed with them in a charming Victorian apartment in Haight-Ashbury, and I ended up spending most of my time with her. We quickly developed a sense of camaraderie and curiosity. We traded stories comparing stripping to whoring. I told her about the rules and the laws, the hours at the gym, the eight-hour shift, the tedious men, and the money, of course the money. She could make in one hour what I'd been able to earn in three. Drew thought dancing was too much work. Maybe she was right, but I knew I could never turn tricks; I'd thought about it.

Besides being a high-price call girl, a position she seemed to genuinely enjoy, Drew held a Ph.D. in Comparative Literature from Berkeley and wrote for *The San Francisco Bay Guardian* and *Mother Jones*. We talked politics over sushi and jasmine tea then exchanged tips on masturbation over chocolates and wine.

A couple of times our discussions about sexual technique led to demonstrations. Drew was the first woman to ever fist me. First she pulled from beneath her bed a sturdy, no-frills vibrator obviously designed with one intent only. She massaged oil into my pussy, flicked on the vibrator, and nestled it between my labia and slid it over my clit. She kept the fingers of her other hand inside my vagina, waiting for me to get really wet and dilate. When I was ready she closed her fingers into a small fist and slid her arm up my cunt to her elbow. She pumped her forearm, slid her knuckles over my G-spot, until I came several times.

After I watched her masturbate—she preferred to use her fingers—I looked around her fringed, pink and red bedroom. I told Drew she'd decorated her room like a nineteenth-century brothel, and she countered that the apartment had indeed been part of a whorehouse back then. She'd kept the faith: silk sheets, down pillows, heavy gilded mirrors hung from the ceiling and secured to the walls at the perfect angle; portraits of her favorite patrons; scented balms. I noticed framed on her bedside table a series of photographs documenting her boyfriend's forty-sixth birthday party (she was thirty-one). He'd too been a prostitute when he was young, and the photographs featured him with Drew and four other women, ranging from nineteen to sixty. Everyone was all smiles, especially him. Marty was joining me in San Francisco the next day to celebrate his fortieth birthday (I was twenty-eight). Now I knew exactly what to buy for him.

I proposed my plan to Drew, who agreed tentatively on the condition she first meet him. A girl who charges $300 an hour can afford to be picky, so when Marty arrived I took him and Drew out to dinner at a trendy diner in North Beach. She introduced herself as a therapist, which is altogether accurate, and proceeded to charm him with her handle on every topic from medieval Saxon folklore to Libertarian economic theory. Drew fluttered effortlessly between the most esoteric subjects to matters of national interest, between talk of up-and-coming poets and the upcoming election (people thought of the 2000 presidential campaign as an election at the time). Before dessert arrived she and I excused ourselves to the ladies' room and solidified our plans. I gave her the money, and seeing how I was a friend and all, she promised not to consult her watch; we had her for the entire night: a bargain!

I left the bathroom a few minutes before her to surprise Marty with our plans. He was bemused, but he didn't seem shocked. Maybe he didn't believe me, or maybe he'd already caught on to her therapeutic specialization and was about to suggest we hire her. After settling the bill we took a taxi back to the hotel he'd checked into that morning.

Up in the room I drank too many glasses of wine, wanting to sustain the lull between the decision to act and the action itself. Somehow I couldn't feel the moment to set this lark into motion, and I realized I wouldn't know how to do it even if I could have figured out when to try. My first really remarkable foray into the wilds of multiple-partner sex had involved casual friends and a man who was a complete stranger to me, and I had done no more than go along for the ride out of curiosity. Years later, on a different coast, this hotel room I shared with a woman I had become oddly close with in just a matter of days and a man I had taken for my husband. This time I had orchestrated the ride and paid for it, too. This was far from a matter of curiosity; I had a present to present, and the gift extended far beyond any monetary or sexual exchange. I was laying on the line my reputation as a libertine, a sex worker, a feminist, a friend, and a transcendentally secure top-rate lay. With so much at stake I froze. Where was I to go now that I had found out where too far led? I drank another glass of wine. Eventually Drew asked Marty what he wanted us to do.

Following his exact instructions, I straddled Drew's face while she masturbated. My arms propped my torso over hers, and I looked down between her legs and saw that her fingers were skating across her clit at the same leisurely pace her tongue was flicking over mine. I watched her clit swell with every stroke of her fingers and when it was really popping Marty reached between her legs, spread her labia further, and then pressed his fingers gently against her clitoris and massaged it in slow, patient circles. I could feel my own clit pulsing against her lips as her tongue slowed into step with Marty's fingers. When I started to groan Marty gently pushed me off of her face and back onto the pillows. He didn't need to ask Drew to continue; she lowered her face between my thighs and resumed licking my clit immediately. I could tell from the hot little puffs of breath against my pussy that he had resumed playing with hers. I soon felt an orgasm building inside me and pressed my cunt up into her soft mouth. As I felt her tongue start to dart more forcefully over my clit I heard her cries get louder. After the last shudder clenched my body and her final moan had bled out to a whimper, Drew raised her head from between my legs and kissed my wetness all over my neck and lips.

When I think past those first sweet moments, the intermingling of our bodies trips through my mind like static images projected onto a screen, and these slides have been sifted through and shuffled so many times I no longer remember the order. This is what it looks like: Drew's fist up my cunt; Marty's cock buried in Drew's pussy, my fingers nestled beneath the ring piercing her clitoral hood; my mouth on Drew's clit, Marty's dick between her lips; Marty's dick deep inside Drew's ass, her lips and fingers clamped tight around my nipples; my pelvis rocking Marty's cock, his mouth sucking her clit. Someone's fingers, someone's cunt, someone's dick, someone's mouth, someone's tits. In this new territory, anatomy overrode ownership. Whose mouth, whose cunt—who cared? The $300 didn't make Drew mine to give any more than a gold band rendered Marty mine to share. Now that I looked close, the boundaries I'd constructed to define "friend" and "husband" and "self" shimmered faintly and evaporated in the hot air surging from my inflated arguments on the sex industry, postfeminism, monogamy, and the lash.

If this essay were one of my pieces of erotica, this would be where, after recuperating from countless devastating orgasms, we all take a sudsy shower together and ring up room service for a late-night breakfast of eggs Benedict and smoked salmon and champagne. We'd toast our accomplishments, laugh over our exploits, and fall into a warm and blissful sleep. But that's not how it happened. Though I won't argue this account can be read with one hand, I want to be clear I'm telling the truth, and the truth is always bursting at the seams; it refuses to be sewn up tight and tidy.

This is how the story really ends: Drew, poor thing, was getting tired and possibly a bit bored. Maybe she felt she'd put in her share of unpaid overtime and was eager to get back to her boyfriend or see another client before the night was over. Quite probably she was accustomed to bringing men to orgasm within ten minutes, and here Marty had taken up four hours. My husband can prolong taking his pleasure, and I knew perfectly well that his procrastination could wear a girl down. Still,

I felt the bottom drop out of my stomach and my chest tighten around my heart when Drew asked, "Do you want me or Stacy to make you come?"

Or?

That choice of contraction brought the borders that had moments earlier faded into my peripheral vision back into immediate and bold relief. The distinction between my anatomy and Drew's could no longer be overlooked. There was my body or there was hers. There was now a choice, and that choice was Marty's. I snapped to the position of the entitled and indignant owner: I had purchased a product for someone, and the act of presenting the gift made the beneficiary all the more mine. As mine, Marty was subject to my control. It should have been my choice—not his—whether Drew or I brought him to orgasm and it should have been my privilege—not hers—to give that choice away. We'd discussed rules before anyone had so much as taken off their shoes. Condoms, gloves, dental damns had been covered. We'd addressed everything that David and I had ignored two decades earlier. But the subjects Dave and I harped on we dismissed. With this threatening question hanging, I desperately wished I'd been a bit more petty from the start. I'd been such a stickler for the latex! How could I have overlooked this more permeable membrane, the ebb and flow of who played which role to whom? I had failed to entertain the prospect that a woman I'd hired to get my husband off might do just that. Why didn't it occur to me that Marty might not come from the friction of my body? Considering I had gone out of my way to make that less than a certainty, why did I care?

And then he said, "You." So Drew jacked off my husband, took a shower, and then took another $25 for a taxi back to the Haight. Then I said some mean-spirited things I no longer remember but still regret and fell asleep. I woke up in the morning feeling terrible for ruining Marty's birthday with my absurd envy and tried to simultaneously apologize for and excuse my behavior. I worried I'd lost face. What did Drew think of my alleged lack of inhibition now that my anxieties had been exposed? How could a woman who had stripped for a living find the exchange of sex for money threatening? What did I care if she got Marty off when she had just days ago gotten me off? What did Marty think of my claims to sexual freedom now that I'd entered into competition with the hired help? And who was a pornographer to get miffed when a whore was only doing her job?

And what was I to make of myself? Was I a generous and indulgent wife who'd arranged for every man's fantasy? Or a nagging hag bent on dissecting every trivial phrase and wringing all pleasure from the most promising of evenings? Was I an adventurous new friend who was open to any lifestyle or a duplicitous excuse for an ally who turned hostile at a word out of line? Was I sharing Marty with Drew or Drew with Marty? Did they end up sharing me? Drew was long gone, the thick hotel drapes struggled to keep out the morning light, but the frustrating dichotomy of *either this or that* only grew more grating and insistent.

After Marty and I returned to Houston, I carefully crafted a long letter to Drew apologizing for vague things like "bad vibes." I hoped that if she hadn't noticed my disgruntlement—an unlikely possibility—that my euphemisms wouldn't tip her off. If she had noticed, I hoped they would serve as admission enough. I mailed the letter and checked the mailbox compulsively for days after.

I received a kindly note that managed to acknowledge my apology without holding me responsible for what I'd apologized for. It was exactly the sort of discretion you'd expect from a professional. She discussed the pitfalls of "free-for-alls" and announced that limiting the behavior acceptable within a marriage strengthens it. Huh? And I'd been thinking that allowing for anything was the test of my sexual endurance. Now Drew was assuring me that the only way to win a race was to draw a line to cross.

And I realized it was neither a matter of anything goes nor out-of-bounds. I wasn't obligated to some romantic or political or ego-bound ideal to reject possessiveness or endorse monogamy or endlessly legislate amendments to The Perfect Marriage. I didn't have to get it right. I saw that somewhere between my logical laissez-faire policies and my actual emotional restrictions lay freedom.

His Scene

by Elizabeth Coldwell

So the car pulls up outside the house a couple minutes before eight, and Jimmy and I get into the routine we go through every time I make an outcall.

"You sure you're going to be okay, Polly?" he asks, watching as I pull out my compact mirror and slick on another layer of cherry lip gloss. "I'll be parked up just round the corner, I've got my cell phone and if you need to get the hell out of there . . ."

"Jimmy, I'll be fine," I assure him. I mean, it's sweet that he cares so much about my safety, considering he's not my brother, not my lover, just the guy I room with in a rundown tenement three blocks from the college campus. But I've been working for Black Cat Escorts for nearly nine months now, and I know how to take care of myself.

Not that I see a problem with this client. The guy's name is Ben Roddick, and he's booked me as a birthday treat for his wife, Jeannie. Well, not me specifically, but Lacey, the house-mother, knows I'm one of the few girls on her books who's happy to do a little femme on femme. I reckon some of them would rather have hot wax dripped on their tits than lick pussy—but then there are guys who'll pay for that kind of thing, too.

I take a last look at my reflection before I get out of the car. When Lacey gave me my instructions for the night, she told me Roddick thought his wife would like it if I dressed "kinda slutty." I'm wearing a very short, pleated tartan miniskirt and a white ribbed vest that has the effect of making my small tits look bigger than they are. No bra beneath the vest, so the dark circles of my nipples are visible through the fabric, and tight little white panties that hug the contours of my freshly shaven mound. Ankle socks instead of nylons, and strappy sandals. That slutty enough for ya, Mrs. Roddick?

A deep breath and I push the car door open. Jimmy is tuning the radio; there's a snatch of Springsteen, a couple of bars of salsa music, then a preacher's voice, partway through some rant about hellfire and damnation, before he finds what he's been looking for—the commentary of the night's big football game. There's a grunt of acknowledgment that I'm leaving, but apart from that he barely notices as I step out onto the sidewalk; the moment Polly Gray, psychology major, becomes Jade, $200-an-hour hooker.

Don't ask me why I settled on Jade. I guess you're thinking it's the image I have of myself, something hard and precious, which is about as far as you can get from reality. Truth is, no one else on Lacey's books was using the name, and it just seemed to complement the hokey, high-class aliases chosen by the other girls: Sugar, Velvet, Sheridan, Tanqueray . . .

Not that I ever really expected I'd be choosing a name to be using with clients. I mean, girls like me don't usually consider hooking as a means of paying their way through college. But there are only so many tables you can wait for minimum wage before you decide there must be ways of taking less shit for more money—and that's where Black Cat came in. Okay, so I told myself at first that I'd just act as an escort, and draw the line when it came to offering sex, but you're naïve if you think that's the way it works in reality. And it's not so bad; I love sex, I get to spend time with some fun guys and I never have to do anything I don't want to—which, let's face it, is more than some girls can say.

And the guys I visit *are* nice—the prices Black Cat charges, it weeds out most of the losers. After all, it tends to make you think twice if you know sending out for a BJ is going to max out your credit card. But I can see that Roddick has serious money; not only is this one of the most exclusive neighborhoods in town, a red BMW convertible and a silver sports utility vehicle sit side by side in the driveway. Do I really need to add that they have his-and-hers vanity plates?

I ring the doorbell and wait. The guy who opens the door is in his early thirties and looks like a catalog model: about six foot, with brush-cut blond hair, sea-blue eyes, and a smile that's clearly the product of expensive cosmetic dentistry. He's casually dressed in khaki chinos and a black roll-neck sweater. His gaze devours my body in a heartbeat, lingering for a moment on the brevity of my skirt. The nonchalance he's trying to effect is spoiled by the nervous vibe he's giving off.

"Mr. Roddick?" I ask. When he nods, I say, "Hi, I'm Jade."

"Great to meet you," he says, taking my hand and shaking it vigorously, as though I'm a business client rather than his wife's lay for the night. "Come through."

"Can we get the messy bit out of the way first?" I ask.

It takes him a moment to catch on, but as soon as he does, he says, "Oh, sure," takes a billfold from his back pocket and counts out the fee. "Don't want Jeannie to know quite how much I'm spending on her, right?" he laughs. Minus the cut Lacey will take, it's still a good night's work.

That done, he leads me down the hall and into the living room. It reeks of understated good taste, and the carpet is thick enough for my heels to sink into as I walk. I suspect someone has styled the place for them, chosen everything from the window drapes to the Klimt print that hangs over the fireplace. There's a petite woman in a simple black shift dress sitting on the cream leather couch, her dark hair swept up into a chignon and a wide silver band round her slender throat. Jeannie.

I smile at her, but she doesn't rise to greet me.

"Jeannie, this is Jade. Jade, can I get you a drink?"

"White wine, if you have it." I'm not a great drinker, but I

usually have one glass, to be sociable, and to kick-start my
juices if the guy I'm with hasn't got them flowing already.

Roddick goes into the kitchen, leaving Jeannie staring at
me. I can't fathom the expression in her green eyes. She makes
no attempt at conversation, and I find it all a little odd. I've
done girls before, and they always want to chat beforehand.
Always. We're going to be fucking soon enough; doesn't she
even want to try to find out what I'm like?

After a few uncomfortable moments Roddick is back, pressing a generous glass of wine into my hand. He hands another
to his wife.

"I have to say, you look great, Jade," he continues, babbling
just a little. "I mean, really great. Don't you think she looks
great, Jeannie? Just what I asked for."

That's when it hits me. That one word. "I" not "we."
Suddenly I realize what is wrong with this picture. It might be
his wife's birthday, but Ben Roddick has arranged this threesome as a present for himself. No wonder Jeannie is so distant
and frosty toward me. When he booked the appointment, he
told Lacey this was what his wife wanted, but I'm not buying it.
This is his scene.

I sip the wine faster than I otherwise might, registering the
oaky taste of chardonnay. I don't need to see the bottle to
know it isn't this year's vintage. Jeannie barely touches hers.

"So tell me about yourselves," I say. Give me some insight
into this weird situation, is what I mean.

Turns out Roddick is in real estate, while Jeannie is a buyer
for one of the big department stores downtown. No kids, not
yet anyway, not while both their careers are still so hot. The
sex between them is great, always has been, but they've been
wanting to experiment for a while. Tonight seemed like the
perfect occasion to live out one of their fantasies—two girls,
one guy. They couldn't ask a friend—well, it might get taken
the wrong way—and using contact ads seemed kinda sleazy,
so they hired me. And all the time Roddick's saying "they," all
I'm hearing is "I."

Raising the glass to my lips, I realize I've drained it without knowing. Roddick offers to get me a refill, but I decline.

"Well, I don't know about you, but I'm feeling horny," Roddick says. "Let's go to the bedroom, girls . . ."

This is the point at which I could stand up and leave. Tell him I don't think his wife is comfortable with what's about to happen, and that maybe it's better if I go, before they do something they might end up regretting. I've already made my rent this month; I can stand to lose tonight's fee. Lacey will understand, and Jimmy will appreciate not having to sit out in the car all night. But Jeannie is already on her feet and heading for the stairs. So I put my wineglass on the coffee table and follow.

There are already candles burning in the bedroom, and the air holds the subtle smell of jasmine. Roddick is slotting a CD into the player, and within seconds the strains of Kenny G fill the room. Either he thinks it will create the right mood or his musical taste is the only thing someone else doesn't choose for him.

It's clear neither Roddick nor Jeannie know quite how to progress. I assume he's lived this fantasy in his head a thousand times—maybe the two of them have even talked it over in bed—but now it's about to happen, it's nothing like he planned. It's clear I'm going to have to take the lead from here on in.

"Come here, Jeannie," I say gently, and pull her into my arms. For a moment I think she might resist; as I press my lips to hers, I feel her stiffen slightly. But then she begins to respond, her mouth opening against mine, and when my tongue snakes out a little way, hers presses back against it in a manner that suggests she finds kissing another woman, at least, not unpleasant.

Roddick has kicked off his shoes and is reclining on the bed, watching as we kiss. "Why don't you lose that skirt, Jade?" he suggests.

Before I can reach for the zipper, Jeannie has reached behind me and is pulling it down. The skirt falls to the floor, and I'm standing there in my vest top and little white panties.

I catch a glimpse of the two of us in the mirrored front of their wardrobe; the elegance of Jeannie's outfit makes my state of partial undress look even cheaper. I wonder if this is what Roddick had in mind when he asked me to dress this way; a whore who so obviously looks like a whore seducing his lady wife. The image sends a nasty little thrill through me, and I realize that despite the strangeness of the setup I've walked into, I'm actually feeling hugely turned on.

I don't need any encouragement to unfasten Jeannie's dress, and she offers no resistance as I slip it down her shoulders and off. Beneath it, she is wearing a matching black lace bra and panty set, a garter belt, and the sheerest of black stockings. The cups of the bra are underwired, forming a breathtaking cleavage from what is a surprisingly generous pair of breasts for such a small woman. Has she dressed for her husband, herself—or me? Whatever, I certainly appreciate the way she looks. It's classy—and as she reaches to lift my top up far enough to bare my breasts, it becomes even more so.

For someone who looked like she was ready to run a mile when I first walked into the house, she's suddenly making all the moves. Her husband isn't guiding the scene, not anymore: He's just lying back, stroking what I can't help but notice is a pretty sizable bulge in his chinos and looking at us like Santa's just emptied his sack a couple of months early. Mind you, the way Roddick's rubbing himself, that's not going to be the only empty sack around here.

I giggle to myself, and Jeannie must be taking the noise as encouragement, because her hands have strayed to my tits. Now, they aren't the biggest pair you'll ever see, but the nipples get really hard really fast, particularly when cool, curious fingers are traveling over them the way Jeannie Roddick's are at this moment. My mind's jumping ahead of itself, wondering what it's going to feel like when she turns her curiosity to what's in my suddenly damp panties, but I'm still prepared for her to back off the second she starts to feel uncomfortable with what she's doing.

"Panties, Jeannie?" I hear Roddick say hopefully, and for a moment I almost want her to tell him to go fuck himself, that she's taking things at her own pace, and that she'll decide when my underwear—and hers—gets removed. But there's still a part of her that's going through this to please him—though I suspect that part is getting smaller by the minute, as her own desire to experiment exerts itself—and her fingers hook into the waistband of my panties and tug them down. She's clumsy, and I shuffle on the bed, doing my best to help her. At last she has them round my ankles, and I do the rest myself.

Her eyes widen when she realizes I've shaved. Maybe she's seen this before, in some porno she and her husband have rented in a typically suburban attempt to spice up their sex life, and she doesn't believe anyone who isn't a model would ever do such a thing, or maybe this is her first sighting of a bare pussy. Whatever, I get the impression she finds it a little intriguing, an impression that is strengthened when she runs a finger down over the soft, pink skin, heading down to the lightly glistening cleft between my lips. I shiver at her inexperienced touch and part my legs a little wider.

"That's it, Jeannie," I urged. "Touch me just there. It feels so good." She does as I ask, finger almost stumbling across my clit as she begins to explore. Maybe I exaggerate my moan just a little to give her the encouragement she needs, but as she begins to rub, I don't need to playact any more.

I glance over at Roddick and notice that he's stripped down to nothing but a pair of tight-fitting gray jockey shorts. The material clings to his swollen cock, and there's a damp circle around the head that shows just how excited he is. I wonder how much further he's going to let Jeannie and I go before he joins in.

Jeannie seems oblivious to him, still tracing gentle little rings around my juicy bud. "Do you want some of that yourself?" I ask, and she nods, almost absently. I know her type: she wants it, but she can't bring herself to ask for it. Nice girls don't, and Jeannie Roddick has been brought up to be a nice girl.

She doesn't protest as I reach behind and unhook her bra. Her big breasts tumble out under their own weight, and I can't resist cupping them and feeling their sexy softness. A touch becomes a taste; she makes a startled little noise as my lips latch round her nipple, but she doesn't push me away.

Roddick sits up, reaches for his wife's panties and gives a tug. He gets them halfway down her ass before she protests. "Ben, no!" Her voice is soft but sharp. "Jeannie's doing me. This is my present, remember?"

I don't know who is the more surprised, her husband or me. With that one little speech, she's just made it perfectly clear that this is no longer his fantasy. He might have let the genie out of the bottle, but it's not going to be his wishes that get granted. He slumps back against the pillows, visibly hurt.

"Why don't you just watch and enjoy?" I suggest, trying to salve his disappointment. "A lot of guys really love that."

And then a couple of Jeannie's fingers push up into the wetness of my snatch, and talking suddenly becomes a little difficult.

Abruptly, she withdraws them. "Lick me," she murmurs. She lies back on the bed, expectantly, and I settle myself between her spread legs. At first, I nuzzle her through the crotch of her panties, until the expensive lace is saturated. Then I push the gusset to one side and my lips make contact with her soft, juicy folds. My tongue pursues her slick clit, teasing it. She's moaning a little and chewing her lips, and I know she's no longer doing this to please anyone but herself.

There's a shuffling on the bed behind me, and then I feel Roddick's hands running over the contours of my ass. I listen for the sound of a condom being unwrapped, hoping he's going to stick that big cock of his into me, but instead all I hear is a rhythmic slapping as he begins to jerk himself off.

Jeannie's moans get louder, and her pelvis is pushing up into my face as she gets nearer to coming, making it harder for me to keep my grip on her panties. Behind me, I hear Roddick say, "Yeah, that's it, that's it," his words punctuated by gasps, and I don't know whether he's speaking to me or talking himself into his own climax.

Then she squeals, he groans and I feel my mouth filling with a sharp, salty wetness at much the same time as hot come spatters on the small of my back. I pull away from Jeannie's cunt and look at her face. She smiles at me, her features glowing and alive. "I never thought it would be like that. Thank you," she whispers.

I'm so horny I'd love to come myself, but the sensible thing to do is just get out of there. What's just happened could change everything between them. Either they're going to bottle their feelings up and wipe tonight from their memories, or they're going to have to sit down and talk about where they go from here, and I reckon it's safer if I leave before they start hurling those expensive gew-gaws in the living room at each other.

I dress in double-quick time, wish them a polite goodnight and make my way out to Jimmy's car. He's still engrossed in the game as I slip into the passenger seat beside him.

"Everything okay, Polly?" he asks, when he finally registers my presence.

"Oh, sure," I reply. "Just the same old same old. Guy wants his wife to get it on with another girl—only this time she ends up wanting it more than he does." I sigh. "You know, Jimmy, I can see the day coming when some guy tries to sue a hooker for screwing up his marriage."

Jimmy sticks the key in the ignition, in no mood for philosophizing. "Why don't we go to O'Leary's? I'll buy you a beer and we can watch the rest of the game."

"Beer sounds good," I tell him, but the restrooms at O'Leary's sound better; I think longingly of the big, quiet stalls where I can sit on the john and finger myself till I get the orgasm I still crave. He turns the car round in the Roddicks' driveway and we head back downtown.

Birthday Girl

by Ludmilla Kryzmska

I suppose I'm naïve. I never thought about spanking.

My husband Claude arranged a surprise birthday party for me. He invited Marcy and Tyler Wright, our two best friends. I came home from work to find Claude setting out a fabulous five-course dinner and Marcy, petite, curvaceous, and lively, frosting a yummy chocolate fudge cake.

We had cocktails first, lots of wine with dinner, and cognac after dinner. We were so full we could barely move, but we made it to the living room, where we devoured the cake, then lay back, stared dully at the remnants of the cake on the coffee table, and sipped our coffee laced with Irish whiskey.

Tyler and I were sitting on the sofa. Marcy and Claude were each in an easy chair facing us. It seemed very hot. Claude, a good-looking man (I think so, anyway, and Marcy has said so, too), unbuttoned his shirt, exposing his hairy, muscular chest. Tyler, tall and thin with a boyish smile and kind blue eyes, kicked off his shoes and rolled up his sleeves. Marcy's blouse was falling open, exhibiting her red lacy bra and fulsome breasts, and her skirt rode up her thigh, but she didn't notice, or didn't care. I found myself staring at her bosom, which was straining against the red lace, and at her thigh, shapely and smooth. I wondered if I should be worried by my fascination with her sexiness. I decided I shouldn't. We always kissed when we met, on the lips, sensuously. My skin tingled after those kisses.

We were feeling pretty uninhibited.

Tyler started telling off-color jokes. Marcy would laugh, her blouse would open more, more thigh would show, and she would grab Claude's hand, as if that would contain her laughter. After awhile, they kept on holding hands, as if they'd forgotten where their hands were. Claude's eyes roamed between her thighs and her breasts. I was a little jealous of her breasts. They looked perkier than mine. But I wasn't jealous of her and Claude holding hands. I knew Claude loved me madly. We told each other everything, even our fantasies of having sex with other people—sometimes people we knew, sometimes people we just saw walking down the street.

Tyler must have seen them holding hands, too. He put his arm around me and hugged me close. I breathed in his provocative aftershave. Tyler and I had always flirted, stolen kisses, even let our tongues play together. He felt me up a couple of times, lightly squeezing my breasts, hugging me close until I felt his penis harden against my pubic area. The last time he did that, Marcy came into the room. Tyler saw her, but he didn't stop. She didn't seem to mind. She felt my breasts as well. We all laughed about it.

And laughed, too, when I told them how sometimes when Claude and I made love I imagined I was riding up and down on Tyler's penis—which, from a few "accidental" touches, I knew was, well, stalwart and audacious—which Marcy confirmed the time she mentioned that her jaw was sore; and how Claude, as his tongue plucked my clitoris, wondered if Marcy's love button (as we called it) was as sensitive as mine. And then Marcy admitted that she got turned on whenever she fantasized Tyler making love to me, and Tyler, laughing, said *he* was turned on whenever Marcy described how she fantasized making love to *me*. I wondered at the time—this was only a few weeks ago—if we would ever act on those fantasies, but I didn't think so. We were really pretty normal people. That's what I thought then, anyway.

Now Marcy had Claude's hand in her lap. She was laughing and moving his hand up and down her thighs. He looked like he was enjoying it. He glanced at me to see if I was upset. Just then Tyler's hand glided inside the opening of my blouse, made its way, as naturally as water flows downhill, into my bra, lovingly to enclose my breast, like a lost bird finding its nest. His fingers gently kneaded the soft plumpness, and two fingers grazed back and forth across my nipple, which immediately stood up, and sent sparks to the base of my spine. Claude merely smiled and pressed his and Marcy's hands deeper between her thighs. The food and the alcohol had wrapped us all in a loving haze. What harm was there in a little playfulness? It seemed impossible that anything could happen that we didn't really want to happen.

Claude's hand disappeared under Marcy's skirt. I was getting as excited watching Claude's hand creep higher under Marcy's skirt, exposing her thighs higher and higher, as I was feeling Tyler's fingers rhythmically squeeze my breast, and his fingertips pinch my firm nipple. It hurt, yes, but it was such a pleasant hurt that I wished he would pinch even harder.

Then Marcy cried, "We've forgotten the best part!"

And Tyler exclaimed, "We haven't spanked Emily!"

I laughed, "You're not going to spank me!"

"How old are you?" Tyler asked. "Thirty-two?"

Before I knew it he stretched me across his knees. I almost got away, but Marcy helped hold me down. "Come on, Claude," she cried, and there was Claude kneeling by my face, smiling.

"One!" Tyler gave me a light whack.

"Harder," Marcy urged.

"Two." It was harder, but it didn't really hurt. I stopped struggling. Much to my surprise, I was looking forward to the next thirty spanks. Tyler's thighs felt warm against my stomach, and his hand on my back, holding me down, was firm and reassuring. He slid his hand over the soft fabric of my blouse. Claude's face was next to mine, kissing me. Other hands—they must have been Marcy's—were slipping up and down my calves.

"Three."

"Oh, Tyler, it's not a birthday spanking if it doesn't hurt a little," Marcy said. Why did her words excite me? I felt my skirt lifted, exposing my bikini panties.

"Four." That hurt a little. I squirmed against Tyler's thighs.

"Five." Tyler's other hand slipped under my blouse. His palm was hot against my bare back.

"Six."

"It's not lucky unless it's a real spanking," Marcy said.

She peeled my sheer blue panties off my fanny. She tugged them down my thighs. She lingered at my knees, plucked them over my calves, got hung up on my ankles, and finally jerked them off my feet. I tried to cover my bottom, but Claude, laughing, held my hands.

I felt naked. I felt exposed. I pictured my bare bottom, revealed to everyone. I squirmed to get free. Tyler held me tight. I squirmed harder. My pussy rubbed back and forth across his thigh. I was getting excited.

"Seven!" Marcy cried. Now she was spanking me.

"Eight!" Her hand smacked my left buttock. "Nine!" Right buttock. "Ten!" I was no longer embarrassed, my bare bottom in the air, everybody looking at it.

"Eleven!" I was proud to exhibit it. It must have been red and glowing.

"Twelve!" Why was it so thrilling to be vulnerable? To not see what was going to happen next?

"Thirteen!" To be at others' loving but unpredictable mercy?

"Fourteen!" Was I weird? Abnormal? Perverted?

"Fifteen!" If I was, I didn't care. I didn't care because Tyler was unhooking my bra. His palms slipped under my breasts. I wasn't struggling to get away anymore. I didn't want to get away.

"Sixteen!" I liked my bare bottom exposed. I liked Tyler's

palms holding my breasts as if they were priceless, fragile delicacies. I liked to rub my naked pubis against Tyler's thighs. I
liked the sensation of my juices drenching his trousers.

"Seventeen!" Marcy's palm stung, sending a quivering to
my pussy, while her other hand snuck between my thighs.

"Eighteen!" Why did I spread my thighs apart?

"Nineteen!" Could Claude see me spread my thighs further? Could he see Marcy's hand reach higher? Did he know
her hand was rubbing my nooky? Did he know her hand was
getting wet?

"Twenty!" Marcy said. "My hand's tired. Claude, it's your
turn."

Marcy kneeled by the sofa. Her blouse fell from her shoulders. Her red lacy bra dropped to the floor. Her breasts were
beautiful, naturally firm, with small pink nipples. (I'd seen her
breasts before, when we went shopping together, and we
shared a dressing room, trying on bras. Marcy eyed my breasts
without embarrassment, and said, "I love your breasts, the way
they swing slightly, and your nipples, so pert and proud. They
excite me." I was a little taken aback, but her compliments
were so genuine and innocent, I could only be flattered. I said,
"I like yours, too." "Do you mind," she asked simply, "if I touch
them?" "No," I said, before I even thought about it. She cupped
my breasts and flicked her thumb over my nipples, which
popped erect. We both laughed. Then the clerk asked through
the door if we needed any help, and we resumed trying on
bras.) Now she slipped her hands under my breasts and
squeezed them. I sighed with pleasure.

Tyler's palm massaged my thigh. Another hand—
Claude's?—slithered up my other thigh. Both hands grazed my
pubic hair, and someone's finger traced the crack of my buttocks down and up, sending shivers up my spine.

But why wasn't anyone spanking me? Every smack had sent
a tingling to my pussy. Every slap had sent my aromatic dew
dripping from my labia.

I kicked my feet and squirmed to indicate I wanted more.

My pubes rubbed Tyler's thigh, sideways, up and down. Goodness knows, I should have been embarrassed to masturbate against Tyler's thigh—but I didn't care. I rocked myself harder and faster. I was beyond shame. By now Marcy and Tyler were more dear, more trusted, than anyone I'd ever known, except Claude.

"Don't stop," I said.

"Don't stop what?" Tyler asked teasingly.

"It's your birthday," Marcy said.

"You can have anything you want," Claude said.

"What would you like?" Tyler taunted.

"Spank me," I whispered.

"We can't hear you," Claude said.

"Spank me," I pleaded.

"Louder," Marcy insisted.

"Spank me!" I cried. "Spank me hard!"

The smack caught me by surprise. But I loved it. "Twenty-one!" Claude cried.

Marcy's tongue flicked in and out of my mouth.

"Twenty-two!" I caught her tongue between my teeth.

"Twenty-three!" I sucked on her tongue. It was like a jabbing muscular penis, a slithery giant clitoris.

"Twenty-four!" Tyler's fingers were slipping in and out of my honey pot.

"Twenty-five!" Tyler's finger rubbed my stiff, pulsing clitoris.

"Twenty-six!" Tyler's fingers filled my vagina. Three fingers? Four? I was full, yet I wanted more. I wanted to be filled, to be packed, to be bursting.

"Twenty-seven!" I looked over my shoulder. Marcy sucked on Tyler's fingers.

"Twenty-eight!" Marcy sucked my tongue into her mouth. She nibbled it, nursed it, feasted on it.

"Twenty-nine!" I sucked my juices off Marcy's tongue. I thought I'd go crazy with these new sensations, all happening so fast, all exciting me so much.

"Thirty!" I wanted a dozen things at once—Tyler's fingers to fill me up, Marcy to absorb my tongue into her warm mouth and nurse it like a baby on a tit, someone to spank my hot and tingly bottom again and again, anyone to thrust their lively tongue into my hot twat and flick their tongue across my teased and tantalized clit, someone's iron cock to plunge inside me and pump me dry.

"Thirty-one!" Someone's fingers rubbed my dripping labia. Were they Tyler's fingers? Marcy's? Could Claude hear the slurps as the fingers slid in and out?

Two fingers pressed the sides of my clit.

"Oh my God," I said.

"Thirty-two!" My clit jerked up and down, fucking the two fingers.

I was almost coming, I was at the brink, I was moaning, I couldn't get over, please help me get over, please—

"And one to grow on!"

My orgasm washed over me over like Niagara Falls. I plummeted from exquisite agony to a shuddering ecstasy that went on and on until I thought it would never end, until I hoped it would never end. Lightning throbbed from my toes to my crown. My fingers dug into Marcy's arms. Hands squeezed my buttocks. I shrieked. I groaned. I kicked my feet.

It lasted a long time, it didn't last long enough, I wanted it to stop, I wanted it to go on . . . my body jerked . . . shivered . . . spasmed . . . hands soothed my buttocks . . . hands caressed my breasts . . .

I lay limp across Tyler's thighs.

Claude sat me up on the sofa next to Tyler.

Marcy looked at Tyler. "Your pants are soaked," she laughed, pulling off his pants. He wasn't wearing undershorts.

Marcy yanked off her skirt, then her thong.

My skirt was bunched at my waist, my blouse was open, my bra hung loose. I took everything off. Only Claude was still dressed.

I pulled down his pants and undershorts while Marcy

peeled off his shirt. "Well," Claude said, "now that we're all naked, what shall we do?"

"You're the Birthday Girl," Marcy said. "You get whatever you want."

Tyler was standing beside me. My fingers encircled his penis.

Claude was standing behind Marcy, his hands reaching around to massage her breasts. Her hands went behind her. Was she playing with his cock?

My bottom still tingled from my spanking, my pussy was still wet, and Tyler's cock was getting harder in my hand.

"We'll go into our bedroom," I said. I pulled Tyler along by his penis. Marcy led Claude by his. "And *I'll* spank *you*," I added, looking at Claude. "And *you*," I said to Marcy. "And *you*," I said to Tyler.

We climbed onto the bed. The three of them lay on their stomachs, their bottoms in the air.

I think we're pretty normal people, don't you? What is normal, after all? Isn't it what feels good, and is exciting, and doesn't hurt anybody?

That's what I think.

In at the Deep End

by Bryn Colvin

We can of course train you to use the various craft. It would be too much to hope that any applicant already had those skills," Dr. Williams said, thoughtfully. Claire nodded, trying not to beam too much. This was her dream job, and it seemed to be falling into her lap.

"In terms of your knowledge base and academic achievements, you would make an excellent addition to our little team," her interviewer continued. "My only concern is how you will fare psychologically. It is more efficient to work offshore in six-week blocks. You have to bond well with the rest of the team and handle the isolation from the rest of the world that you will experience. There's no reliable way of testing for this one, not that I trust, so I must ask you to think long and carefully. You must know yourself; please consider how you might handle the psychological challenges that joining this team will represent."

Claire took a deep breath: She was at heart a very sociable creature, and a genius where balancing work and play was concerned. Unlike most of her fellow students she had maintained both an active social life and good grades throughout her various courses. Being trapped on a boat for six weeks at a time with no access to friends, parties, and nightclubs was an alarming prospect, but then, this was one of the few jobs in existence at the cutting edge of marine archaeology and she didn't want to waste her extensive qualifications in some dull office.

"I'll be honest with you and say I don't know. I like to be sociable. I guess it would depend totally on how I got on with everyone else. It could work, I mean, I'm pretty laid-back. I don't get stressed readily so six weeks shouldn't be a major problem."

"And of course," he continued, "There is the question of your personal life—mobile-phone connections are unreliable at best, and we don't have any post, as you can no doubt imagine. It means leaving your loved ones and not getting any contact for the duration."

Claire shrugged. "Not an issue. I don't have any serious ties."

"I think you may fit in nicely." And for the first time, Williams smiled. Claire felt the tension ease out of her shoulders: The job was hers. Mulling it over, she thought that six weeks in a boat with this man would not be such a terrible thing. He had the firm wiry physique of an accomplished swimmer, coupled with the aura of distracted intelligence that haunted most of the intellectual highfliers she had ever encountered.

She spent the following few months in training, learning how to manage the main boat and its entourage of smaller craft, the hoisting gear, and an assortment of implements she hadn't seen before. While the crew included an experienced sailor and two other people who had long been on Williams's team and knew the gear intimately, the doctor made it policy that everyone who went out should have at least a basic handle on how everything worked. It could make the difference between life and death in an emergency. Equally, he required all of his crewmembers to have a grasp of basic first aid, radios, and local marine wildlife. During her training, Claire saw little of Williams, and nothing at all of the rest of the people she was to be working with.

The sticky heat of the day was only slightly relieved by a soft wind off the sea when Claire boarded the *Merry Maiden*. Williams greeted her on the deck, his usually somber suit replaced by a loose T-shirt and baggy shorts that revealed his tanned and muscular legs. Once she had deposited her bags in her tiny cabin, he gave her a tour of the boat and introduced her to the others.

They met Tania in the galley, her blond hair swept up in a scarf, and her slender body minimally adorned by a bikini and sarong. She had the kettle boiling, and turned to greet them with a warm and open smile. Eric was concentrating on taking them out and barely grunted a hello, although Claire noticed that he took his eyes away from his work long enough to look her up and down. He was a tall, broadly built man with a sheen of dark hair on his chest and a series of tattoos down his arms. Nadine was a petite and dark-skinned beauty, who could have come from almost anywhere, although Claire found herself thinking that the woman would make an excellent mermaid, with her high, firm breasts and cascade of hair so dark that in some light it almost seemed green. The final crew member, Ian, looked like he might be more at home in a music shop or in front of a computer—unlike the others his skin was very pale, with the pasty sheen of someone who does not venture outside often. His hair was long and dark, his face gaunt and dominated by the most remarkable cheekbones Claire had ever seen. Everything about him seemed slightly delicate. He was softly spoken, and she stopped to talk to him for a while. Like her, he was on his first trip out.

"I'm guessing you're the new girl," he said.

"What gave it away?"

He looked her up and down.

"You're as overdressed as I am."

They were both wearing jeans. Claire had opted for a strappy top that showed a moderate amount of cleavage, but Ian was displaying even less skin with his long-sleeved shirt.

"I figured, given how much we'd be in the water during the

day, I might as well bring stuff that'll be comfy for the evenings," she said.

"Well, I'm glad to find it's not just me. I guess they're all used to each other. They seem like one big happy family up there."

"I guess we should probably go up and make a stab at being sociable."

Ian nodded his acquiescence.

On the deck, Tania was making the most of what little leisure time they would have. She lay stretched out like a cat, her pert breasts exposed to the warm sun and her eyes closed. The expression on her face was blissful. Sitting beside her, Alex was reading over his notes while Nadine rubbed sunblock into his back and shoulders. As she finished, she tickled him playfully in the ribs. Hearing their approach, Nadine turned her head.

"Are you joining us?" she called out.

Claire walked over to them, conscious that Ian was a little behind her and slightly uncomfortable. He wouldn't be the first guy who had found himself slightly on edge at the sight of exposed female flesh.

"It is glorious out here," Claire commented, her eyes taking in first the vivid blues of sea and sky, then the more immediate visual feast of human beauty. With practiced ease, she kicked off her shoes.

"I suppose I should go and dig out a bikini or something," she said.

"You could just ditch the jeans," Tania suggested. "We aren't going to be bothered."

Claire had always been relaxed about her own body, and on a ship this size, things were inevitably going to be quite intimate. She slipped out of her jeans, folded them, and turned to place them on the narrow bench behind her. Ian was blushing slightly. She smiled reassuringly at him.

"Are you going to join us?" she asked.

"I'm not much of a sun worshipper," he said. "But if you

lot have no objection, I'll just sit here in the shade and letch quietly."

Tania laughed, and Claire found herself smiling as well. Still facing him, she pulled her top over her head, freeing her well-rounded breasts. She moved her shoulders slightly, watching his expression, knowing full well that she could be in his bed any time she wanted to be.

"More sunblock!" Nadine called out.

Alex stood, pot of cream in hand.

"May I?" he asked.

Claire nodded and settled herself on the deck. His hands were strong and firm as they worked over her back and shoulders, rubbing the sunblock in and massaging gently as he went. She breathed deeply, blissfully at ease and feeling very indulged. Slowly he worked down the backs of her legs. She could feel the warmth of the sun on her skin, soaking into her body. She knew he was taking his time with the cream, but didn't mind; she was enjoying being touched.

Claire dozed pleasantly for a while, tasting the sea air and listening to the sounds of the boat and to the light banter among her companions. She had no real sense of time passing, but after a while rolled to expose the front of her body to the sun's rays. Within seconds she felt Alex's hands on her legs again, and opened her eyes to see him kneeling at her side, applying yet more cream to her calves and thighs. He paid a great deal of attention to the tops of her legs, fingers straying dangerously close to her sex but never actually touching. He moved on to her stomach, then her face and shoulders, before applying himself to her bosom. His touch was gentle and skilled and she found herself hoping that he would brush those long fingers of his against her nipples, but he didn't. When finally he had finished, she opened her eyes. He caught the faint look of disappointment on her face, and smiled, raising his eyebrows slightly.

Claire caught a glimpse of Tania's long legs as she moved past.

"I think our new boy might be feeling a bit left out."

Claire raised herself onto her elbows in time to see Tania straddle Ian on the bench. He wrapped his arms around her waist and lowered his head. Claire could not see clearly, but imagined he must have his face in Tania's breasts. This was more forward than anything Claire had experienced before, but she was finding it liberating.

"Is there anything you'd like?" Alex asked her softly. She looked up at the older man. She had grown used to thinking of him as an employer and mentor, but realized he was offering himself to her in a very different capacity. Nadine was watching them with unabashed interest. It was an easy decision to make: Claire sat up into a kneeling position and placed her arms lightly round Alex's shoulders.

"Anything?" she asked, her tone playful.

"Well, within reason."

She kissed him, pressing herself against his chest and delighting as he began to run his fingers over the curves of her hips. He tasted of sea spray. Claire felt a hand on her shoulder and broke away from the kiss, to find that Nadine had joined them. Alex turned to kiss her and Claire knew this was nothing new for them. Her heart began to race as the erotic possibilities of her situation became more evident. When Nadine and Alex separated a little, she offered her own lips to the beautiful, mermaid-like girl.

They traded kisses back and forth among the three of them until Nadine said, "Time to initiate the new girl I think."

Claire didn't have to ask what she meant as she felt her panties being pulled down her legs, and her body showered in kisses and caresses. She lay back on the deck, all thoughts erased by the pleasure of sensation as Alex and Nadine sucked and teased a breast apiece. Her sex dripped with anticipation and her stomach fluttered between fear and desire.

Being a slim but well-rounded girl with an outgoing nature and a pretty face, Claire had enjoyed the company of more blokes than she could easily count since losing her virginity at fifteen. Even so, she had always been spoilt for choice and had said "no" at least as often as she had said "yes." However, she had never so much as kissed another girl. There was something incredibly provocative about looking up to see Nadine running fingers and tongue across her skin. Alex was watching them both, his expression rapturous.

"I knew you'd like her," he said softly, and Claire was unsure which of them he was speaking to.

When finally Nadine dropped her head, applying her sensuous mouth to Claire's sex, the new recruit opened her legs and surrendered herself gladly to this most exquisite of pleasures. She was conscious of the stillness around her, the vibrations of the boat as its engine chugged onwards, and the sensation that every eye was upon her. Enjoying the knowledge that she was fully on display to her companions, she gave voice to her pleasure, arching her back and pushing forward with her hips as Nadine slid cool fingers into her hungry body. Deeply aroused by her circumstances, Claire came quickly and repeatedly, until she had to beg Nadine to stop and let her rest. The dark-haired woman surfaced, eyes shining. Looking up, Claire could see Alex, his eyes closed in pleasure—while she had been distracted, he had included himself in their play, and was now working himself furiously against Nadine's posterior. Nadine bit her lip, clearly enjoying these ministrations.

In a sudden rush of inspiration, Claire slithered down between Nadine's legs, until her head was between the other woman's thighs. It was cramped and hot, Nadine pressed down close on her, and Claire could see Alex's cock thrusting between the engorged lips of her vagina. She negotiated her hand between them, caressing his balls and stroking the sensitive skin between scrotum and arse. It was easy enough to imagine herself being the happy recipient of that superb organ. With her tongue, she began to gently stimulate Nadine's clitoris, returning the favor she had been given. Hot fluids dripped onto her face as she listened with delight to the now ecstatic lovemaking that was going on above her.

When finally they rolled apart, Claire was drenched with
sweat and other juices, her hair plastered against her scalp and
her body once again wracked by desire. Looking around she
saw that Tania was mounted on Ian, the two locked in a private
ecstasy. Alex and Nadine had fallen into a comfortable
embrace, and she felt suddenly isolated, a fifth wheel in a
world that had unexpectedly become filled with couples.
Everything seemed to have changed, the light was low in the
sky and she realized that the noise of the boat's engine had
ceased. Everything was still, save for the rocking of Tania's
body.

Eric wandered nonchalantly onto the open deck area at the
front of the boat, and looked around at the sated and the still
indulging.

"I see you started without me," he said, sounding amused.
He looked down at Claire.

"Have the good Drs. Williams totally worn you out yet?" he
asked her.

While she knew he'd said something significant, her mind
was too full with thoughts of sex to do much more than say,
"Not quite," and open her legs slightly, inviting him to look. At
that moment she wouldn't have cared who he was: The need
to be laid was almost overpowering. She could see from the
look on his face that he was feeling as frustrated as she. She sat
up, pulling down his shorts and taking his already stiffened
member into her mouth, teasing him with her tongue. He
swelled until she could barely accommodate him between her
lips. Coming up for air, she tilted back her head to look at him.

"Do you want me?" she asked.

"Yes."

With her back once again on the deck, Claire opened her
legs wide to give this broad and powerful man full access to
her body. With just a few strokes from his cock, she was sent
back into the transports of pleasure Nadine had already
invoked. Her body swam with orgasmic delights. She was
vaguely aware that with another orgasm or two she might lose

consciousness altogether when Eric's body tensed and trembled in a single convulsion that sent the final waves of pleasure through her exhausted body.

Late the following day they reached the drowned islands that were to be the focus of their research. Work began in a very ordinary way, with no one commenting on the extravagancies of the previous night. Claire worked in a daze, still bathed in a hazy afterglow of sexual pleasure. She watched the four established teammates go about their work with relaxed confidence, but took some comfort from the fact that Ian looked about as bemused as she felt. In the aftermath of that encounter, she felt the need to talk to someone, to try and make sense of her reactions in the context of another's perceptions. She had never embarked on anything like it before, and while the sex had indeed been glorious, she could not begin to make sense of her current emotional state, nor to unravel where this left her as a person. Her first encounter of lesbian sex, voyeurism, and threesomes in the space of one evening was a lot to grasp. Looking at her companions, she could not decide who best to approach or confide in and the creeping sense of being isolated in what was otherwise a tight-knit group started to gain a hold of her again.

After the evening meal, she offered to wash up and retreated to the galley. She could hear occasional sounds of laughter from elsewhere on the boat, and found herself wondering if variations on the previous night's themes were being played out in her absence. She didn't even hear Tania arrive.

"How you doing?"

Claire looked up and smiled. It seemed slightly easier encountering the two people on the ship she hadn't actually opened her legs for.

"I guess we dropped you in at rather the deep end last night," Tania observed, her voice warm and tinged with concern.

"I'll admit it wasn't what I'd expected from this job," Claire

said, blushing slightly. "I mean, I've never . . . I'd not done anything like that before."

"Neither had I until a few years back."

Claire waited, sensing that Tania had a tale she might be
willing to tell.

"Alex was working in the Med then, interviewed me,
offered me a job, took me out for a meal. I can't have been
more than a year older than you are now, and I was quite an
innocent, I can tell you. I ended up going home with him. I
was butt naked with his dick in my mouth when his wife
walked in."

Claire had the sense of pieces falling into place.

"I, of course, was totally embarrassed, but Nadine just
walked over and said 'You want a hand with that?' and before
I knew where I was, we were both playing with him. And that
was me hooked."

"So this is normal for them then?" Claire asked, carefully.

"Pretty much. They like to experiment, and I'll admit
they've given me something of a taste for it as well."

"It can't be easy to live with, though," Claire mused aloud.
"Being the unrecognized third party in someone else's marriage."

"And not always that," Tania shrugged, but there was a hint
of sadness in her voice. "I'll be honest with you, this is a much
easier lifestyle if you are playing as a couple, if you've got
something stable to fall back on, someone to share it all with."

Claire had no idea how to respond. More than a decade of
serial monogamy had not prepared her for this—she was struggling to understand how such open relationships might work.

"Don't they ever get jealous, Nadine and Alex?" she asked.

"Oh, it happens," Tania smiled, "He'll be dead pissed off
that she got to make you come on your first day and he hasn't
got any with you yet."

It turned out to be a quiet night because Nadine was working on something. Tania had told her that Alex seemed to have
a real talent for finding the bi-curious, individuals who had not

yet tasted the pleasures of same-sex love, but who would be willing to try.

"He's never yet recruited someone to work with him who hasn't wound up in an orgy before the end of their contract," she said, with a certain amount of pride.

Claire gathered that Eric and Alex had some kind of bet on to see who would manage to seduce Ian first.

Claire awoke from her sleep, but at first did not know why.

"Claire?" There was someone in her room, but her weary brain failed to immediately recognize the voice.

"Wassup." She sat up, pulling the covers up around her shoulders. Whichever one of the guys it was, sat down on the end of her bed.

"Sorry to wake you."

"S'okay, what's the problem?" she asked, her mind starting to focus.

"I just needed someone to talk to, and I thought . . . I hoped you wouldn't mind." She realized the voice was Ian's, and he sounded quite fragile.

"Talk away," she said. "It's been a bit odd for me as well . . ." she tailed off, thinking about what Tania had said.

"Alex and . . . and Eric . . ." he began.

"Ah."

"I just don't know what to think right now. I mean, it wasn't a bad experience really, it's just not who I thought I was. I don't know what this makes me. I mean, I'd always thought I was the marrying and settling down type, and I've never liked keeping secrets. Well, you're a girl, would it bother you that I'd, you know?"

"I guess not," she said. In the darkness, she shuffled closer to him on the bed and put an arm round his shoulder. His body was rigid with tension.

"Did you enjoy it?" she asked.

"At the time, yes," he admitted. "They both of them . . . had me. No one's ever done anything like that to me before."

"Are you feeling guilty?" she asked.

"A bit, I suppose."

"And a bit dirty maybe, like you've done something that marks you?"

"Sounds about right."

"I've been feeling the same way, you know, not sure what to think of what I've done. You didn't see most of it; you were too busy with Tania."

"I saw you with Eric. I'd never watched before either, but I thought that was really hot. I felt quite envious of him really."

"Stay with me?" she asked him. "You don't have to do anything, but it sounds like you're feeling as insecure as I am, and I'd like someone to snuggle up with. Yesterday was great for me, but there was no emotional intimacy in it, you know? I'm not sure that's what I want."

"Okay."

The bed was small, but they curled up in each other's arms, each lost in their own doubts and reveries. Ian gently stroked her hair and shoulders as she lay with her head on his chest. She kissed him on the chin, then the lips. Cautiously, they began to explore each other's bodies. Ian was gentle and tender with her, taking his time to get to know her shape, to relax and comfort her into a sweet and tender arousal of the senses. There was no force or urgency, but a slow and intimate coming together, rich in kisses and words of reassurance.

"I want to make love to you," he confessed.

She rolled him onto his back, wrapping her legs around his slender torso and lowering her face so that his lips met hers. It was remarkably easy to slide herself onto him, taking him deep within her body. They lay still for a while, before she started to move her hips slowly against his. She took her time, savouring him, pausing for long kisses and to allow him access to her breasts. She came a little before him, resting her head on his chest again and enjoying the sensation of having him in her.

Claire woke in the faint light before dawn and contemplated the man who had shared her bed. His long hair was fanned out around his face, his expression in sleep tranquil. This made more sense to her, a slightly unfamiliar man who might stay for a night, or a week, or maybe longer. Someone to talk to, someone to get to know, to explore carefully and who would learn how best to please her. The session on the deck had been fun, but it lacked something that she didn't quite know how to name. She began to make sense of the things Tania had been saying. It would be easier to go and play with the others if she could come back to this bed and this man, to talk, to enjoy the simpler comforts of touch, the more modest pleasures of tender sensuality. In a sea of flesh and possibility, it would be good to have something reliable to cling to.

Ian opened his eyes and for a long while they simply studied one another.

"Hello," he said.

"Hello yourself."

He reached out to stroke her thigh, his face warmed by an affectionate smile.

"I think the next few weeks are going to be a bit crazy," he observed.

Claire had just taken off her swimming gear and was heading for her room and a change of clothes when Alex pounced on her. He grabbed her from behind, pressing himself against her as he smothered her neck and shoulders in kisses. Caught off guard, Claire struggled briefly. She had been thinking that morning that maybe it would be nice to try and get into a proper relationship with Ian. The intimacy of their sleeping together had changed things for her. Further encounters with her crewmates had not been part of her latest vision and she had planned to avoid them. Already her body was betraying her. She could feel her nipples hardening as Alex worked his hands over her stomach and up toward her chest and she gasped in spite of herself. He caressed her clitoris fleetingly.

"Now, are you going to be a good girl?"

"Yes, Dr. Williams," she said submissively, not knowing

what else to do. He hoisted her up, lifting her onto his shoulders before heading back toward the deck. With a sinking feeling she realized that it would not be enough for this man to fuck her; he had to do it publicly so that all of the others would know. The thought of Ian observing this sent a flicker of fear through her.

The others had gathered on the deck, all clearly aware of what was going on. Claire briefly saw herself as some human sacrifice, her body about to be offered up to some prehistoric god of carnal pleasure. Part of her wanted to resist, but she was fiercely aroused and finding herself unable to fight the desire that was taking hold of her. Alex dropped her unceremoniously onto the deck, and before she could move, Claire found herself covered in fingers and lips. Disoriented, she had no sense of who was who. She wondered why they were so keen to do this with her, and why she could not resist them. She felt herself surrendering, her breath coming in short gasps and her senses reeling with escalating delight. Suddenly, she was pinned to the deck, a firm hand on each arm and leg. Tania was standing over her, brandishing a dildo.

"Do you want this?" the naked blond asked her.

Claire wanted to resist. Nadine and Eric had each secured one of her legs. Glancing sideways she could recognize Alex's hands on her arms. She tried to see Ian but had no idea where he was. Nadine used her free hand to stroke the insides of Claire's thighs.

"Yes or no?" Tania persisted.

"Yes," Claire confessed.

She watched, fascinated as Tania lowered the implement toward her waiting sex. The thing was impossibly huge, but Tania worked it with skillful hands, gently prising Claire open. She felt more full than seemed possible, shivering with pleasure as the dildo rubbed against her G-spot. When the thing was as far in as it could go, Tania nodded and her co-conspirators rolled Claire onto her knees. Claire waited, willing once again to let them do as they pleased with her. Alex continued to hold her down.

When Ian emerged, naked and blindfolded, she realized that he must have been complicit in what was going on. Tania and Nadine fell on him, and Claire felt an unmistakably pang of jealousy as she watched the way in which he responded to them both. The three of them were undeniably beautiful, the darker skin of the women sharply contrasted by Ian's pale flesh, the swathes of hair, the athletic limbs. They moved with grace and sensual ease, licking and sucking at each other's bodies. She watched Ian bring first Tania and then Nadine to climax, eventually too caught up in the spectacle to think of envy. He was too good to watch. Each shiver of sympathetic pleasure made her clench slightly around the dildo, sending intense rushes of sensation through her body.

It seemed as though they must be working to some pre-planned script, for when Eric stepped forward, the women backed off. There was no mistaking Ian's willingness, and Claire watched with fascination as the cock that had so recently pleasured her own body was worked slowly but surely into another man's arse. She could tell that Ian was nervous, but it was evident that he wanted this experience, that it no longer troubled him as it had on the previous night. From the expression on Eric's face, he was clearly enjoying himself. It had not occurred to Claire before that a man might get so much pleasure out of being penetrated—she had assumed that it was just a submissive thing, a desire to be filled, but Eric was blatantly fast approaching a state of sexual ecstasy. He groaned with pleasure, gushing a hot stream of semen onto the deck before Ian came himself. He pushed off the blindfold and saw Claire, prone as she was.

"Having fun yet?" he asked her, his voice playful. Something in his tone, in the brightness of his eyes reassured her.

Alex gave her a playful slap across the buttocks, and she clenched her muscles involuntarily. She gasped as her vagina clamped down hard on the broad toy within her. After a few seconds, a second slap came, then a third and fourth. The sting of the slaps and the shock of squeezing the dildo were almost more intense than she could stand. The spanking continued slowly, determinedly, until she had worked herself into a frenzy of need and lust. Alex reached between her thighs, grasping the dildo and turning it in her, edging it backward and forward. She closed her eyes. It didn't matter what anyone else was doing or who was watching. Gradually, Alex worked the dildo out, leaving her empty and unsatisfied. Before she could complain, he filled her instead with his own warm member, only a fraction narrower than the toy had been. She almost cried in relief as he began to thrust himself deep into her. Opening her eyes, she looked up at Ian, taking in the rapt expression on his face. She was going to come with him watching her, with him watching as someone else fucked her, with him enjoying seeing that. She forgot her doubts and her previous intentions, sharing her pleasure with him as Alex drew one quick and shuddering orgasm after another from her body. She collapsed onto the deck, her head spinning from a surfeit of hormones.

Sweaty and undignified, she crawled over to Ian. He welcomed her with open arms, a warm refuge in which she could recover from the violence of her passions.

"You were amazing," he said softly. She nestled against him, glad that she had been able to share that encounter with him, and realizing that watching him in a new sexual experience had been a rare privilege. What she wanted to do most, after cleaning up, was retreat to the quiet privacy of her cabin, and get him to tell her everything—who had planned what, how it had been for him. She wanted to talk about what had happened. Maybe do more than talk if he wasn't too tired from his previous efforts.

Claire lifted her head and saw that Tania was watching them. She felt a pang of sympathy for this fellow traveler who had lost her heart to a married couple. *Too easy to get hurt in this game,* she mused, but even so the possibilities were so intoxicating that she knew she would keep coming back for more, just as Tania did.

Balance

by Helena Settimana

Please Nona, please Nona, please Nona, please."

Shit. I hate that kinda talk. Beggin' for it; whining, wheedling, like the world's gonna end if the bastard doesn't get him some. Not from *me*, no way. That isn't my style. I'd never be rid of a guy like that. Give him some an' he'd be making wedding plans. *Shit.*

'Dru was like that; always steppin' to me, never mind where it was, pushing up, testing my patience, wheezing like an asthmatic dog. Little beads of sweat were on his upper lip, and he kept wiping his hands on his clothes. He looked like Jiminy Cricket, too, or like one of them candy Easter bunnies you get in Wal-Mart, but with the ears bit off.

"Gimme some. I won't tell."

"Tell who?"

"I dunno . . . whoever he is . . . I'll love you to death."

Yeah, that's what I am afraid of.

Crap like this gets my blood up; raises my ire. I can't help myself. *Shit.* I like what I like, I like things my way, and I can't abide a dude who's whinin' over his blue balls, especially if I got nothing to do with it. To me it shows no confidence. No self-respect. I can't even *think* about laying down with that.

I got a theory about confidence. I never met a guy with sexual confidence who didn't have a cock like a mule. I think it is a sort of natural selection thing: a display like the puffing of a pigeon. Even if we can't see it straight off, he knows it's there and he walks like a gunslinger on account of it. I bet 'Dru had a dick like a cocktail shrimp.

Andre wasn't like 'Dru. Andre knew his own score, which is why he was so easy to get with and why he *messed* with me so. Andre walked like John Wayne, with a six-shooter on each hip. He wasn't so handsome, but looked like a prince all the same; something in his bearing did that. He'd stand in a room and hold his own court, mostly—like he expected the world to come to him. I like that in a man. Always had a circle of admirers; some men, but mostly women hanging on to what he said.

I think he intimidated men. A lot of them didn't much like him 'cause he topped them without working at it. Andre acted like it was a given that I or anyone else would just want to take him home, and it didn't matter who suggested it, so long as he liked what he saw. He could smoke me with his eyes and take all my shit out of me so that I didn't even think of bein' a bitch except *for* him, not *to* him: you know what I'm saying? He'd push up, too—but not to beg. He had balls.

He'd go, "You know I like you, Nona, so why haven't we done it? You 'fraid of me?"

It hung out there like a red flag in front of a bull. "*Afraid*." Christ, I got like I was eight years old or something, and all red and hot, first time he did that. I figured that the smoke was rising offa my face. I didn't feel like walking all over him like I did with most guys. I knew I couldn't. Fact: I was a bit scared, and that tripped me up, but I'd never admit it. Not to him.

He told me to come by and check out his place, and maybe have a beer or something. I figured I knew what the "something" was going to be and went anyway, a little messed about not having control over myself, or him. That drove me nuts, deep down, all the while he was "having his way," as the saying goes. I just lost my cool. I let him. I kept telling myself that I really hadn't lost my hold on the situation, but I had.

He was like, savage; like nothing I had ever crashed into before. Letting go like that, the way he made me do, is easy with guys who have some art in their loving, the ones who'd come to worship me with their cocks and tongues, and hands. Worshipping is different from begging. You go to church. You don't necessarily want to live there; know what I mean? Anyway, he didn't come to worship. He was the idol. *The man.*

First thing I know is that he had his hands all twisted in my hair and his stump in my face, and there's this sweaty, ballsy smell taking up air in the place, but it shouted of nothing but sex, and lots of it. Motherfucker was making me choke on it, and was pinching my nipples and slapping my tits; none too gently either.

Hell if I could understand it, but I was just full of want. The insides of my thighs were greased with juice. We were stinking up his couch: The fucking thing was covered in plastic and it made farting sounds as we slipped on it. I had figured him for a guy with better taste.

He messed me up. Jesus, with all that twisting and slapping, I was hotter than I had been in my whole life and in my mind I was begging him to put his mouth on me. I finally got fed up and started to holler, "Fucker, EAT ME!" but he just kept right on like he was deaf, until he pulled me offa his dick by my hair and pushed me around so he could have a go at me like "Rover." I didn't recognize myself asking for it like that. My damn face was stuck to the plastic wrap on the sofa seat.

He was gonna split me in two. I felt like I was stuck like a dog and I kept pulling away as he was jamming it in, trying to save myself some of my insides, but he kept at it, and in a bit it wasn't hurting no more. Motherfucker made me scream with just his cock. The neighbors started banging a broomstick or something on the floor overhead.

I cried that night, but not 'cause I was hurt.

This sort of shit went on for months: I felt like a baby. Weak. No power. It was sort of liberating, and sort of disturbing all at once.

Then one time he had a friend, a pretty-boy named Leon, come visit and crash on that stupid sofa for the night. Leon was almost a brother, who lived outta town. The two of them were tight, and when Leon was there, they drank and smoked together, and I got made to take the backseat. I even got to fetch the beers—lucky me. So, late, Leon finally crashed, and Andre and I went to bed and started fooling around a bit. We lay in his room, and he began to cajole me to go and make sweet with Lee. Said the scene would turn him on.

"Nona, it's not fair I have my friend visiting and he has to sleep on the couch . . . go get him."

It surprised me a bit, that kind of reasoning. He had this sort of weird look in his eye. I wondered if Andre'd be sharing his bed with this dude if I wasn't there; if he would think it was so unjust, but it made me kinda hot, all the same.

So I went.

God, that Leon was gorgeous: tall and smooth. I stared down for a while at his face while he slept and thought about what it would be like to scene with him. Very fine. So I woke him and without telling him what was up, asked him to come with me. I figured he could suss it out since I was butt naked. He had a hard-on before we reached the bedroom.

Leon was the kinda guy I used to go for, gentle, sensual, with a soft, full mouth that loved to commune with a body. Big, kinda sad eyes. I could handle him, and whisper what I wanted. He'd give it to me. Andre's biggest defect was that he wouldn't eat pussy or use his hands to get me off. Not that I usually missed it, you understand: But Leon ate my face, chewed my tits and my pussy until his damn fine mug was soaked. He had a soft touch.

Leon had me wrapped around his head, screaming while Andre slid "it" between my teeth. He really seemed to get off on watching while I twisted on his friend's tongue and babbled like I had a bad fever. He was just staring like he had gone nuts, staring mostly at Lee, at what he was doing to me. I had a hold on one of Andre's legs and could touch his balls and the sensitive ridge of flesh between them and his asshole. I figured he'd bust my face if I ever touched him there, but when Leon pushed my legs back over his shoulders and started fucking me, my middle finger found Andre's ass and I heard him moan out loud for the first time, ever. I could work it in a bit at a time, slicked up with my own wet, until the palm of my hand was wedged between the hemispheres of his butt. It surprised the hell outta me. Then a light kinda went on in my head.

I swear to God he was thinking about Leon's cock being in him instead. Something about the look on his face telegraphed that. He'd stare at my mouth stretched open to take him, and then down to where he'd catch a glimpse of his friend's wood smacking into me, and rest there, transfixed, and his asshole relaxed even more.

Leon's breath got ragged. He was rocking on me really tight and deep and hard; up close, up tight, up inside of me. I don't know if he ever came, though, funny as it sounds.

But Andre came like that, with my hand wedged in his ass. He pulled outta my mouth which I didn't expect, 'cause that was his favorite party trick. That's when I knew for sure that there was a bit more to this than I had allowed myself to see. He started cussing him, talking dirty, like he was talking to me, but he wasn't. He was gonna top dog Leon same as he did everyone else. He took aim—swear to God—and his ass tightened round my hand like a steel band. Damned if he didn't shoot a wad like Silly String into Leon's pretty brown face. It hung in opalescent gobs off of his cheek and the wedge of his beard, like tinsel. Leon didn't even blink. Stuff was falling on my tits. Next thing I know is those two were sleeping like babies. When I woke up, Andre was touching Leon's shoulder, like by accident.

After that, I looked at Andre differently and the balance of our relationship changed. This "latent" thing bugged my ass; not because fag stuff bothered me *per se,* but because it felt sneaky, and my vision of Andre was not like that. I realized I had some kinda big power over him. I could be the key that allowed him to unlock this desire he held in so tightly. Through me, he could make it all right; let it slip out like no one would notice—except me with my hand in his butt.

Leon came to visit a few times, but I wouldn't always play. That pissed Andre royally. He wasn't used to not getting his way. He got really chill for a long time. I wasn't impressed.

When Andre started begging me to do Leon, I knew for sure that I had been mistaken about him knowing his own score. I told him to fuck Lee himself. He lost all my respect.

Shit.

Sex with His Ex

by Jennifer Whitlock

I like to say bisexuality means never having to say, "I'm jealous." Don't hate her because she's beautiful—fuck her because she's beautiful. It's a win-win situation. And when your husband's there, it's win-win-win.

It's really true. Contrary to what "normal" wives might believe, seeing my husband make sweet love to a hot, juicy woman does not make me jealous. Not when I get to savor that lovely morsel myself. I'm secure that my husband will never leave me—even more so *because* I bring home gorgeous women. Sharing *adds* to my allure—it doesn't take away a thing.

And then there was Janet, my husband Will's ex-girlfriend. Maybe it was jealousy, maybe it was some kind of pissing contest. Whatever it was, she became less "Janet" and more "That Bitch."

I first met Janet when we visited Amsterdam, Will's hometown, to announce our engagement. I wanted to like her because Will said that she was bisexual, and that she went to a sex club that used to be a horse farm. I imagined her on her hands and knees in a hay-lined stall, bucking and whinnying. Surely I'd hit it off with a woman with such cojones, and I'd have my first three-way with my then-fiancé.

Um . . . that's not what happened. No hay, no threesome, and no hitting it off. Will thinks the whole thing was a misunderstanding, but I think she was sinking her weasely little claws into my guy. Whatever it was, she kept talking Dutch with Will in front of me, even though she knows English, and she knows I don't know Dutch. I interpreted her use of language as a deliberate attempt to leave me out.

And when she did speak English, she wasn't much better. She chose conversation topics such as how Dutch culture is better than American anything. And when we announced our marriage, she said, "Why would you ever get married? It takes away your freedom!" in the same disgusted, bewildered tone I might use when wondering why anybody would ever want kids. Except that I *wouldn't* use that tone in front of a pregnant friend—I would congratulate her to show support and good will because that's what nice people do.

Once I placed That Skanky Ho Bitch on my shit list, I found I could take any deficiency that I would excuse in a friend and add it to her growing list of faults. Poor dear. She must not have used enough sunblock throughout her long lifespan. Doesn't she know that sun damage is one of the top causes of wrinkles? That and smoking, and—it's so unfortunate—she must be a chain smoker.

It's so much fun being Catwoman! But I love my husband, and I would not demand that he give up old friends. So when we were planning another trip to Amsterdam six years later, I encouraged Will to e-mail her. Go ahead! Visit her! I just didn't want to see her myself.

Until she invited Will and me to attend a swinger's club with her and her boyfriend. She e-mailed links to two clubs. These places make my life seem rather tame, and that's no easy task, believe you me. I learned that Showboat is a "giant float-ing erotic palace" with two floors, one of which lies beneath the water. Mistress Manita monitors the S and M room, which crackles with whips, chains, and "a variety of pain and pleasure tools." I've never done that kind of thing, but the novelty made it even more exciting. And Mistress M. looked as fetching as she was menacing. Oh Mistress Manita, I've been so bad!

The sauna room featured a decadent fountain with a naked cherub pouring water onto a huge seashell. The copywriter said the following about the orgy room: "For gangbangers we have a special treat. One giant red bed five by five meters sur-rounded by pillars and mirrors, scarily lit, heavy moaning and entangled bodies . . . Join in or watch it from close by . . ." The photo revealed a naked woman with four guys servicing her. As if I weren't curious enough, the website promised, "The ladies are in charge and no one else." Hmmmm. Me and Manita. Ruling the Lust Boat. On your knees, worm!

But let's not be too hasty—Fun 4 Two looked a lot more chic, in a bordello boudoir type of way. It boasted a shiny yel-low bar, crimson lacquered walls, blood red velvet sofas, baroque chandeliers, animal-print chairs, art deco floral lamps, golden cherubs, murals of naked women, a pool, a sauna, a dance floor, orgy rooms—the works. The website explained that guests begin the evening wearing "appropriate" outfits (no T-shirts or sneakers). But when the DJ plays the "lingerie tune," everybody must change into exotic lingerie, putting their cloth-ing into their lockers.

This is not a friendly suggestion; it is a requirement, the website emphasized. "Sometimes we notice guests walking around in regular everyday underwear, which in our opinion, is totally inappropriate in a club that people visit for erotic rea-sons. Some of our guests might be insecure, or doubtful that their figure is suitable for wearing sexy lingerie. From our experience we have seen that wearing nice sexy lingerie, which helps to 'disguise' those worrisome spots, can be the differ-ence between night and day . . . We do everything we can to help create the most erotic atmosphere possible for our guests, and we expect that our guests in return will also put an equal amount of effort into achieving this."

At this point, I was ready to give Janet another chance. I was just so curious about these foreign worlds of lingerie, gang bangs, scarlet paint, and animal prints. So many taboos and basic rules of society are flagrantly violated in places like this. Rules such as: Do not have sex with somebody other than your spouse; Do not have sex in public; Do not watch other people having sex; Do not wear lingerie in a nightclub; Do not have sex with your friend's boyfriend; Be jealous of your husband's ex-girlfriend, especially when he's having sex with her. Here, these rules are thrown out the window, and basically we have to remember: Women are in charge, and put on lingerie when you hear the song.

I felt particularly interested in rule breaking because after being married five years, I felt I could use a little variety. Back in the day, I never really was single—I was more multiple. I enjoyed that lifestyle, but I love my husband and I want to stay with him. This was one way to get that old sense of adventure back, I thought. Even if we didn't participate, it would be an exciting show. Just being there could produce enough images to improve our sex life for the next few months.

We could have gone on our own, but we really would rather go with a tour guide who knew the ropes. Question is— would Janet exhibit major bitchiness, which would be a major buzz kill for my little fantasy? I had to perform a taste test.

So Will made arrangements to scope out Janet and her boyfriend ahead of time. They wanted to take us to a bar by a beach, but I refused. As much as I like the beach, and as much as I wanted to hit it off with her this time, I needed an escape route. Once we were kilometers away, I'd be marooned. And if Janet was annoying, I'd be stuck with a fake smile pasted on my face, glassy eyes, slamming down martinis to relieve the bore-dom as I heard dissertations on the deficiencies of America and the inadvisability of marriage. No thanks, or *nee danke*, as they say in Dutch—I think. No bitch by the beach!

So we met them in Amsterdam, where we were staying, to allow for a quick getaway if necessary. We had it all planned. Instead of embarrassing Will by bitching back, I'd develop a headache. Will could stay—I didn't mind. We set up signals: if I left early, but still wanted to go to the sex club, I'd say, "See ya Saturday." I'm a genius, huh? And if I left early and *didn't* want to see their ugly faces again, I'd say, "Nice meeting you again." We had a plan.

My misgivings didn't stop me from dressing sexy that night. Just in case. It's like when I go on job interviews, I always dress and act as though that job were my first choice. I might decide not to go for it, but at least I improve the chances they'll want me. Keeps my options open. So I wore my thigh-high boots with cutoff shorts and a bohemian embroidered shirt that showed a peek of cleavage.

Janet wore a classy black dress and was friendly and gracious. Her boyfriend, Ward, kept showing me pictures of her in lingerie stored on his digital camera. Damn, she was busty underneath those understated rags. And get this—when the others spoke in Dutch, she told them to speak in English so I would understand. She was trying, gotta give her that. I don't know what made the difference—the fact that she had a boyfriend? The thigh-high boots? The cleavage? The fact that she might get a piece of my husband? I don't know, but I enjoyed it.

Now that she was on my good side, I could focus on her charming qualities. She had short pixie brown hair and mischievous playful eyes peeking behind her glasses. Made me wonder what was up her sleeve behind her restrained exterior.

So we were on. We'd go to a club not included in the e-mails, the Nieuwe Country Club, with another couple, Gerard and Georgette. "You'll like her," said Janet. "She's lively, like you." And she was. Raven haired, gap toothed, red lipsticked. Beautiful but with a pleasant sense of loopiness. You could tell she had a sense of humor just by looking at her face. The guys were okay, but guys are guys. Let's face it. Women are prettier. Besides, Will was not comfortable with me being sexual with other guys; why aim my desires where they'll remain frustrated?

This country club was in the Middle of Nowhere, Holland, right by a windmill. From the outside, it looked like a plain old warehouse. But inside, the mood lighting really did an instant Botox job on all of us—we were all over forty, and that lighting must have subtracted ten years apiece. I was fascinated by the series of sex rooms upstairs. As with the other clubs, crimson

and animal prints predominated in the rooms with padded
floors and peepholes and velvet couches. Condoms were
everywhere, and a note by the dildo mounted on a stool stat-
ed that condoms were required when mounting the fake penis.
Bad sex partners could have their head and wrists restrained in
the stocks, or their arms chained over their heads by the dance
floor. But the sex swing is what grabbed me. I wanted to swing
back and forth, weightless, legs spread wide, sliding back and
forth, impaling myself on my husband's majestic penis.

But first, downstairs for drinks. The admission price included all you can eat and drink. The only stipulation was that after
a certain time, they would not serve drinks unless you were in
lingerie. So there we were, three couples sitting on a scarlet
velvet couch, wearing sexy underwear and drinking alcohol. I
didn't know what to do, so I got silly and cocky.

When Georgette bent over to get something on the table,
and I saw her luscious ass peeking out from under her
camisole, I grabbed me that butt. Everyone on my side of her
butt took my lead and grabbed along. It was deliciously
naughty. I got away with that, so I lodged my face in
Georgette's ample bosom and gave her a smooch. I wouldn't
want to leave out Janet, so I pulled her nipple out of her lacy
black bra and gave her a nibble. Just like that. Not only did they
let me, but they seemed to like it too. Georgette let out a grow-
ly purr, and Janet smiled big, as her eyes flashed more mischief
than usual.

"What's that bulge beneath your husband's boxer shorts?"
Janet asked.

I reached in and pulled out his fully extended cock. And
before you know it, all three of us women were stroking it and
admiring it. "How beautiful!" "And big!" I leaned down and
kissed it, and the other girls took their turns. This, in a nightclub with a few dozen patrons. This may be tame stuff to them,
but I felt audacious, wild, and daring!

I wish I could tell you more about who did what. But it was
hard to keep track. I suppose if I had a sober secretary follow-

ing me around and taking notes, I would be able to report more details. But somehow, one act flowed into another, and before you know it, I was in the red orgy room, swimming in a sea of breasts and hands and cocks and mouths. I do remember at one time, I reached down to play with my clitoris. This is a standard practice I do to enhance whatever my partner is doing to me. But this time, it didn't fly. "You don't have to do that," someone—I don't know who—said, and took over for me. I remember having all five people touching me at once, parting my thighs, putting fingers in my drenched pussy, sucking my taut nipples, licking my swollen clit, kissing my hungry mouth, and then, my husband fucking me. What a rush! I felt the deep love, trust, and familiarity I have with my husband, along with the excitement of being with new people in such an exciting situation. The sea of body parts enveloped me, and I came in a giant red explosion, crying out hoarsely.

I lay down in my syrupy soupy state, enjoying the views. Georgette was sucking Ward's cock. I love to watch women give blowjobs, and she did it with such gusto. Janet told me, "I'm going to go for your husband, is that okay?" I gave her the go-ahead, and watched her straddle my husband's face and ride it. I felt no jealousy—after all, she asked for my permission, and I could still withhold it. But why should I? They both helped me come, and they looked so sweet together. A guy across the room was fucking a blond long-haired woman doggy-style. So porno movie!

Then our horse and carriage turned into a pumpkin. Gerard came upstairs and upon seeing Ward fucking Georgette from behind, noted that no condoms were involved. Gerard yelled something in Dutch, and went downstairs. After that, I heard that Ward hit Gerard, and took off in the car without us. We were kicked out of the club because Gerard was in the fight too, and we don't abandon our friends. So here we were in the middle of nowhere without a ride, and I hadn't even been on the sex swing!

So we took a taxi home. Janet was bummed. "I'm never

going to talk to him again," she vowed. But she kept saying, "I'm fifty-two! I'm too old to start all over again. I thought he was nice! I even met his father!" We called up Janet a few days later, and she was giving Ward another chance—if only so that she could make him suffer before she broke up with him for real. She added that he was sorry.

The moral of this story can't be that swinger's clubs—and group sex—are antidotes to jealousy.

What puzzles me is: How could I ever have been jealous of her in the first place? Look at all that venom I wasted, for nothing! I think that once she threw down the gauntlet, I wanted to win, even if I used words, not swords. Which is kind of silly because I already won. She might have acted like she had her claws in my husband, but I know the score. Thank God I gave up that catfight, because it would have robbed me of a pretty fantastic experience.

I think I also imagined that she had something I didn't. Early in our relationship, Will read me a piece of erotica that he wrote just for Janet. He never wrote erotica for me. When they were dating, she visited him in New York and he visited her in Amsterdam. What kind of passion would be so ferocious as to span the continents? That rumination compounded my misery.

I later found that my husband and Janet never even were in love. They had sex when he was visiting his family in Amsterdam, and again when he visited his family again. She did visit him in New York. But that's about it. It made me feel better. But the truth is, what does it matter? I've loved others, and he's loved others. So what? We chose each other. It was easier to not care about their past when she was sweet and loving to me. I have to remind myself not to let another person make me feel less loved. I masquerade it as cattiness, but underneath it all, it's old-fashioned insecurity.

Finally, I think that she spoke my hidden fear—that marriage would take away my freedom. But what has her freedom gotten her? She's clinging onto an asshole she can't trust. And why? Because she doesn't want to be alone as she ages. It's true that I gave up the freedom to fuck other men. But I get a loving, devoted husband who will stay with me forever and be a designated driver for me and my friends. And I have seduced some vivacious, voluptuous vixens, who have become dear friends. It's the best of both worlds.

Burn

by Tenille Brown

1

Mitch released Eve from an embrace that was three-hours old. He watched her cower far on her side of the bed, so near the edge he was sure she would spill over onto the carpet, the dull thud disturbing their eighty-year-old downstairs neighbor. As he did every night, Mitch allowed Eve to go into that silence, that peace she slipped into long after he should have been asleep. And though his arms ached to reach out and pull her back to him, he allowed the space between them to grow until there was nothing there but an emptiness that neither she nor he could grab onto.

With her back to him, her shoulders shook softly. It was the first time he had known tears to escape her eyes. He wondered how long she had been crying when he wasn't there, while she was at her office or locked in their bathroom, free to feel what she had promised she wouldn't, what neither of them ever thought she would.

"Are you thinking about her, Eve?" This he said after turning to face the window, to watch the heavy raindrops latch on for a slow ride down the pane.

Mitch heard her take several breaths, felt her tussle on top of the sheets and when he looked over his shoulder, she was facing him, tears streaking her dark face. By the light of the moon, her dark naked body resembled an onyx statue and when she looked at him, her eyes spoke what she otherwise could not say.

He nodded, having known the answer for two months.

"I know what we promised," Eve said, "but sometimes I just can't help it."

"Do you think about her a lot?"

Mitch was on his back now with his arms folded. He stared at his locked fingers, how pale they seemed against the dark hair on his chest. In the emptiness above him he could almost see Lorn's face, the woman they had both foolishly thought harmless. He could almost smell the dime-store perfume that had lingered on their sheets and in the atmosphere of their apartment long after Lorn had left. In the distance, he was sure she was laughing at him.

"Eve?"

Mitch felt her jump, startled. He wondered where she had gone in just that quick moment.

"I've been thinking about her more lately, I guess," Eve said finally. "Don't you? Think about her I mean?"

"Sometimes. But only when I'm wondering about you, if you miss her. If you want her still." He turned to her. "You wouldn't go to her, would you?"

"No," Eve said all too quickly. "No. We said we wouldn't and I won't."

"Okay."

Eve batted her eyes and tucked in her lips. She pulled the sheet up from the foot of the bed so that it draped over her hips and hung at her waist like a loose white skirt. "I'm done with it now, Mitch, I promise." She said this while wiping her eyes, as if a simple brush of her hands could sweep away all thoughts of Lorn, all desire to be with her again.

And of the validity of Eve's promise, Mitch wasn't sure, but the deepest parts of him wanted it to be true, wanted this thing to have never happened at all. He extended his hand to his wife and she crept toward him so that he could grip her waist. He pulled her toward him, filling the gap between them so that never again would there be room for another. He circled her

small waist with his arms and sank his face into her hair and
only when he heard her exhale and felt her hands rest on top
of his, did sleep find him.

2

The still of the apartment unnerved him and Mitch loosened
his tie and undid the top button of his shirt so that he could
breathe in the stuffy thickness of their home. He had spotted
Eve's car out front as he approached the building, but when he
walked into the apartment, she wasn't standing in the kitchen
fixing her lunch, or sitting on the sofa flipping through talk
shows after deciding to take the afternoon off. There was no
evidence of her presence at all except for the hair clip that lay
abandoned on the counter and the scent of her sweat clinging
to the atmosphere like glue.

The silence rang in his ears like sirens and like a fox he
crept toward the bedroom door that was closed except for the
inch of space that allowed him to peek through. What he saw
inside made him drop the tie he had been clutching so tightly
his hand had gone numb and made him stumble backward to
maintain his balance. He felt his lips form their names, but his
shock wouldn't give voice to the words.

He watched Eve lay naked in their bed, her back support-
ed by a stack of pillows, her knees drawn up to her chest and
parted. She threw her head back and parted her burgundy
kissed lips in a silent scream of pleasure. Lorn lay comfortably
between Eve's legs, bare from the waist up, her jeans undone
and the lace edges of her black panties exposed. And though
Mitch couldn't see past the mass of curls that shielded Lorn's
face, he knew she was smiling that wicked smile.

They looked much the same as they had that night, Lorn
and Eve complementing each other's body in a slow dance. But
now the sight of Eve's dark frame silhouetted by Lorn's yellow
skin burned in his mind like a bad memory. He had loved them

that night, thought the two of them beautiful together, but they now shared something he was no part of, a passion only the two of them could know, and it left Mitch to question what he had done, to question what his and Eve's marriage had become.

For a moment Mitch allowed himself to wonder how long he had been simmering in his naivete, then he decided it didn't matter. He reached for the knob, wanting to throw the door open and demand that they stop, wanting to snatch the door closed and walk away as if he had seen nothing at all. But instead he did neither and stood idle as Eve thrust wildly about amidst the disheveled sheets and Lorn moaned softly as she pleased his wife.

When his knees were no longer dependable, Mitch backed away from the scene as silently as he had approached. He walked back to his car, forgetting the vital thing that had brought him home in the first place and remembering only the foreign look of bliss on his wife's face and the emptiness that lingered in the pit of his stomach.

3

It was the liquor that gave him the courage to come. He had grown tired of pretending that Eve's innocent longing for Lorn hadn't gone from nights of silent crying to her sneaking away from her office in the afternoon or taking long trips to the grocery store. At Sal's he sought solace in an endless trail of cheap vodka on the rocks but it had served no purpose other than to send his mind and his car to the other side of town.

As he approached the door, he considered turning around, walking back to his car without knocking. He thought of pretending he had never traveled this street or stopped in front of this house, but before he could come to a decision, the door opened and Lorn stood there in an open purple robe, the sash dangling against her ankles.

His drink-hazed eyes focused well enough to grope the smooth space between her breasts, her flat stomach and her

belly button that protruded slightly on one side. He watched
the small circles of her nipples press against the satin of her
robe and his nostrils were invaded by that awful dime-store
perfume. He pondered the purpose of wearing such a scent to
bed when he came back to himself, noticing Lorn observing
him with a crooked smile, and he felt awkward and silly.

For a moment Lorn stood there, staring, knowing. Without
Mitch asking to come in or her saying anything to him at all,
Lorn stepped back to allow him inside.

She spoke first as had been her way the night they met. "If
you've come to ask me to stop fucking your wife, I'm afraid
you've wasted twenty-five minutes and some very expensive gas,"
she said, her arms folded across her chest as if already victorious.

"Why won't you . . . *sh*top?" Mitch slurred as he stumbled
into the house.

"It's not that I won't, Mitch," she said, closing the door.
"You see, I'd gladly stop if she wanted me to." Lorn lit the
Marlboro she had been holding loosely between her fingers
and took a drag. "But she *doesn't* want me to. You know that,
don't you, Mitch?"

"I know you've done something to her!" Mitch pointed a
shaky finger close to Lorn's face and half shuffled, half stumbled toward her. "You did it that night and now she doesn't
know up from down. It's some sort of power you have over
her, and she's your puppet . . . your . . . fucking puppet!" Mitch
gripped his temples where they throbbed with the onset of an
alcohol-induced headache.

Lorn turned her face away from Mitch's breath. "Why don't
you have a seat or something? You're drunk as shit."

"Don't you tell me what to do. I don't need a goddamn seat!"

"Fine." Lorn blew smoke circles in his face and Mitch
fanned them away, coughing.

"Yeah I know it's fine."

Lorn sucked her teeth and mashed her cigarette out in a silver ashtray on the counter. "You know, Mitch," she said,
"maybe you should have taken a good, hard look at yourself

before you brought your drunk ass over here accusing me of
stealing your wife away. I didn't fuck up your marriage. It
appears you didn't need any help there at all."

Mitch laughed. "Maybe, Lorn. Maybe I didn't. Maybe *I'm*
fucked up. Can't even please my own wife without bringing in
another broad to help things along, right?"

"Aw, come on, Mitch. The self-pitying thing really isn't you."
Lorn clamped her cherry red lips tight on the end of another
Marlboro, uncrossed her arms and took Mitch's hand, which
he promptly snatched away.

"Don't fuckin' touch me."

"Hmm, those aren't words I'm used to hearing and you certainly didn't have a problem with me touching you that night."

Mitch spat on her hardwood floor. "It was one night and it
wasn't one for the history books from where I was sitting, so I
wouldn't get all cocky."

Lorn laughed. "And bitter, too," she said. She ran her hand
across his flushed cheek. She traced his lips with her fingers
and parted them playfully, then held one just beneath his nose.

"She came to me today," Lorn whispered, her breath burning his cheek. "She was on her lunch break. She kept her skirt
and heels on."

Mitch swallowed the lump that had formed in his throat
and concentrated on keeping his lips from quivering.

"I want this to stop. This thing between you and Eve," he said.

"Then Eve is the one of whom you should be making this
request. She's married to you; I'm not. And isn't that a good thing?"

Lorn pressed against him, her long, slender body melting
into him, searing his chest and thighs with her heat. She
brushed her lips against his neck. Mitch didn't want it to feel
good, her wavy brown hair tickling his neck, her nude body
rubbing against his chest and crotch. He didn't want the feeling of sweet remembrance to rush directly from his head to his
briefs, but his cock defied him, stiffening and rising against his
trousers. And although Mitch longed for the strength not to, he
reached for her, held her tightly by the hips and pressed

against her, willed her to feel the mound between his legs pulsating against her bare thigh.

She smiled of victory, she smiled of power. She put out her half-smoked second Marlboro and removed her robe, shaking her head at him as if he were pathetic.

But he would not be pathetic.

Mitch pushed Lorn against the door and pressed his lips firmly against hers. His teeth bore into her lips until her snide smile twisted in pain. He tasted her blood. She giggled against his mouth.

His tongue plunged deep into her throat and she sucked hard as if to show him that roughness bore no weight with her. He fumbled with his belt buckle and zipper and she pushed his hand aside, undoing his trousers with ease. They fell down his thighs, past his knees, and around his ankles. She freed his raised cock from his boxers and lifted her leg, pressing her foot flat against the door so that her knee rested against his hip, holding him in front of her. He bent slightly to push himself inside her and he held on to the doorknob to keep his balance. The heat from the inside of her torched his cock and the sweat dripped from his temples down his cheeks and dripped from his chin onto her breasts.

She bit down on her bottom lip, smiling, daring him to take his eyes away from hers. "You're showing me, aren't you?" she said in a throaty growl. "You're a man, right, and you can fuck me better than your wife. Is that your point, Mitch?"

His answer was in a swift and hard thrust into her that caused the arch in her back to flatten against the door. She gasped. He pulled out of her swiftly and suddenly and turned her to face the door, lifting her hands above her head.

Over the sound of their hurried breaths, he heard her snicker.

He used his finger first, shoved it into her ass so that she tightened and quivered and followed with his cock without warning. Lorn released a small shriek but soon relaxed and closed her eyes and moaned against his thrusts. Her pleasure provoked his frustration and his frustration provoked his pounding hard against her back until her ass was slick with her juices and his cock slid free against his will, against his thrusting, and hung soft and heavy between his legs.

"Fuck!" He looked down at his shriveling disappointment. Damp from her juices, it lay limp and lifeless against his thigh.

Lorn exhaled. She lifted her hand and studied something small and foreign beneath her fingernails. She sat on the bar stool, picked one of her discarded Marlboros from the ashes and relit it, dragging slow and long.

"Geez, look at you, you're all red! You done here, Mitch, or do you just need time to restart your engine?"

"Fuck you!" Mitch screamed at her, his finger in her face.

He stepped clumsily into his boxers and pulled his trousers back around his hips leaving his belt loose and his shirttail hanging out.

Lorn playfully applauded. "Way to go, Mitch. That'll show me to fuck your wife when you're not around!"

"Fuck you, Lorn! And stay the fuck away from Eve!"

He struggled with the doorknob until he was finally able to snatch it open and escape from Lorn's ridicule. In the car, his breath came fast and hard and he pounded the dashboard, screaming an endless stream of profanity as he backed out of Lorn's driveway.

4

Mitch sat in shorts and a torn T-shirt on an old recliner in the darkest corner of the living room. Rubbing a bristly beard that was two weeks old, he watched Eve slide through the slightly cracked door, set her purse down on the floor, and step out of her heels. As she removed her coat, she glanced about the room. She reached for the wall switch.

"Don't." His voice was raspy, louder than he had intended.

"Why are you sitting in the dark?" Eve asked, giggling, nervous.

"I like the dark," Mitch said, "Besides, I was just waiting on you."

"I told you I would be late."

Mitch rose from his chair and walked toward her. "I know. I knew you would be late. I just wanted to see that pretty face as you came through the door. That's all. You didn't go to her today, did you, Eve?" He hadn't meant to let the words escape his lips but they lingered on his tongue all the time now and even if he didn't ask, he would always wonder.

"You're being silly, Mitch, really."

"Am I?"

"Yes." Eve looked at him as if he were foolish. Then she continued. "I thought we were through with this business with Lorn. I told you, it was over months ago. I don't see her at all anymore. Not after work, not at the corner store . . ." She turned her face to him and he caught her lips between his.

"Then why, Eve, why can I taste her?" he said, pressing his fingers against her lips.

"Taste her?"

"Yes taste, her . . . her cunt on you."

"Come on Mitch, I can't do this. Not tonight."

"I swear she's all over you," Mitch said, slowly circling Eve as she stood terribly still. "She's on your clothes, in your hair even."

"That's ridiculous."

"When did you see her? If it wasn't after work, when? On your lunch break? Did you meet her in the parking lot and let her eat you in the backseat of her car?"

Eve laughed and in his ears she sounded much like Lorn had that night and this made him feel silly, childish that he had let it come to this. He let his hands fall at his side.

"I'm crazy, right?" His head hung low; his chin touched his chest.

"You're not crazy, Mitch."

"But aren't I? I mean, was I a fool to think we could bring something like this into our marriage for only one night and neither of us would get drawn into it?"

"You weren't a fool. And I was the one who got drawn in."

She lifted his chin with her finger. "But I'm not anymore. You have to believe that."

Mitch nodded and wrapped his arms around her. He lay his head on her chest and held tightly to her, inhaling her hair, tasting the day's stress on her neck. He let his hands relax on her back, then brought them around and cupped her breasts, rubbing them softly through her blouse. He looked to her for confirmation that it was okay and she nodded slowly, giving her silent permission for her husband to love her.

Mitch's legs weakened beneath him and he slid down the front of her until his bare knees met the rough carpet. He fingered the last two buttons on her blouse, opened them, and touched the cave of her belly. He lay his cheek there and inhaled her and suddenly he didn't smell Lorn there anymore. He tugged at Eve's skirt and pulled it down over her hips. He pushed her panties aside and gently licked her where she was covered with a fine layer of jet black hair.

Mitch lifted his head so that his mouth met her cunt again and his tongue explored her in ways it hadn't since Lorn had invaded their lives, invaded their bed. And Eve tasted the same as she had every time before they met Lorn, before they became what they were. He gripped the insides of her thighs, rested his cheek against them.

He felt Eve relax against him and when her knees weakened she fell against the wall, grabbing the back of his head. She tossed her leg over his shoulder, her heel resting against his back. And as he tasted her, loved her, reclaimed her, his knees bore in to the carpet twisting and turning, burning with his need for her.

On the gray carpet he released himself, upon his lips she trembled. He looked up at her and kissed her belly, looking over to see the slight stain of cherry red smeared on the front of her blouse, inhaling the faint scent of dime-store perfume. And tired of fighting against something that wouldn't let him win, tired of clinging to her like life, Mitch let go of Eve, his hands falling at his sides, and cried.

How Can I Help You?

by Sage Vivant

nicholas had teased her about finding the kind of bar in San Francisco that made the city famous; a place where sexual preference was irrelevant, gender was mutable, and public displays of everything short of fornication were common.

They settled for Café du Nord, a hip, slightly rundown establishment furnished and lit by more than enough bordello red. The patrons ranged from shy geeks to outrageous performers but the atmosphere held enough mystery to keep Nicholas and Claree there for several drinks.

The tables varied in size, and each had its own arrangement of (formerly) plush seating. As the couple snuggled in a faded rouge Victorian settee, Nicholas whispered into her hair.

"Check out Miss Lonelyhearts over there." He tried to nod in the woman's general direction but with Claree behind him, it took her a few minutes to figure out which woman he meant. When she located the subject of his remarks, though, she knew exactly what he referred to and giggled. The blonde with two wispy streaks of blue to frame her pretty but painted face pouted on her perch at the bar. She caught Nicholas and Claree looking at her but instead of turning away, she held the gaze and let her mouth slide into a mischievous grin.

"Oh, now you've done it," Nicholas teased. "She's noticed us."

"I think she's just noticed you."

"Well, in any event, we're about to get a visitation."

The odd but intriguing woman approached. The slow, studied sway of her walk accentuated the cinched bustier's effect on her slim waist and rounded hips. Her tits nestled firmly into the cups of the garment but with every step she took, they jiggled just enough to communicate their preference for freedom. Hollywood would have considered her overweight but Claree knew that Nicholas would find her on the tasty side of luscious. Claree was surprised to note she shared that opinion.

The woman, who finally arrived after a breathtaking but nearly interminable saunter toward them, pointed to the space on the settee. She raised her eyebrows and pointed to the space. There was room for one more body, so Nicholas gestured that she seat herself next to Claree.

Up close, the woman's skin—from décolletage to hairline—had a dewy, delicate quality that contrasted sharply, almost comically, with the heavy kohl of her eye makeup. She was Heidi in Transylvania. Despite the jarring streaks of blue in her hair and the burgundy slash of color at her mouth, there was a disarming sweetness about her. Her age was hard to pinpoint—Claree guessed somewhere in her early twenties.

Nicholas's arms were still wrapped around Claree as she leaned back into his warm chest, which had become decidedly warmer with the arrival of goth angel. He extended a hand to the woman, probably to elicit words from her but also because he was an outgoing kind of guy.

"Hi, I'm Nicholas and this is Claree."

She smiled, thereby subtracting yet another five years. "Laura. I think you don't live in San Francisco."

They laughed politely, even though the comment irritated Claree. What was Laura trying to say? That they looked like hicks or something?

"No, we're here from Suisun City."

"I could tell because you look too happy."

"Well, we are," Claree agreed, relieved that her assumption about Laura had been wrong.

"I love that. It really turns me on." Laura's big blue eyes—

a disconcerting visual echo of the stripes in her hair—widened earnestly. Her breasts heaved slightly and Claree couldn't help but watch them reassert themselves back into place when the sigh had passed.

"Do you like big tits?" Laura's head tilted and she awaited a response from either Nicholas or Claree or both.

"Yes," they answered in unison, laughing at their timing.

"I'm glad. I like them, too. Yours are nice," she nodded at Claree's formidable pair. Claree blushed, more out of pride than embarrassment. "I have a dildo in my bag. Wouldn't it be fun to use it?"

Claree decided to leave this one up to Nicholas. They'd often talked about a threesome. Well, more of a slave situation, really, but Laura seemed a far cry from a dominatrix, so perhaps this was the opportunity they'd been waiting for.

He turned around to look directly at Claree. The bar's red lights and furnishings cast rich depth to his brown hair and eyes and made his tanned skin appear darker. She read his interest as well as his caution. The angle of his eyebrows told her he needed her encouragement.

"I think we have time, don't we, honey?" Claree asked.

Laura led them to a third-floor walk-up about two blocks away in the Castro neighborhood. Like its owner, the flat spoke of fairy tales, death, sprites, and crucifixes. Turquoise, heart-shaped pillows were strewn below an Edward Gorey print, while a tarantula sat patiently in its terrarium. A Britney Spears compact disc lay on the stereo. Claree imagined Laura's under-wear—days of the week scrawled in blood.

Laura took her time lighting candles. As she moved about the room, she told the couple they could get naked if they wanted to.

"As soon as I'm finished here, I'd really like to fuck you both up the ass," she said, as if announcing what ride she planned to enjoy next at Disneyland.

Nicholas and Claree undressed themselves down to underclothes. The cool San Francisco night floated through the room, chilling Claree slightly. She looked over at Nicholas, whose erection was as stiff as her nipples.

"Oh!" Laura exclaimed when she noticed Nicholas's bulge. "Won't you take those off so I can see you?"

Nicholas glanced at Claree, who nodded and grinned. He stepped out of his briefs quickly, revealing all eight glorious inches of compliance.

"And I know you don't want to hide those pretty titties," she smiled at Claree, who instantly unhooked her bra and flung it off happily.

Laura unsnapped her skirt and waited for it to whoosh to the floor at her feet. Then, she kicked the garment aside and knelt before Nicholas. She didn't attempt to remove the bustier. With no fanfare but surprising concentration, she swooped down on his cock. He nearly teetered at the sudden intensity of her sucking.

From where Claree stood in tingling awe, the finesse with which Laura made Nicholas's cock disappear and reappear again between her dark lips was uncannily like the method Claree herself used on him. How did this woman know exactly what he liked? Come to think of it, how did she know they would respond positively to her invitation to anal play?

Nicholas's groans interrupted her musings. As Laura sucked, he thrust himself in and out of her mouth, fucking it in long, deep motions. Seeing him abandon himself to this stranger stirred something in Claree and emboldened her to step toward Laura and stand next to her with her legs in a wide-open V.

Maybe Laura caught her scent. Maybe she couldn't resist unencumbered pussy. Claree willed the young woman's hand to her creaming lips and in seconds, that's exactly where they were. Laura diddled Claree as she sucked Nicholas. The couple watched each other's arousal catapult to a fever pitch—they'd never seen wild-eyed horniness in one another that they hadn't been responsible for.

Claree desperately searched for something to grasp as the throbbing pulse between her legs intensified and rendered her knees useless. Laura's shoulder was closest. The moment she clutched it was the moment the tremors claimed her body. Her shouts filled the room and even as she collapsed in stages beside Laura, her orgasm persisted, twitching and twisting its way to a close. Laura instinctively moved her hand from Claree's cunt to her asshole, spreading the juices from one hole to the other. After several applications of her own natural lubricant, Laura's finger rimmed her asshole, causing Claree to position herself on all fours. Her face was inches from the carpet, which smelled of patchouli and wet dog.

"Prepare to get fucked," Laura said.

Claree had her back to them but knew that if Laura could speak, she was no longer eating Nicholas. So, when his thickness pushed at her ready hole, she grinned and winced with a new wave of pleasure. While he inserted himself past her forgiving sphincter, Laura got up and stood before Claree and Nicholas. The couple fucked and watched Laura strap on the aforementioned dildo, which was the same shade of hellish red as her lipstick.

But she was watching them, too, and with every penetration, she stroked her dildo as if it were her very own cock. Her eyes glistened with ethereal delight. Her breathing was shorter, like a man's would be as his balls tightened with excitement.

"How can I help you?" she rasped. The submission in her voice came out in a plaintive purr.

"Fuck me in the ass, like you promised," Nicholas blurted out.

Claree couldn't remember who moved whom in what position, but she found herself on her back, with Nicholas now entering her pussy. Her big tits bumped and jiggled as she absorbed his pounding.

Out of the corner of her eye, she saw Laura get behind Nicholas, where the man's body now obscured her movements. A minute or so passed, during which he pumped Claree's pussy, ramming himself so deeply inside her that he nearly tickled her spine.

But she knew when Laura's dildo poked its way into his hole. He paused, bit his lip, shut his eyes and stifled a high groan. Once Laura was in—and fucking—he resumed his pumping, matching Laura's rhythm. He'd slam into Claree, Laura would slam into him. Damp skin met and slid against damp skin. Squishing, slippery noises sputtered throughout.

His abdomen tensed and his posture changed. Suddenly, his shoulders were larger. His chest rippled with muscles Claree had never noticed before. Laura's little grunts punctuated every new push up his ass. Claree knew he was close.

He roared when he came but the sound was nothing compared to the colossal pounding he directed into Claree's pussy. He trembled with demonic fervor, and seemed to want to pass that fervor along to his wife. Or was it too much for him to contain and he *had* to share it, else it destroy him?

Claree came, too, but the intensity of his orgasm blurred with her own and she couldn't distinguish which pulses emanated from him, and which from her.

Laura extracted herself from Nicholas slowly and got to her feet. She walked out of the room while her guests let earthly concerns gradually invade their thoughts. After several minutes, Laura returned, smiling, still wearing only her bustier.

"Take your time recovering. I think I'll just go to bed now, if you don't mind. Just go ahead and let yourselves out when you're ready."

Nicholas's eyes darkened. He looked like he wanted to say something but didn't know how. Laura recognized his hesitation and asked him if everything was all right.

"Oh, yes. Everything is fantastic," he replied. "But, I was, uh, wondering . . . Do we need to leave you any money?"

Claree hadn't considered the possibility that Laura did this for a living. Or a supplement to a living. She hoped Nicholas's question wouldn't offend her.

Laura smiled. "No, I don't do this for money."

Though her answer seemed to satisfy Nicholas, now it was Claree who was curious. Laura hadn't come at all during the night, which made her voluntary participation all the more mysterious. What was in it for this strange woman with the tarantula roommate?

"So, why do you do it?" Claree ventured.

A beatific grin spread across the semi-goth girl's smeared lipsticked face. "There are very few lovers out in the world," she said quietly, zipping up her skirt. "They are so rare—like endangered species. When I see people who are happy, I want to experience that happiness, know that kind of love. When I saw the two of you, I knew I could not only fulfill some of your fantasies but satisfy my own need for ecstasy, even for a few seconds." She walked toward the door, then turned to the couple one last time.

"Thank you for letting me inside." She closed the door behind her.

Claree looked at Nicholas, mute with understanding. Laura had gotten inside them in ways they'd never imagined.

Author Biographies

Jayden Blake lives in western Massachusetts with her partner, dogs, and cat. A librarian by day, Jayden's colleagues have no inkling that she moonlights as a pornographer. "Jessie's Girl" is her first published story.

Chris Bridges, benevolent dictator of HootIsland.com, has delved deep into the pits of ecstatic passion and discovered it to be pretty funny, especially if a bicycle horn is involved. His silly erotica has been collected into a form that is easier to hold in one hand, the book *Giggling into the Pillow*.

Tenille Brown resides in South Carolina. Her first novel, *What It Looks Like from the Outside*, will be released in 2004. Her work will be featured in the anthologies *Chocolate Flava* and *Best Women's Erotica*, also to be released in 2004.

M. Christian is the author of three best-selling collections: *Dirty Words*, *Speaking Parts*, and *The Bachelor Machine*. He has edited nearly twenty anthologies and his short fiction has appeared in more than 150 anthologies, including *Best American Erotica*, *Best Gay Erotica*, *Best Lesbian Erotica*, *Best Fetish Erotica*, and . . . well, you get the idea.

Elizabeth Coldwell is the editor of the U.K. edition of *Forum* magazine. Her stories have been included in *Wicked Words 6*; *Leather, Lace and Lust* (here at Venus Book Club); and *Best SM Erotica*.

Bryn Colvin is an English author fascinated by anything out of the ordinary. She has been writing for some years, in a range of genres, including romance, fantasy horror and some nonfiction work. In the rest of her life, she has a small child, a folk club, a band and a strong interest in green living.

Debra Gray De Noux was the longtime associate publisher of Pulphouse Publishing. Her fiction has appeared in magazines and anthologies in the U.S., Great Britain, and Germany. Her erotic fiction has appeared in dozens of men's magazines. She is the editor of *Erotic New Orleans* (Pontalba Press, 2000) and the forthcoming *Erotic Women* (Alex Books, 2004).

Odysseus Eleftherios writes fiction and drama, not all of it erotic, and continues to do anything for his beautiful wife.

Florence Hoard is a piano teacher with a penchant for erotic writing. She is a writer at Custom Erotica Source and her work has been published in *Naughty Fairy Tales* and *Wicked Words*. Though she swings both ways, she doesn't do it often.

Ludmilla Kryzmska lives in the Midwest, likes to swim, volunteers at a food co-op, and looks forward to her next birthday.

Jennifer Maer is an advertising copywriter who finally turned to fiction because it offered a more realistic view of the world. She lives in San Francisco with her partner, Lotus, and a laughably enormous cat named Sophie.

Bill Noble, fiction editor at Clean Sheets.com, has published more than 150 works. *Three Crows Yelling* won the National Looking Glass Award, and he's been nominated for the Pushcart Prize. His work appears in *Best American Erotica* (including a Best Erotic Story of the Decade), *Best New Erotica*, and elsewhere.

Randy Panache, an American living in permanent European exile, works as an editor at an international consultancy. She previously worked as piano teacher and accompanist. Her leisure activities include learning Bach fugues, writing reviews of classical concerts, reading aloud to her stepdaughter, and attending swinger clubs and parties. Her sex writings are at www.randy-panache.de.

Julia Rebecca is a writer, artist, and sailor who, along with her husband, lives on a small island in the Caribbean. She is a theoretical bisexual and polyamorist, as well a practicing monogamist. Her work can be found on www.literotica.com, in *Closet Desire IV*, and in the forthcoming *The Many Joys of Sex Toys*.

Stacy Reed's essays appear in *Binary*, *Illness and the Academy*, *Diverse Words*, *Whores and Other Feminists*, and *First Person Sexual*. Her fiction has been featured in *Flasher*; *Leather, Lace and Lust*; the *Herotica* series; and *The Oy of Sex*; as well as online at *Peacockblue*, *Mind Caviar*, and *Dare*. She writes for Custom Erotica Source.

Jason Rubis lives in Washington, D.C. His fiction has appeared in *Leg Show*, *Variations*, and several anthologies, including *Desires*; *Guilty Pleasures*; *Sacred Exchange*; *Leather, Lace and Lust*; and *Fetish Fantastic*. He is the author of several fetish novels from Pink Flamingo Publications (www.pinkfla mingo.com) and MTJ Publishing (www.mtjpub.com).

Helena Settimana lives a dull life in Toronto, Canada. Writing about sex and the people who have it livens things up considerably. Her work has been featured in the *Best Women's Erotica* series and *The Mammoth Book of Best New Erotica, Volume 2*. She is Features Editor at the Erotica Readers and Writer's Association (http://www.erotica-readers.com).

Joy VanNuys is a chef and a writer who lives in Brooklyn, New York. Her work has recently appeared in *On Our Backs*, *Nervy Girl*, *Best Bisexual Women's Erotica*, and *Best American Erotica 2004*. She makes excellent sausage. Visit Joy on the Web at www.JoyVanNuys.com.

Sage Vivant operates Custom Erotica Source, the home of tailor-made erotic fiction for individual clients since 1998. Her work appears in numerous anthologies. She is the author of *29 Ways to Write Great Erotica* (www.29eroticways.com), and coeditor with M. Christian of *Leather, Lace and Lust* and *Binary: Bisexual Erotica*. Visit Custom Erotica Source at www.customeroticasource.com.

Jennifer Whitlock (a.k.a. The Divine Ms. J) is a psychotherapist in New Jersey. She has written for *Men's Health*, *The Philadelphia Inquirer*, *Allentown's Morning Call*, and *Prevention*, when they had old people in the cover, and she wasn't allowed to say "fart" even when writing about fiber. Edit this, Rodale!

Swinging Resources

Websites

Lifestyles Organization (national organization) http://www.lifestyles.org

MathesPlus.com http://www.matchesplus.com/

Fun 4 Two (swinger's club in the Netherlands) www.fun4two.nl

Showboat Swinger Club (Netherlands) http://showboat.nl

Swing Connection U.S.A. http://www.swingconnectionusa.com/

Connection Online (worldwide links to swinging)
http://www.connectiononline.com/

Swingers Online http://www.swingersonline.com

Erotic University (class and FAQs on swinging)
http://www.eroticuniversity.com/classes/ask-swing.htm

Don's Real Offline Sex Resources http://www.donsworld.com/swing5.htm

Carousel Couples Club (swingers club in New York City)
http://www.carouselclub.net/

Wife Swapping Guide
http://www.wife-swapping.org/

Books

The Lifestyle: A Look at the Erotic Rites of Swingers by Terry Gould

Recreational Sex: An Insider's Guide to the Swinging Lifestyle
by Patti Thomas

The Ultimate Swingers Guide by Tia Minell

Swinging for Beginners: An Introduction to the Lifestyle by Kaye
Bellemeade

Together Sex by Ed and Dana Allen

Considering Swinging by Ed and Dana Allen

Threesome: How to Fulfill Your Favorite Fantasy by Lori Gammon

The Ethical Slut: A Guide to Infinite Sexual Possibilities
   by Dossie Easton and Catherine A. Liszt

Polyamory by Dr. Deborah M. Anapol

Open Marriage: A New Life Style for Couples by Nena and George
   O'Neill